MW00917617

# Seize the Crown

## The Kingmaker Series, Volume 2

## Gemma Perfect

Published by Gemma Perfect, 2017.

SEIZE THE CROWN

**First edition. January 1, 2017.**

Written by Gemma Perfect.

# Lanorie

I CANNOT SPEAK. OH, well, you know that's not true. I can speak, but I can't believe what I'm saying.

Everleigh was meant to be Queen today. It's all she's talked about all week, since she made the river rise. It's all I've thought about since I told her secret. I know, I know. I feel awful. I'm not proud of myself.

I told Everleigh's secret, then I tried to end it all. Stupid, I know. But it was a dreadful week. Will was hurt, and the King was dead, and it was all my fault.

So Everleigh has been destined to die since she was born. I've known her since I was seven, and she was nine. I'm her handmaiden. I have spent most of my life looking after her.

Then everything changed. She was told she would live.

And now it has changed again. Her brother is King.

The old King is dead, killed by his own son. Then he – Macsen – was killed by his brother, Millard. And he, well, he'll kill you as soon as look at you, I reckon.

It's all I ever wanted; Millard to be King. When I thought Everleigh would die and her blood would crown a prince, I wanted it to be Millard. Everyone thought it would be. He's so handsome, so clever, so nice. We know that's not true now, of course. He sat by and watched his brother kill their father, and he thought he killed Everleigh too. Didn't lift a finger to stop it. Then he killed Macsen. And Halfreda.

Halfreda was the wise woman. Old as even the oldest thing and scary, but I suppose I must admit, nice. She saved me when I tried to... you know, and she made sure I was better. I feel sad that she's dead. It was an awful thing to see. He just stabbed her in the heart, in front of everyone.

Then he killed Archer. Oh, Everleigh had fallen hard for him, let me tell you. She never thought she would find love, what with dying so young and being a princess, all protected and that. She wasn't a splendid catch really, as beautiful as she is.

Then Archer turned up. He was related to Halfreda, and he was a knight, only young but a right wonderful fighter. Well, he wasn't good enough. Millard killed him.

Millard's a madman. I don't want to even look at him, in case I'm next.

Poor Everleigh, she put her cloak over Archer, and then as we walked away, her knees just went. She sobbed that hard. Will and I kept her up, but she started screaming about Archer's body. She didn't want Millard to send him to the Ashes – where the dead bodies are burnt. She wanted him to be sent out to sea, like her father was.

I took her to Halfreda's rooms; it was the only place we could think she might be safe. If Millard sees her, he will probably kill her. What she will do next I don't know. I'm glad it's not up to me to decide.

So, Will went back to fetch Archer. They need to wrap his body up and then we can take it to the little island to send him off.

Oh, it's been a scary and horrible day. Every time I shut my eyes I see Macsen's head flying clean off his body. There was so much blood and upset today. How any of us will sleep I don't know?

Poor Ginata had to crown him after all that – what else could she do? I don't know her well, but I feel awful sorry for her. I don't go to the village much and when she came to the castle; it was to visit Halfreda, and I wouldn't join the pair of them.

She looked so petrified as she crowned him. And I knew she was hoping he wouldn't finish her off too. I was the same. I didn't want to catch his eye in case I gave him an idea. No one is safe here.

Cook just knocked, guessing where I was – she's wilier than she looks, I reckon. She said that Wolf's taken Addyson off to the tower. Wolf is Millard's henchman, though everyone thought he worked for Macsen. Shows you what a sly one he is, changing his tune like that. I'm to take food up to Addyson. What is this place coming to? I know she's the cursed princess, but she shouldn't be locked away. And what about Everleigh? She told him she'd kill him. He won't want to see her at breakfast. Next time he sees her, one of them's not long for this world, I tell you. Who will live and who will die, I wouldn't want to guess.

And Cook was full of it. Seen nothing like it in her lifetime. And now we all know he's crazy, none of us wants to go near him. There's to be a feast tonight, and Cook reckons he's already talking about a proper coronation next week, one without a headless corpse watching him – his words, apparently!

Everleigh's just sitting in front of the fire, watching the flames and crying. I don't know what will snap her out of this or who will look after her. Poor dab.

# 1

EVERLEIGH'S DRESS IS wet through from crying; tears flowing continuously down her face, with no move made from her to stop them. Her nose is running, and she's dribbling. The wailing has stopped; her heartbreak is silent now. She doesn't care what a mess she must look, or that Millard has probably put a price on her head. Everything has gone wrong.

Lanorie and Will stand together watching her, in Halfreda's rooms, the only safe place they could think of to steer her to, away from Millard. "I have to go." Lanorie's voice is a whisper. "Cook wants me to take food to Addyson in the tower."

"He *has* locked her up then?" Will asks, but it is more of a statement. They both know how terrible things are. Lanorie reaches for his hand.

"Where's Archer's body and the others?"

"I asked the pages to wrap them up. They know Halfreda and Macsen, but I explained that Archer was covered with Everleigh's cloak. There are some other dead bodies – some fighting went on after the coronation – but they'll be taken to the Ashes. They'll put the three of them on the island and leave them there till we decide what to do with them. I can't imagine Millard giving them any thought."

"He may want their heads on spikes."

"Then I am glad I moved them. Bad enough that so many are dead today. He can't play with their corpses."

Lanorie shakes her head, upset, and Will pulls her close, hugging her, giving and taking some level of comfort on this awful day.

Everleigh is rocking as she watches the flames. She has lost everything is; least importantly, her crown.

Her father is dead, murdered by her oldest brother, Macsen. And Macsen. Her sweetest brother. Dead before she got to confront him. He tried to kill her too and if her best friend Will hadn't put his own life before hers, she would have been dead at his hand.

Halfreda – the wise woman – saved Will.

Her happy, close knit family of only a week ago, is now altered irrevocably.

Her emotions and lifelong loyalties need time to catch up with the facts of what has just happened.

Her entire life long, from when she was old enough to understand her role, she has known she would die at seventeen. All Kingmakers did. Learning from Halfreda, that she would live and rule as Queen has changed her life for the good but ended up being the downfall of all that she loves and cherishes.

Macsen, desperate for power had been plotting to kill their brother Millard at the sacrificial ceremony – when the Kingmaker's throat is slit and her blood decides which prince will be King – instead of drinking Everleigh's blood he had planned to give Millard a death draught. He tested that draught out on their father, King of the Realm.

Letting her mind go there was painful. Wondering about her father's last moments. Had he known it was his own son who killed him? She hoped not. She hoped that he had been oblivious. Can there be a greater crime than a child killing their own parent? Maybe a parent killing their own child?

Macsen had then learned that Everleigh would live, or had it been the other way around? Had he learned that she would live and killed their father to get the throne, no one would ever know the order, or how his murderous mind had made something so awful seem like a logical next step for him.

Whatever happened, he decided to kill her too. She could never repay that debt to Will. Always her best friend, he had done something she would never have dared ask of anyone; taken her place in her bed and almost died for his trouble. Thank goodness Macsen was a clueless soldier and thank goodness that Halfreda had saved Will.

And then Millard. Her tears flow afresh when she thinks about him. Her other wonderful brother; acerbic but funny, blunt but loving, always there for her, if not always on her side. He had turned out to be worse than Macsen. She can hardly believe that's possible.

Millard had known of his brother's plan to kill him during the sacrifice. He knew that he had bought the death draught. He knew Macsen had killed their father, and he knew – or thought he knew – that Macsen had killed Everleigh, and he had just sat back and done nothing.

With archaic law decreeing that the eldest son – Macsen – be King if the Kingmaker wasn't there to make the choice the traditional way, Millard had stepped in during the coronation and killed Macsen, his own brother. Sliced his head clean off, so he could be King instead.

She was glad she missed it. She had been hiding in these very rooms, such a short time ago, so happy and ready to be Queen, to take on her birthright. That was when Lanorie, hysterical, took her out of hiding.

She had tried to claim her crown, and that was when Millard killed Halfreda, who she had known and loved her whole life long – as had he – and then he had killed... her mind almost refuses to go there, but she forces herself to. He deserves her to remember him. He had died for her. The ultimate sacrifice and what every knight promises to do for their King or Queen. She just never thought it would happen. Even after Ginata's vision where she saw him get hurt, Everleigh had thought he would win. She had let him die, and she hadn't been able to help him or save him.

Archer.

Her tears are sobs now. Her body pained by the wracking.

Lanorie whispers to Will, "I need to go now. I need to check on Addyson. Maybe it will help Everleigh if she knows she's safe?"

"Excellent idea. I'll try to talk to her."

They both look doubtful and Lanorie gives his hand a squeeze before she goes, shutting the door quietly behind her, even though Everleigh has shown no sign of knowing that either of them are in the room with her.

Will steps softly towards her. He is sure Millard is busy doing other dastardly things, but he can't help but worry that he will come looking for his sister. He will not want her alive, not while she threatens his reign.

He sits down beside her, his princess and friend. He rests a hand on her arm, wanting to touch her, to help her. "Everleigh," he says. "Everleigh are you all right?"

He knows she is not, even as he asks it, but he needs to say something.

She turns to face him and looks surprised to see him. "Will." Her voice sounds scratchy from all the crying she's doing.

"Everleigh. I don't think you're safe here."

Her gaze is blank.

Will tries again. "I think Millard will try to kill you."

Gaze still blank, tears spilling over, she looks back at the fire.

Will wishes Halfreda was here, she would give Everleigh some potion or other, something to help her. She's suffering from shock. And heartache. And stress. And no wonder.

He is silent but still touching her arm. She feels stone cold, and he rubs her skin, trying to warm her up. She is unaware of him once more, lost in her memories, lost in the trauma of the last few hours, the last few days.

He locks the front door and moves through to Halfreda's work room. If Millard's soldiers come, the lock won't stop them, but he will hear them. He cannot bear the thought of her being slaughtered like a defenceless lamb, unaware that anyone has even come for her head.

Halfreda had many rooms within the castle, and several rooms here too, just outside of it. She had accumulated a lot of stuff in her long life; she was the oldest person Will had ever seen or known and he has no clue of her actual age. She was older than ancient when he was young and older still when she died. He can hardly believe she is gone. It seemed like she would never die, just become older and older and older, but he knows everyone dies, eventually.

Her work room is full of herbs and potions, bottles and books. He would never know what to give Everleigh but is hoping that Halfreda will have something bottled and labelled, something that might help.

He cannot bear seeing his princess in so much pain. It relieves him she is alive but needs her to snap out of her maudlin thoughts, this inertia, before Millard sends an axe for her.

Eyes roving along the bottles and jars, he sees something labelled as 'Lift.' Another as 'Sleep.' Another as 'Boost.' While she could do with all three, he just needs her to have enough energy to get away from the castle. He doesn't know where he'll take her, but it won't be long before Millard looks for her. Maybe he will enjoy the night, revel in being King of the Realm, but come morning, sober and concerned about his crown, surely, he will hunt her down like a dog and kill her. Or lock her up. Alive would be the best outcome for her, but she would still be a prisoner. Will wants her safe, with or without a crown on her head. Millard may want her dead, regardless.

He picks up the bottle labelled 'Boost', opens the top and puts a drop on his tongue. He doesn't want to inadvertently kill her with a mislabelled bottle of poison. He doesn't drop dead, and so goes back to Everleigh's side.

# Ginata

WHAT A DAY. AND IT has not ended yet. It is the worst day I have ever had the misfortune to live through and yet I cannot thank the gods enough that I *have* lived through it. Several times today the gaze of a madman rested on me and I have feared my time was over.

But here I am.

I knew something was wrong this morning, but I did not understand how wrong. Maybe Halfreda could have seen it if she hadn't been so close to the end of her life, and yet her love for both boys had coloured her vision of them and what they might be capable of.

I have no such alliances; I had seen them a handful of times on visits to the castle and had only met Macsen when he was disguised in a cloak, buying a death draught off me. If only I had been down at the river the day he came calling, or next door enjoying an ale with Della, or anywhere else where he wouldn't have found me.

And yet he is not the problem anymore.

With one prince dead, one princess in a tower, one Kingmaker on the loose, we have a new King. A mad and murderous one. And he has called me to his room.

Standing with him now, while he tells me, the new wise woman of the castle, what he expects from me, I dare not let my attention wander for a second, but my heart is still beating too wildly.

First Macsen and then Millard; two insane brothers had me in their sights and twice I have been saved. When I crowned Millard, I was sure he would run me through straight after having fulfilled his need of me.

And yet here I am. I cannot quite believe it. Am I a lucky witch? Maybe.

Halfreda was not. I dig my nails into my palm to stop any tears from sprouting and giving my emotions away to this monster before me. And a monster he is. A beautiful monster, so handsome and affable. Now he is King, he laughs and jokes and waves and smiles. But earlier on he pierced Halfreda's heart with a sure sword. He pierced Archer's beautiful heart without a pause.

I feel Halfreda's loss like a physical thing, a discontentment in my heart. I am sad about Archer but I knew him not. I know Everleigh will be beyond distraught and I wish I was with her now instead of here with Millard. I want to serve her, not him.

I will serve her. I will be as false to him as he was to his family, his sisters, his brother, his father. I will pretend to help him and obey him, but I will be an agent for the other side. I will assist and aide Everleigh in any way I can until the crown is on her head.

Halfreda was a wonderful friend to me, especially after my parents both died. She always looked out for me and imparted all her knowledge to me. I will use her knowledge now, her wisdom, for a cause of my own.

Millard's wish has come true; I crowned him King of the Realm. Now, he sees me as an ally and I will gain his trust and abuse it. Willingly.

I take the drink and smile at him. It's easy to smile at his handsome face. It's easy to pretend to like him. He pleases my eye even though his touch repulses me. As his fingers brush mine when he gives me the goblet I contain a shiver through pure mental control.

He cannot know what I think when I see him or how much he upsets me. This monster must believe that I am only here for him.

"So," he says, his eyes tender. "Quite a day..."

He lets his words hang in the air and I am unsure how to respond to him. "Indeed," I say, noncommittal, but hoping he doesn't mind. If he minds, I am all too aware, I may die.

"Do you think ill of me?"

Again, what would he have me say?

I take a deep breath. If I am to work with him, convince him of my worth and loyalty, I need to speak to him, engage with him, push away my fears and commit to this path I've chosen.

"Your Grace. I am a witch, but a simple one. I have lived my entire life long in a small square house, just two rooms, with my parents. After they died, I lived alone. I wash in the river; I sweep my own floors. I eat what I can, when I can, but some nights I go to bed with a pain in my stomach from hunger. I cannot imagine the life of a prince, the call to power and leadership. I aimed to serve and help in the village and it's all I can try to do now. I am not clever or learned or wise like Halfreda, I am a simple witch but if you let me stay I will put my mind to helping you, serving you."

Is it enough? I worried about mentioning Halfreda's name, but I wanted to speak plainly. I have let him think I am more naïve than I probably am. But I don't think there's any harm in it. I look him in the eye, no fear, well plenty of it, but hopefully well hidden.

A beautiful smile breaks out over his face, and he looks genuinely relieved. "Power and leadership," he says, nodding at me. Happy with my answer. "Exactly. Only those raised to be Kings could understand. Thank you, Ginata. I feel better. You make me feel better."

I smile at him. I am relieved and pleased. I do not want to die.

"And now for your rooms. Halfreda had rooms in here, but also outside. They weren't the best, or the fanciest, but I think you should live inside. I will have the old King's rooms made up for you, fit for my closest advisor."

I do not want to sleep in a dead man's bed, but I cannot show my repulsion or fear. If this man wants me close, and that's what it takes to stay alive and win the crown for Everleigh, then it's what I will do.

"It would delight me," I lie.

"One other matter, before I let you rest. I am sure you are tired out. It's been a busy day. And still the feast later."

I nod my agreement but stay quiet.

"I want another coronation. A proper one. Today was a farce, really. It should have been Everleigh's death day, then Macsen's coronation, and then finally mine. I want a day that's just about me."

I am literally speechless. This King murdered his brother without flinching, killed his lifelong mother figure without hesitation and then stabbed the man his sister was in love with, all without missing a beat and now he worries about having a day to himself without the attention on anyone else.

It hits me then; this King is still a child. A spoiled little boy. He wants to be the star, the chief attraction, all eyes on him.

I am nodding so he will not know what I'm thinking. "I think that's a sensible idea. A coronation should be a grand affair, something people will remember for the right reasons."

He grins at me, so pleased with what I've said. The key to winning over this man is to always be on his side, or at least let him believe you are. And, actually, this self-involved madness might help us, might give us a chance to get Everleigh her crown back. Halfreda's words echo in my mind: you can only have a coronation with witnesses of more than a hundred, or any mad man could have himself crowned. Well, a madman has had himself crowned, and we will help Everleigh take his crown away.

"I will get it arranged and you can crown me properly."

I nod along. I have a feeling I will do a lot of that.

# 2

GINATA HURRIES THROUGH the castle corridors, heading outside to Halfreda's rooms. She is only guessing, but it's the only logical place she can think of for Everleigh to be hiding. But she won't be safe there for long.

The door is locked, so she knocks. "Everleigh, Will? Lanorie?"

Will rushes from Everleigh's side and opens the door, and Ginata slips inside. Being inside Halfreda's room, away from Millard's side, she finally breaks down. Will leads her to a chair, and she sobs with her head in her hands.

Will is quiet next to her, Everleigh doesn't even look up. She has drunk none of the potion yet; he cannot get her to snap out of the fog she's in. Maybe once Ginata is all cried out, they can help her together. He is sure Lanorie will come back once she's fed Addyson and together they can come up with a plan.

He pats Ginata's shoulder as she cries, keeping himself calm by wondering what they will do next. He may only be a fool in the making, but it doesn't take a genius to work out that life has changed for all of them. Irrevocably.

Ginata takes a deep breath and wipes her face. She smiles up at Will. "I needed that. I've been with Millard. The King."

It was treasonous the way she was thinking; that she would help someone steal the King's crown and take his place. If I could read her mind, she'd be hung for what she was planning to do. She was safe enough in Halfreda's old rooms, but everywhere else she would have to watch what she said, how she said things, her reaction to what others said, even. This man did not need good reasons to end people's lives. He was quick to the temper and slow to regret.

"Are you all right?"

"Yes. Well... he expects me to take over from Halfreda, which I knew. He's moving me in to the King's old rooms – that I didn't expect. Or like." She shrugs. What choice does any of them have? "How is she?" Ginata nods her head towards Everleigh who hasn't moved for more than an hour.

"Not good and I don't think she's safe. Did Millard say anything about her?"

"No, but he wants another coronation next week. He wants one without all the other stuff detracting from him."

Will laughs, although it is not funny. Not really. But he can't help it. "Really?"

Ginata nods. "Really."

"What did you say?"

"I agreed with everything he said. I am not willing to die, no matter how much I want to help Everleigh. Halfreda believed she should be Queen; that's enough for me. But I won't die for her. I think another coronation is perfect. It will let us crown her this time, plan it all properly, do it right. And I will help, but I don't want to die for my trouble."

Will couldn't argue with her. He would die for Everleigh; he almost had. But they had been friends their entire life. She was more than a friend to him; she was family.

"She hasn't moved for ages. I tried to give her one of Halfreda's drinks, but she won't take it. What can we do?"

Will is glad Ginata has come back. She'll know how to help Everleigh. They must get her to wake up, focus, move. They need to get her to safety.

"I can help her," Ginata says, moving over to Everleigh's side.

"Where will we put her? Where can she go? She's not safe if Millard wants another coronation. He won't want her turning up again and spoiling things."

"I was thinking about my cottage." Ginata takes hold of Everleigh's hand. "I don't think Millard would ever think of going there. I'm not sure if he even knows where it is."

"Brilliant." For the first time since they walked away from the massacre, Will feels himself relax. He's not solely responsible anymore. They will work it out together. He sits on one of Halfreda's comfy chairs and lets Ginata take over.

"Everleigh." Ginata's voice is loud, but Everleigh doesn't move. "Everleigh!" Louder again, accompanied by a shake of her shoulders. Everleigh looks at her, smiles faintly, turns her gaze back to the fire. Ginata shakes her again. "No, Everleigh. Stay with me." She takes hold of Everleigh's chin and turns her head, holds her face in both hands. Everleigh tries to turn away, but Ginata won't let her. Her grip is too firm.

"Everleigh."

"Yes?"

Will moves to the edge of his chair. That's only the second time she's spoken, but she sounds more like herself.

"Everleigh. We need to get you out of here. You're not safe. You need to snap out of it."

Everleigh nods, but her gaze is vacant again.

"Everleigh." Ginata's voice is harsh this time, sharp and loud. "Everleigh. Your brother is dead. Halfreda is dead. Archer is dead." Everleigh lets out a cry. "Archer. Is. Dead. Sorry, Everleigh, but he is. But Addyson is safe. She's locked up. She needs you. The Realm needs you. You need to snap out of this fog. We need to move you."

Everleigh's eyes focus on Ginata. "He killed them all."

"Not Addyson. Not me. Not Will. Not Lanorie. And not you. You are alive, Everleigh. We need you."

"Why didn't I save him?"

Ginata shakes her head. Everleigh discovered that she was the Kingmaker who would live, written in a prophecy, the day she made the river rise. It was the test to prove if she would die or rule. A ruler, a true King or Queen, could command mother nature. Everleigh was even more special. She could move things. Inanimate objects. She had moved an arrow to stop it hitting a deer, and she had moved Millard's sword when he was fighting Archer.

But she hadn't moved it on the final fateful blow.

"I'll never forgive myself."

"Everleigh. Your magic, your power is new to you. You don't have control of it yet. You cannot blame yourself. You can't."

Everleigh shakes her head but shifts her position, stretches out her arms and then her legs, then stands. Will jumps up, hugs her. Ginata passes her the drink Will found earlier. "Drink." She holds it up to Everleigh's lips, not allowing her to refuse.

Everleigh drinks, wipes her tears away. "What do I do? One of you tell me. Please."

"First thing's first. You're not safe. We must move you. To my cottage."

"Then we need to rescue Addyson. Millard might turn on her any minute," Will says.

"Then we need to get the crown on your head," Ginata finishes.

Everleigh shakes her head. "I don't even care about being Queen anymore. I just want to be safe. Just me and Addyson."

Will and Ginata exchange a quick glance. Will takes her hand; he knows her the best. "Everleigh. If you don't take your crown, why did your father die? Or your brother? Or Halfreda? Or Archer?"

At his name, Everleigh's eyes flood over with tears again.

"You can't let their deaths be for nothing. Be pointless."

"Where are they?"

"On the island, by now. Waiting for us to send them out."

"We need to do that today. We can't leave them there in the cold. Can you do the ceremony, Ginata? Do you have time?"

Ginata nods, she's not sure what Millard is planning to do for the rest of the day with his newfound Kingship, but she expects she can sneak off for an hour.

"Let's go."

"Shall we wait for Lanorie?" Lanorie is never far from Will's thoughts. He has been half in love with her for years and the only good thing he can think of that has come from today is their sudden affinity. As the two people left who are closest to Everleigh, they have a bond; they both look after her in their own way and they both want the best for her, and they have taken some comfort from each other these past few hours.

"Where is she? Addyson?" Everleigh is coming fully around, becoming more aware of her surroundings and what's going on. The look of panic on her face is growing as she thinks about her sister. "You said we have to rescue her. Where is she?" Lucid suddenly, Everleigh is full of agitation, upset marring her face.

"She's in the tower."

"The tower. She's not dead?"

"Not yet."

Will glares at Ginata. "Not at all. He never wanted to hurt her, he said so."

"He hurt everyone else," Everleigh says, her voice tinged with anger.

"Not you or Addyson."

"I wonder why..."

"We can't hope to understand him." Ginata takes her hand. "We just need to get you to safety, rescue Addyson and get you crowned as our Queen. You can question him or kill him then, as you prefer."

"Kill him." Everleigh's voice is hard with anger.

# Ceryn

I DROP A DEAD RABBIT on the chair and then I pull off my mask – a swatch of leather with ties, that I never leave home without – and throw it on the table. The fire is low, so I pile more logs on, satisfied when the flames lick higher.

Something is wrong. I don't go for all that magic claptrap they love to bang on about in this Realm, but I know my friend and I know something is wrong.

I am waiting for Weaver and I reckon he'll agree with me, or else I'll make him. There's ale in the jug so I slosh some in a mug and down it in one go. I've had a busy morning and I'm thirsty.

I prepare the rabbit while I wait for him, skinning it and then gutting it. I throw the head out for the dogs. I don't have any dogs myself, but there's plenty of them around here and I'm happy to chuck out my scraps for them.

I stab a fork into the body and start roasting it over the fire. Weaver will be hungry too and he'll be glad not to wait. He might have some spoils from his morning too. We'll have a feast and decide what to do about Archer.

Ah, Archer. We are a band of brothers, us three, despite my unfortunate gender, and we roam the Realm together, hunting our feed and helping the common man. We give our extra meat and fish to the poorest families; we make sure the King's men are being just by keeping our eye on them and what they're up to. Only last week they had three adolescent boys in the square, all lined up to some end, waiting to punish them in some cruel way, when Weaver shot his arrow straight through one of their bags of gold, collected from some poor farmer or other. The coins streamed out, and in the pandemonium of half the square fighting over the money, the boys ran off. They'll not catch them again; one urchin in this Realm looks the same as another.

The King's men. All utter hooligans, they are. They reckon they serve the greater good, the ruler of the Realm; mostly they serve themselves. Well, we three wage war on them, best we're able.

Well, we did until last week.

Archer's kin Halfreda came to visit; she's the King's wise woman, lives at the castle, doling out her mumbo jumbo. He reckons he'd had some dream of a Queen. Poor Archer, he's the softest of us three. Likes to dream and imagine a different world to the one we live in. Just because he can fight and beds down in a fancier place than mine or Weaver's, he can't see the bad in the world. But he wins his jousts, and he dishes out most of what he wins; it's a good contribution to our cause. We keep a little pot that we all chip in to – I'm an expert hunter and once we've given away what we can; we sell some of the best cuts to the people who can pay for it. Weaver can sew like an old woman, so he mends things for free for the people who can't pay and charges those who can.

We try our best to make our little corner of the Realm better. But Archer's been gone a week. And I don't know why.

He was all a bit hush-hush when he left, reckoned he was just visiting his kin. But in the week leading up to the Kingmaker's death, I don't reckon it's a coincidence.

I taste some rabbit. Tender and rare, just how I like it. I tear strips off, burning my fingers, and cram them straight in my mouth, pour more ale and eat and drink my fill. I leave plenty for Weaver and close my eyes while I wait for him.

I must have drifted off, a nice snooze after dinner, as Weaver slamming the door wakes me. The rabbit is cold, but I pull off a bone and suck on it.

"You've been ages." Most of what I say to Weaver comes out as a complaint. I'm not known for my cheery disposition, but I'm a happy grouch. I won't whinge about the hand I was dealt by fate or any of that crap. I had a rubbish start to life, but I'm doing all right.

"A bit of fighting in the square, couple of men drunk in the morning, taking swings at anyone who came too close. They're snoring in a ditch now. Nice rabbit?"

"Lovely. I think there's something wrong with Archer."

He places two rabbits on the table: show off. His eyes narrow. I don't think he'll dismiss me; I'm not one to worry or become hysterical.

"He didn't say when he'd be back..."

"True. But it won't hurt to take a ride up to the castle."

Weaver chews on some rabbit, grease dribbling down his chin. "It'll take a few days."

"True." Stating facts isn't meant to dissuade me. He likes to mull things over, Weaver, make sure he knows what's going on, reach the right decision.

A knock at the door makes us both jump. Weaver waits for me to pull on my mask before opening the door. One of my neighbours: "Thought I smelled rabbit. Brought you some ale."

We happily swap our wares, and he heads away, eating as he goes. I skin another rabbit. If we eat our fill before we go, we won't have to waste too much time on the road hunting down our dinner.

I put the rabbit on the fire and take off my mask; it's too hot to keep on inside, and Weaver has seen my mark a million times.

He won't stare, or point, or throw me out.

He won't mutter spiteful things about the devil's mark or shrink away from my touch.

I don't think he even notices anymore.

We share the rabbit and make a plan.

## 3

MILLARD TAKES A LONG swig of his wine, raises the goblet to
Wolf, who grins at him, and then drinks the rest.

"My man," he greets his closest friend and ally.

"Your Grace."

"So, it is done. I am King."

Wolf bows low. "You are. We knew it."

Millard nods. "Only because you betrayed my brother..."

Wolf nods. "I would do anything you asked me to."

"You serve no other?"

Wolf shakes his head; the truth.

Millard pours more wine into his jewelled goblet. He offers
nothing to Wolf. Wolf stands, hands clasped behind him, waiting.

"I'm in a pleasant mood, Wolf, but I have to say I was worried
about you."

"Your Grace?"

"You betrayed my brother so easily, you spilled his secrets as
easily as I pour this wine. How do I know you won't do the same to
me?"

"Your Grace, I served Macsen only because you told me to, I
spilled his secrets because you asked me to. I serve no other."

Millard nods, watching Wolf over the top of his goblet. "I think
I believe you. But I need to be wise, Wolf. I need to know that my
trust isn't in vain. That you are my man. I'll be watching you. Fetch
me the fool's boy."

Wolf nods and turns to leave.

"Bring me Everleigh's handmaiden too. I may trust your loyalty
for now, but can I trust theirs?"

Wolf nods and leaves.

Millard smiles as he surveys his room; he won't move into his father's old rooms. The witch can have them. He likes it where he is; he won't sleep in a dead man's bed or walk in his shoes. This reign is his own, and he plans to enjoy it.

KILL HIM.

Everleigh's words fall heavy in the quiet room and while Will and Ginata nod at her words, they are both scared. They all know that Millard must die. Not only because of what he's done today, but because of what he will do to Everleigh when she takes his crown. He won't accept it or agree to her being Queen and so death or prison are the only two options and after what he did today, they can both see why Everleigh is suddenly steely in her decision to end his life.

"We need to go to the island first. I'll do it when we come back."

Will takes her hand, stopping her from pacing the room. "How? I know you're furious with him. Understandably, but he'll be heavily guarded. How will you kill him?"

"Quickly."

Will and Ginata laugh, some tension in the room dissipating.

"Wonderful idea. But practically, how?"

Everleigh shrugs. She doesn't really know how, only that she wants to do it, needs to do it. Too many people have died and Millard is too unstable to rule the Realm. She needs the crown that is rightfully hers on her head, before too long, before he causes any more damage and before she sinks into another gloom at the mention of Archer's name, or the thought of his eyes, his smile, his mouth on hers...

"I'll think of something. I must. I have to do this, don't I?"

Will and Ginata nod, none of them feeling old enough or wise enough, or in any way equipped to decide here, or to properly guide Everleigh.

"For Halfreda and Archer. For my father. I have to avenge their deaths, and someone has to rule the Realm. Look after all the people, my people. I can't trust Millard to do anything. He's not all there in the head."

They both know she is right.

"Ginata, you said you can perform the ceremony on the island?"

Ginata nods, she has all Halfreda's knowledge and the authority to do so as the new wise woman of the castle. "I would rather do it quickly, so that Millard doesn't find out."

Everleigh nods. "Let's go."

"Without Lanorie?"

"Yes. Millard can't know that Ginata is assisting me. So, we need to be quick."

The knock at the door makes them all jump.

"Open up."

Everleigh ducks out of sight in the other room. Will stays by Ginata's side.

Ginata opens the door, an affable smile on her face. She almost balks at the sight of Wolf, flanked by two heavy-set guards, swords aloft, but she keeps her smile pasted on.

"You." Wolf points at Will, who turns white. "With me."

Will's feet won't move, but Ginata squeezes his arm and her touch seems to wake him up. Reluctantly he leaves the warmth of Halfreda's rooms and follows Wolf.

Wolf pats him on the back, almost knocking him over. "A page said you was with the witch. Come on, the King wants you."

As soon as the door shuts, Everleigh rushes to Ginata's side. "What will he do with him?"

Ginata can only shrug. Any sort of sixth sense or instinct has run away from her. She needs calm to see things, and this day has given none.

"What can we do?"

23

Ginata takes Everleigh's hands in her own, wishing she was as wise as Halfreda.

"Nothing. We can only wait and hope. Why don't we go to the island? Rather than stay here worrying."

Everleigh nods, and Ginata finds her one of Halfreda's old cloaks. Everleigh tucks all her hair away and then sits the hood down low over her face.

Ginata checks the way is clear and takes Everleigh's arm. She is risking her own life and future by having anything to do with her, but she cannot turn away.

They walk in step to the island, and Ginata pulls out the boat, helping Everleigh to climb in.

The three bodies are laid out, Everleigh's murderous brother Macsen, Halfreda and Archer. Only one of them can be Archer – the tallest of the three – and Everleigh almost drops to the floor at his side. Ginata senses it and holds on to her arm.

"It's all right," she lies and Everleigh nods, wishing she could believe her. Wishing it was true.

Ginata gives her no time to fall apart and starts sprinkling white powder over them; a cleansing herb to help them on their way. Then, while Everleigh silently weeps, she chants. Everleigh walks to her brother, drops to her knees, touches him. She cannot see him, nor would she want to now, his head cruelly separated from his body, dusty from rolling on the floor, and she cannot quite believe all that's happened. That this funny, loving boy, her brother, her favourite brother, did this. He killed their father and would have killed her. All for a crown. All for her crown.

She pushes him into the water and turns to Halfreda. Grief is an unfamiliar emotion; she was young when her mother died and so she missed her but never really grieved properly.

Seeing Halfreda's body bundled up hurts her physically, it takes her breath and punishes her. She wants her back; she wants to hear her voice, and see her smile, touch her soft cheek, conspire with her. She smiles at a fond memory and cries harder as the pain turns sharp in her belly; she knows who is next.

Archer.

She pushes Halfreda in to the water and walks to Archer's side.

A perfect young man, one she barely knew and yet felt so deeply for. The first man to turn her head, the first man to kiss her. The first man to wake emotions in her she thought she would never get to enjoy.

Archer.

So handsome, so brave, so willing to fight and die for her.

She drops her head on to his chest, bundled as it is, and sobs.

When she learned that she would live and rule, she had been so happy. And so naïve. She thought her father would be happy, her brothers would be pleased for her, the Realm would celebrate and that this man, this beautiful man, would rule beside her. Her King and knight, her lover and protector.

And now he's gone.

She is all but alone in the world.

The unfamiliar feelings Archer had awoken, now stripped and trampled and ruined. All that was left now: death.

Loneliness and death.

She reaches for the little silver brooch he gave her, a tiny replica crown, and is about to unpin it, to send something of her away with him, when she hesitates. This is all she has of him now, the one gift he had given her, apart from a feeling that she could have a future, a love, a happiness of her own. She leaves the brooch pinned on her dress and puts her hands on him but cannot bear to push him away. She cannot bear that he is gone and that he will never be back. His shock of red hair gone. Her cries become louder until they are a wail. Ginata sits beside her, rocking her, letting her cry, letting her get it all out. She needs to cry, needs to rail against the cruelty of the events of the week. Ginata takes her hand. "It's time."

Everleigh shakes her head, but Ginata takes her hand and helps her to push, to push Archer away, to let him rest in peace.

Everleigh collapses onto the dirty floor, and Ginata quietly watches her.

# Lanorie

I'VE NEVER BEEN IN the tower before and I can tell you I was right scared just standing outside. Cook reckons I'm the best one to take up Addyson's food for the first time, someone she knows, someone to reassure her, and take word to Everleigh that she is alive and well. Cook pretends all she likes to do is gossip and knock the pages over the head with her rolling pin, but she's got a good heart. Hers is an excellent idea, and almost immediately I get an idea of my own.

I run to my room and grab the one bit of my daily dress that I hardly ever bother wearing, a little cap. I tuck my hair into it.

It might be a good idea, but my knees are knocking together thinking about it. I rarely have plans. I'm happy to do as I'm told, never have to wonder, never have to think. Go here, do this, do that, yes princess, no princess... not having a choice is easy, but sometimes the easy option doesn't feel right anymore.

I messed up my friendship with Everleigh when I spilled her secret. She won't say it, but I know it. And I must make it better, somehow.

So, the tower's separate to the main castle and so high that even bending my neck, I can't see the top. Stood right in front of the door is one of the King's men, holding a sword, ready to strike. Frightens me so much the tray of food shakes, ale spilling everywhere.

He looks over at me, a massive scowl on his face, an ugly face he has too. "What?" he says to me, all grumpy.

My voice is a squeak, I'm not ashamed to tell you. "Food. For Addyson." I want to ask him what the heck he thinks I'm doing there with some dinner on a tray. I'm obviously not there to feed him. Fat pig.

He bangs three times on the door with his spare fist and then opens the door. I am shaking as I pass him, hoping he won't attack me and shaking the entire way up the stairs. I have no clue where Addyson is, what room she's in, or anything, but after three lots of twisting stairs and plenty of spilled ale, I come across another one of the King's men.

He's stood in front of a door, facing outwards, a grumpy look on his face. Poor Addyson must be well past petrified, being guarded so closely by these thugs. What Millard expects her to do, I don't know? She's only eleven, hardly an enormous threat to him and all his soldiers.

So, he lets me in and slams the door behind me, happy to leave me on my own with her, after all, I'm no threat, either.

I don't know her half as well as I know Everleigh, but she drops in to my arms straightaway and I hold her tight. I'm not that much older than her really, but I feel older. Her little body is cold, and shaking, her face wet from crying. "It's all right, it's all right, it's all right." I repeat myself, reassuring myself as much as her, I reckon.

"Everleigh's safe. And I'll get you out of here."

She cries even louder then, probably with relief. "I hate it in here. It's so cold, and I'm so hungry. The guards are scary."

"Quiet," I whisper. Poor cursed princess, she may not be well liked in the Realm, people are right superstitious around here, but she's just a little princess. She's always been well looked after. This tower must be the worst thing for her. It's not much warmer or fancier than my little room off the kitchen.

I nod my head. Decision made. Everleigh is my Queen even without a crown on her head, and it's partly, or maybe all, my fault that her father is dead, and her brother and Halfreda and Archer. I told her secret and the stupid boy I'd been kissing went back and told Macsen and Macsen tried to kill everyone before Millard killed everyone else. It's all a mess, and it's all my fault.

I don't want the pigs guarding her to know anything, so I hold a finger to my lips. "I'll swap places with you." Her eyes are wide, mouth open to protest or thank me, I don't know which, but I shake my head quickly.

"I need to do this, then you need to go to Halfreda's room, knock the door and call Everleigh's name. If she doesn't answer, call Will. You need to be quick, and you need to be quiet. Though I don't think those guards are all that smart, and I don't think they'll be expecting anything like this."

I reckon everyone's still a bit shocked by the day's events and I reckon I can do it. I feel sick and excited at the same time. I don't do brave things. I don't do anything. I serve and I wait on people.

But ever since Millard took the crown I have felt like I need to make things better, make what I did wrong better and if I free Addyson I reckon I'll be well on the way.

On the way to Everleigh trusting me again.

I pull off my maid's livery until I'm just in my slip, one of Everleigh's old ones and made of beautiful silver silk. I help Addyson undress, hoping that the guard won't open the door. I don't think he will, why would he? But my movements are clumsy as I untie her laces. Her dress is gorgeous, made of thick embroidered velvet and I will be glad to wear it.

Although we are not much different in size, she looks like a little girl playing dress up in my clothes. She looks so frightened and unsure; but I know I have done the right thing. With her father dead, I have to reunite her with the person who loves her most. It's not fair that that Millard has locked her up.

She smiles at me, her eyes full of unshed tears. "Keep your head down," I tell her, as I tuck her hair into my cap. She'll do it, if she's quick and brave. She'll do it.

"Be quick and brave. Go to Everleigh."

She nods at me, face white and eyes huge.

Before either of us can change our minds, I knock on the door, then sit in the corner, nibbling on the food I brought for Addyson. I hope he will not look too closely at either of us and I whisper, good luck, just before he opens the door.

She walks out with more bravado than I would have in her position and I take a big gulp of ale, hoping I've done the right thing, and hoping Millard won't slice my head off when he finds out what I've done.

# 4

WILL WALKS AS SLOWLY as he is able without angering Wolf, who has a tight hold of his arm, pointlessly trying to delay the inevitable. Though he has no idea what the realities of the inevitable will be; he's sure he won't like them.

Being Everleigh's best friend, but still having a role within the castle – learning the way of the fool – Millard and Macsen were always just her brothers who he tried to entertain. He doesn't know them well at all.

What he saw of Macsen and Millard yesterday has left him quaking, though.

Seeing how Wolf handled Addyson and Everleigh is also making Will nervous.

The walk from Halfreda's room to the new King's room takes an age as he imagines one heart-stopping scenario and another and another, but the walk is also too short.

Two burly guards open the doors when they see Wolf coming; not wanting to keep him waiting.

Millard is standing looking out of the window and turns to greet them.

Will smiles and bows low.

"Will!" Millard sounds pleased to see him and while Will keeps the smile on his face, he feels his insides shrink, as though he wants to make himself smaller; less of a target; invisible. "Where's the handmaiden?" he asks, looking at Wolf.

Wolf shrugs. "Can't find her."

"Send someone to find her. Tell them to keep looking."

Millard strides across the room to Will and claps him on the back.

Will coughs. "Your Grace."

"I can't get used to that," Millard says laughing. "Your Grace. It seems so formal."

Will is silent but smiling; fearing he must look very much the fool.

"So, Will. I saw you helping my dear sister earlier, so chivalrous, so gentlemanly."

Will feels like he is being tricked. Millard is being too nice.

"Where is she?" Millard has his hand on Will's back again, less of a clap, more of a grasp.

Will opens his mouth but cannot force any sound to come out.

Millard grips him harder. "Where is she?"

Wolf steps closer to them. Will does not want him to join in.

"I don't know," he lies with a stammer, and knows he doesn't sound convincing.

Abruptly Millard lets go of his shoulder and paces in front of him. "Let me explain things to you, Will, since you are a fool in the making, maybe more of a fool than less, I'm not sure how learned you are, how bright you are, how clever you are, how much you understand."

He stands still, facing Will. "I have been planning my reign for a very long time. Since I was a little boy. They would talk of Everleigh's role in choosing who would rule, the magic of her blood, the sanctity of the Kingmaker, and as much as I love her, I knew I couldn't let her have a say in choosing who would rule. It couldn't be a random decision made by her blood. I couldn't let her live, sadly. People had to think the blood had chosen me, but I was working out how. Then Macsen, dear Macsen, saved me a lot of trouble, and really... Ha, I've never thought of this, but how similar we were, how alike. He had the same idea as me, and I let him carry on. I didn't realise he'd kill our father, I regret that. He didn't need to die for me to rule. For either of us to rule. And, of course, he'd found out Everleigh's little secret, too."

Will nods along as Millard talks, taking in every word. He doesn't want to be caught out.

"But she lived. I need to know if she will cause me a problem. I need to know where she is. I want to enjoy being King. I want to reign in peace. And though I let her go earlier, I cannot rest, I cannot relax, I am uneasy. Have I got a problem, Will? Is she going to hunt me down, like she said? Put my head on a spike? Let the birds feast on my beautiful face?"

This is a trick. There is no right answer that Will can give here.

"Your Grace." He bows low. "I cannot speak for Everleigh. I am her close friend, but I serve at your pleasure. She has disappeared; I am sure she knows the castle cannot be safe for her. Your Grace, she is your sister, but you are wise enough to want to protect yourself. No one would blame you."

Millard paces again before halting right in front of Will. He moves closer, uncomfortably close. "You say what I want to hear. But is it what you really think?" Closer again, peering at Will's face, trying to see a lie. "How much of a fool are you?"

"I am a fool through and through, but the fool is often the most honest of men. All I say is true."

Millard steps back, mollified. "And you do not know where she is? If I asked you to lead me to her, so I could put her safely with our sister in the tower, would you take me?"

"If I knew where she was, I would help you. I would much rather she was locked up than hurt in any way."

"I know that is true. If I find out you have played me false, Will the fool, you will find that a fool cannot laugh in every situation."

Will bows low again. "Your Grace."

Millard looks at Wolf and nods at him. Will watches him leave. Millard hasn't said a word, so this is a pre-planned move. Will feels uneasy. His ordeal is not over.

"When you said that I am wise, you were so right. I must know for sure whose loyalties are mine and who still serve my sister. After I have spoken to you, I will speak to her handmaiden. You two are closest to her; it hasn't escaped me. Would you like a drink while you wait?"

Wait for what? Will wants to ask, but shakes his head. His stomach is twisting now, and he wouldn't be able to drink anything without spilling it or being sick.

The silence is thick, and Will tries to calm his breathing, tries to think of Everleigh and Lanorie and how, together, they will crown Everleigh and live happily ever after.

The doors bang open and Wolf is walking towards them, with one of the King's men, Brett, struggling to hold on to the fool. Will's father.

Will's father, whose given name is Eldrin but who is only ever referred to as the fool, is upset. He is an affable man, full of silliness and fun, who has never been poorly treated in all his time at the castle. "Unhand me, Wolf man."

Millard nods at Wolf and Brett, who let the fool go. He straightens up, pulling at his funny clothes until he is as smart as a fool can look. He drops into a low bow, the bells on his clothes giving him a musical accompaniment, which would be comical if Will wasn't feeling so sick.

"Your Grace. Is this a lark? Tell me it is."

The hurt on his face makes Will tremble, but he doesn't make a move to reach his father's side; Millard killed his own brother earlier today without a heartbeat of hesitation. Will knows he will kill him if he needs to. As would Wolf, as would Brett, or any of the guards scattered around the room.

"Fool. I apologise. I do, but I must know how loyal my subjects are to me. I hate to use you, but..." Millard shrugs.

The fool looks at his son, his child by fate, and nods his head, just the tiniest movement. It speaks volumes to Will. He nods back.

Millard paces around, reaches for a goblet, takes a deep slug before turning back to them.

"Tell me again, Will. Do you know where Everleigh is?"

Will shakes his head, forcing his words out. "I do not."

Wolf slips his dagger from its holder and brings it to the fool's neck.

"Where is she?"

Will takes a deep breath, apologising in his head to his beloved father, no fool at all, and speaks his lie again. "I do not know."

Millard nods to Wolf, who gently pricks the fool's flesh. A trickle of blood rolls down his neck, staining his skin.

"Where?"

"I do not know."

Millard nods to Wolf once more, and, after several beats of hesitation, he pushes the fool away from him, to the floor. The fool clutches the wound on his neck, tiny but still bleeding. Will wants to drop beside him but stays upright.

"I believe you," Millard says. "And as you know so little, you truly are a fool. Your father can retire from his duties. He was my father's fool, not mine. You will be mine and I expect you to make me laugh. Always."

# Ginata

WE SIT ON THE ISLAND for what seems like hours, but I know from the sun isn't long at all. My heart wants to break for this young girl, not so much younger than me that I could be her mother, but young enough that I feel maternal towards her. She has been cosseted all her life, looked after and mollycoddled. She cannot look after herself and yet she will have to.

I think my idea that she should go to my cottage is good. I don't know why I didn't think of it sooner. I don't think she's safe to even stay a night here. Who knows how long Millard will be happy to let her live. Who knows with this changeable, difficult, spoiled child of a King?

Della can look after her to a certain extent, but she will have to wash and dress herself; how ridiculous that she cannot even do that. I have lived a long time on my own, since my parents died, and I enjoy my self-sufficiency, love my independence. This princess does not understand. They bring food to her, her bed is warmed for her, they manage her in everything she does.

I need to get her back to Halfreda's and I need to get her cleaned up and then we need to move her. If I send her on her way with a few sleeping draughts, some potions to pep her up, maybe Della can keep her safe and well until Millard's coronation.

It's not long.

The courtyard is relatively quiet, and we sneak back to Halfreda's rooms easily. Will is back, brooding in front of the fire.

When he sees Everleigh he bursts out crying, something I've never seen him do. Everleigh runs to hug him and I think it's good for her to have to take care of him; it will help her come out of the fugue she's been in today.

"What happened? What did he do?"

"Nothing, nothing." Between sobs Will tells us about his father and the threat to his life, about Millard's questioning of him and his new role as the fool.

"You are safe. You are safe. You are safe." She whispers it like a mantra, and I realise again how much she has lost in such a brief space of time.

They hug, and I busy myself in Halfreda's bathroom, getting some water from the jugs on to the fire to ready a bath for Everleigh. The last one she will have for a while. She has blood on her clothes, and her hair is matted. She will feel better if she looks better and she can be on her way.

I realise that I have quickly slipped into Halfreda's role of caretaker, caregiver. I am quietly taking charge of this little band of people, and I care about them. I have been alone for a long time, with enough friends – Della, Finn, Halfreda – that I never felt alone. It's never been an issue; I like my own company.

I feel responsible now for these three youngsters, four if you count Addyson.

There's a knock at the door and I go through so that Everleigh and Will can hide.

"Everleigh!"

Even I recognise Addyson's voice, but I am not quick enough to stop Everleigh rushing to answer the door. It might be a trap, is what I'm worrying, but she runs to the door and lets her in. Only her.

Addyson is dressed in Lanorie's clothes, and I cannot help but smile. I would never have thought it of Lanorie, after spilling Everleigh's secret and her stupid stunt of trying to kill herself. She hasn't struck me as clever enough or loyal enough or nice enough.

Maybe she is trying to atone for all that has happened. She's done a wonderful job.

Everleigh is beaming. "How?" Even as she asks, I see her come to the same realisation as I did. And she laughs. "She took your place?"

Will has turned almost green. "He will kill her."

I hadn't thought of that, but of course he will. If Millard finds out about the deception, he will be furious. He won't worry about killing some little handmaiden, when he was happy to kill his brother, to kill Halfreda, to kill Archer. I mustn't forget in the quiet aftermath of such an awful day what he is capable of, my new King, my new master. A chill runs through me.

"We'll get her out." Everleigh puts her hand on his arm, looking right into his eyes. "We'll get her out. I'll make sure of it."

I cannot think how, but she is right. We have to help her; we have to rescue her. She cannot let Lanorie die for her sacrifice, the same as she didn't let Will.

Everleigh holds Addyson tightly, and I can tell she doesn't want to let her go. They are both crying. "Did Wolf hurt you?" Everleigh's voice is harsh. We all feel the same about Wolf. I remember him leaning nonchalantly outside my little cottage waiting for Macsen. Macsen wouldn't have known he had been betrayed. Not a loyal man or a good man. Serving the King happily for now, but could he trust him? I know I won't. If I have anything to do with him. I'm now living in a state of high alert, keeping my wits about me will keep me alive.

"A little, but only when he tied me up and pulled me about. He wasn't cruel."

"This has to end. Today." Everleigh's voice is hard and I move towards her. I need to get them moving. I need to keep them both safe. We must get them to my cottage before too long. The sun is setting, the dusk creeping in.

Everleigh hugs Addyson tight to her again and then sits her in front of the fire; I can see her shivering, but I don't think it's from the cold. Poor baby is probably petrified. I go to fetch her a little something to help her from Halfreda's bottles and jars.

"Do we have food?" Everleigh is asking. It's an age since we ate breakfast, too much has happened to think about food, but suddenly my stomach rumbles like thunder.

Will shakes his head. "I'll get some."

"Be careful."

"I think I've faced the worst for now."

He slips out of the room.

"We need to get you both away from here." My voice is quiet; I don't want to frighten Addyson. "He has forgotten about you, but he will remember. He'll kill you both."

Everleigh shakes her head. "Not if I kill him first."

# 5

"NO!" GINATA'S VOICE is sharper than she intends and Addyson whimpers.

"Ginata, I have to try."

"Trying will get you killed. You don't *try* to kill a madman like your brother. If you're going to *try* you better be damn sure you'll succeed, or he will kill you. You can't have a doubt. He will not keep you alive for love, or loyalty, or sibling nostalgia. You must know it."

Everleigh nods; she knows it, but since she has come back from the island, since she pushed the people she loved into the water, a tightening has been forming around her stomach. She can barely breathe for the knowledge that the man who did this, the man who killed her brother, Halfreda, Archer, is laughing, joking, eating and drinking, full of merriment at his newfound Kingship at so many other's expense. She cannot live while he lives. She cannot rest. She must do this.

Fury will help her win this. She is sure.

Will slips back into the room. They hadn't even locked it after him.

Ginata puts a hand to her heart. "See! We have gotten sloppy just in the last ten minutes. He will kill us all if he finds us here. Eat something and we'll get you away from here."

Will, unaware of Everleigh's declaration of murderous intent, passes around bread, cheese and some sweet honey cakes. Ginata brings a jug of ale and some cups.

Ginata talks while she eats. "We need to get the two of you away from here. My neighbour, Della, and her brother will look after you. I don't think Millard would think to look for you there. Will, you can ask Cook where they keep the clothes for the servants –

not the livery – just the most basic of slips and dresses. I've got water warming for a bath. We need to rush but if we can get you both cleaned up and dressed and out of here, Will and I will get to tonight's feast and Millard will be none the wiser."

Will is nodding while he eats, pleased that someone else is taking control. Pleased that Everleigh and Addyson will be safe, but still worried about Lanorie. "What about Lanorie?" he asks. "We can't just leave her in the tower."

Ginata shrugs. "I really don't know. I know we need to get her out of there, but I'm not sure how. I need time to think."

"She is probably safe for tonight, at least," Everleigh says as she wanders over to Halfreda's work space, nibbling on a honey cake; she needs a weapon if she will kill her brother and she knows Halfreda kept a sharp knife for cutting plants for her potions.

"I agree," Ginata says; Will looks unsure. "He will make merry; he believes Addyson is safely locked up. He won't visit her tonight."

Everleigh finds the knife in a drawer, bone handled, with a viciously serrated edge. She slips it in to the folds of her cloak, ready to take away with her. If she can kill her brother tonight, she can rescue Lanorie and take her crown. If she has her way, her brother won't even get to wake up one morning as King.

Will goes to fetch clothes and Ginata helps the two girls wash and dry. With great care, Everleigh unpins the brooch from her beautiful dress that she should have been crowned in, and when Will brings the clothes they will wear when they escape, she pins it to the plain and slightly shabby uniform, just under the hem where no one will see it.

Wrapped in cloaks, they sit together in front of the fire. "I'm so scared," Addyson whispers.

Everleigh takes her hand. "Me too."

She must fix this. Addyson may be the cursed princess, but she has never been frightened for her life until today. She has lost both of her parents, felt the hatred from her father because of her awful curse, lived with other people's fear and suspicions for eleven years, almost twelve. Everleigh has to protect her.

Ginata brushes and plaits Everleigh's hair first and then does the same for Addyson.

"How do we look?" Everleigh asks when Ginata's done. She doesn't look like a princess or a Queen, but that is what they want.

"Will, you stay here, I'll take them to my cottage. I can introduce them to my neighbours. They'll look out keep for you both."

The longer they are at the castle, the more likely it is that he will find them.

Will hugs Everleigh tightly, and then hugs Addyson too. "Be safe. I'll come down to see you tomorrow."

Everleigh nods. She has never slept a night outside of the castle her whole life long. She feels stripped of everything that makes her, her. Her clothes, her family, friends.

Everleigh is no more and someone needs to pay.

"Ginata, could I have a few sleeping draughts, please. I'm not sure how we'll sleep tonight."

Ginata fetches half a dozen vials and then they quietly slip away.

The walk to the cottage is eventless, which is what they all wanted. "At least you will be at peace here, no need to fear every knock at the door. The entire village knows by now that I have moved to the castle, so you won't have anyone looking for a love potion."

"Good." Everleigh smiles. Maybe a few hours of peace will help focus her mind and heart on what she needs to do. Kill her brother and rescue Lanorie. "What are your neighbours called?"

"Della and Finn. Brother and sister."

"And they're nice?"

"Wonderful."

"I'm scared."

"I know..."

Ginata opens the little cottage up and leaves the front door wedged open. "Get some fresh air in here."

She opens the window and starts setting a fire.

Everleigh looks around. The cottage is tiny, but clean. Most of Ginata's things have been moved, so the shelves are all but empty – there are a few bottles and vials, a big copper-bottomed pan – and the place looks bare. But Everleigh can see that it would have been comfy and cosy. As the flames in the fire lick upwards, she can imagine how nice it would have been for Ginata living here. No stress, no worries, no duty. Answerable only to herself.

Free.

"It's lovely, Ginata. Really. Thank you."

Ginata smiles and hugs Everleigh and then Addyson. They sit on the only two chairs there and Ginata pokes at the fire, stoking the flames.

"I'll tell Della that you're here and explain things."

Ginata leaves them alone and Everleigh reaches for Addyson's hand. "I'm so sorry. For everything. For father. For pretending I was dead. I had to. I wanted to tell you, but I couldn't risk you knowing. Risk Macsen hurting you."

"I hate our brothers. I'm glad Macsen is dead."

"Addyson!"

"They never loved me like you loved me. Father never loved me either. How can I mourn a father when I never really had one?"

Everleigh's heart breaks at the words. She thought she had felt so much pain on this day that she could feel no more. That she would be numb, immune from it. But Addyson's words have hurt her once again.

Her father had been a wonderful father to her, Macsen and Millard. She knows he wasn't fair on Addyson; it's why she has always felt so maternal towards her.

"I'm so sorry, darling."

Everleigh holds her arms out, and Addyson sits on her lap, cuddling in close.

They sit, giving each other strength and support while they wait for Ginata.

"I will always look after you. I will always do everything within my power to keep you safe. I hate that you hurt. I hate your curse."

"I hate my curse too. But I love you and I know I'm safe with you."

They have never really talked about Addyson's curse. What was there to say? The same as Everleigh's role was Kingmaker, Addyson had always been the cursed princess. Since their poor mother died giving birth to her, the Realm, her brothers and the King most of all, could not forgive her or look past it. She is cursed, and that gave them all the excuse they needed to abandon her. They were always there, but they never loved her or cared for her; never showed her genuine affection or consideration. She was just someone to put up with.

"Will people ever see past it? My curse?"

"I do. Others will. Ginata doesn't seem to care. Nor Will. Nor Lanorie."

Addyson doesn't reply, just cuddles in closer.

Everleigh watches the flames; she can think of so many reasons to kill her brother but none to keep him alive.

# Ceryn

SO IT'S DECIDED. I knew it would be. I can't say any of us is in charge, but Weaver is happier to go with the flow, than either me or Archer. Weaver's a thinker, I'm a doer. Archer probably sits between us.

Both of our rabbits are gone, bones sucked dry, dogs munching on what's left. The skins are drying outside, on a line, and no doubt Weaver will use them for something. We waste little; don't have enough to waste.

I have packed up a bag, with some flasks of water, a blanket; I have my bow and arrow, a dagger in my boot. I tie my mask on and I'm ready to go.

Weaver has gone to gather his stuff and we'll meet back here before heading to the castle. He reckons a few days; I reckon we can do it faster. If we don't hit trouble and ride through tonight, I reckon we'll get there tomorrow. It'll be late, but we'll make it.

Halfreda will look after us, we'll probably sleep wherever Archer is and come home with him the next day.

I head out to my horse, Pitch – she's as black as Archer's, but his horse is called Ink. I scratch her behind her ear and ask her to ride us safely to Archer. She whinnies like she knows what I'm saying, maybe she does, and I pat her softly, singing to her, cooing to her. I like her best out of anyone in the world. Maybe I like Weaver and Archer just as much, probably less. I don't like many people. Many people don't like me.

Weaver trots up on his horse, his bag strapped over his back, a smile on his face. Life is wonderful for Weaver. Even the King's men, who hate us, like Weaver.

"Ready?" He asks, though he can see the answer.

"Absolutely."

"We may have news of the new King further along the road."

"True."

We don't get to hear much of what goes on at the castle, nor do we care to hear it. The King's men cause us enough trouble in the tiny villages they torment, we don't care to hear of their jousts and plays and feasts.

Riding along together, I can feel Archer's absence keenly, and I know I am right to worry.

We hit our first bit of trouble just ten minutes from my cottage and it angers me. Trouble will only slow us down, and I want to be quick.

The scene is all too familiar: since the King's men love to lord it over the villagers, the villagers like to get their own back in small, anonymous but irritating ways. They cause aggravation and there's no way of knowing who did it, so the King's men are angry but impotent and the villagers enjoy a moment of quiet victory.

Today, they have tied all the horse's legs together; cruel to the horses, but the villagers don't care, when the King's men are so cruel to them.

The King's men have finished their business and gone to ride away, the horses have fallen in a heap of tied together limbs and the King's men are roaring in fury, embarrassment and pain last of all.

We slow to a stop next to the jumble of men and horses, both trying not to laugh.

"It's not bloody funny." Brett, one we've had several run-ins with shouts as he staggers to his feet. He pulls a dagger from his boot, though it obviously pains him – both hands are bandaged tightly – and starts cutting the ropes away.

The villagers come to observe the fun, forming a circle around the scene. The children are laughing and pointing; the adults acting only slightly more grown up.

One little boy throws an egg, before ducking out of the way.

The yolk runs down one of the King's men's faces and he howls out a threat. An empty one, we all know, but the anger is mounting.

"Leave us alone, you bunch of bullies," someone shouts, and again, you couldn't tell the culprit; they all look alike, sound alike, are as angry as the next.

We grin at each other, we're used to this and hoping that it will fizzle out, as most of the troubles do, when a stone lands at Brett's feet. He jumps back, looking around for whoever did it.

Someone throws another one, and even from up high on my mount I can't see who did it, but it lands with more accuracy, hitting another one of the King's men on the knee. Brett jumps up, brandishing his dagger.

Weaver hops down from his horse and calls for the crowd to move back; most of them listen; they like us because they know we aim to help them. Sometimes a fight isn't what's needed; sometimes words work and there's no point causing trouble for the sake of it, and I love a good fight.

"Back off, back off," Weaver calls out, and again the crowd move back. Brett cuts the rest of the ropes and the men help the horses to their feet. Nobody is injured; the men are just annoyed, but they mount up quickly. Probably wanting to leave before anything else is thrown at them.

As I turn to watch Weaver jump back on his horse, I see a flash of movement and, thwack, someone throws another stone, more of a rock, and it cracks down on Brett's horse, right in its eye. The horse neighs in pain and drops to the floor. Brett is thrown off again, and this time his fury is palpable. A bit of me doesn't blame him.

Weaver rides his horse at the crowd, which is thinning, and people seem happy to back off. Looking around, they seem as upset as Brett is. No one likes the King's men: there's a definite feel of 'us versus them', but ultimately, they are just doing their job. Things rarely escalate like this, and few of the villagers would hurt a horse; they aren't at fault at all.

"Who did it?" I shout out, angry, and upset.

I know it was an accident to hurt the horse, but whoever threw the rock was stupid enough not to be sure of a true aim before they attacked.

No one answers me, but I knew they wouldn't. A joke or a prank against the King's men is one thing, but it's stupid to start a fight. They are all armed; they are all trained in fighting and some of them are nasty, just looking for something to rally against.

This is the last thing we need.

Maeve, one of the nicest villagers, hands up in surrender, moves to the horse. It's probably been blinded in the one eye and is jumpy. Maeve coos to it and smooths along its nose. Her daughter brings her some water, cloths, ointment.

Brett nods at her and she works on the horse, trying to patch it up so it will have a more comfortable ride back to the castle, or whatever inn the men are staying at.

"Can we leave things peaceful here?" Weaver asks him, as I watch Maeve at work; the horse is calm and accepting her tending to him.

Brett nods, but he's angry. "Only because we didn't see who did it and no doubt they're too cowardly to own up."

I agree with him again, and it worries me. I have little in common with the King's men, usually.

"Any news from the castle?" I ask, patting his horse. "Which prince was crowned?"

I know the princes from their travels, they like to visit the villagers, mingle with the common folk, not that I've ever sat and dined with them. Nothing like that. "Did the Kingmaker cry when her throat was cut?" The Kingmaker I never met; she had no reason to travel to our village, and I had no reason to travel to her castle. Unlike Archer.

"The Kingmaker is alive," Brett says, pushing his dagger back into his boot. "One of the princes killed his brother and so we have a new King."

"Really?" Weaver looks surprised, but only because he can't imagine anyone looking for trouble like that. Despite what us three get up to, Weaver is the most placid person I know.

"The new King is Millard."

I shrug, as does Weaver. Which one of the cosseted princes has a bigger crown on his head now isn't really a concern to us. Whoever is in charge will tax the poor and look after his own. We will still have to battle the King's men, who cause so much trouble for us, whoever wears the crown.

We are back on our horses and ready to ride off. "We are headed to the castle, looking for a friend of ours."

"Good luck," Brett says, grinning. "There's even more people there than there was for the feast. Everyone wants to meet the mad King."

Again, who is or is not King doesn't matter to me, nor how mad he might be. We just need to get moving and moving quick.

The crowd has completely cleared and so with a nod to the men we head to the castle, hoping the way ahead is clear.

# 6

GINATA COMES BACK INTO her little cottage with a woman in tow. She is older than Ginata, but not old enough to be her mother. She is as fair-haired as Ginata is dark-haired, and has a kindly face, and soft eyes.

"This is Della, Della this is Everleigh, and her sister, the princess Addyson."

Della bows to them both and then takes Addyson's hands. "You must have been so scared. You too, my Queen, but you more little lamb."

Everleigh smiles. She loves this woman already. No one ever pays more attention to Addyson than to her. No one ever touches Addyson unless they have to. No one has ever spoken so kindly to her, who wasn't related to her or paid to.

"Ginny's told me everything, I hope you don't mind me knowing, Queen, but I will do everything I can. I will look after you both until whatever happens next."

"Thank you." Everleigh sits down, watching Della chat to Addyson in front of the fire, touching her plaited hair, laughing at something she says and for the first time since Archer's death, she feels a peace settle over her.

There is plenty to do, but for a moment she closes her eyes. She is safe. Will is safe. Ginata is safe. Addyson is safe. Lanorie is the only one she has a slight fear for, and yet, she thinks it's unlikely Millard will get to her before she does and so she smiles.

It's been an awful day, but by the time the sun comes up tomorrow she will have done it. She will risk no one else's life; she will go to the castle alone, once Addyson is sleeping and she will kill

Millard. Before he does any more damage, and more importantly, before he finds Lanorie or Addyson or her.

She tunes out of the quiet conversation around her, slipping into a dream, then a word or a laugh wakes her up, before she drifts off again. In this world between waking and sleeping she is calm, can pretend that all the horrible things that happened this week, didn't.

Would it have been easier for everyone had they had sacrificed her as any other Kingmaker? Definitely. Her father would still be dead, though, and Millard would still have killed Macsen to become King, and so not everything would be better. But she wouldn't be here to feel the pain, that would be better, but then who would protect Addyson? No one else but her.

There are always reasons to want a different outcome to what there is and yet she is glad to be alive. Addyson's laugh nudges her away from sleep and her smile widens. Della will be wonderful for Addyson. Everleigh thinks she could ask her to move into the castle when she is Queen. Addyson needs people in her life that aren't frightened of, or repulsed by, her curse. Della is obviously neither.

They are talking a little louder now, all feeling safe and more relaxed, away from the castle, away from Millard, away from the death of the day.

Della is talking, her voice is low and lilting, musical, almost, to listen to. Ginata didn't mention any husband or children for her, only a brother, but she would make a superb mother, bedtime stories would be heaven with her sweet voice.

Everleigh tunes in and out, her body sinking so deep into the chair, she doubts she could move if Millard ran into the cottage brandishing his sword. Her limbs are liquid, and she feels happy for the first time since she opened her presents that morning. Is it still her birthday? That doesn't even make sense.

Archer died on her birthday. How would she ever enjoy another year's passing again?

She opens her eyes. "Ginata, I've just remembered the stupidest thing."

"What?"

"It's still my birthday." Suddenly Everleigh is both crying and laughing, smiling and sobbing, as both Addyson and Ginata hug her, both laughing and crying with her.

"I'll be glad when it's over. Your birthday," Addyson says, wiping at her tears. "By your next birthday things will be better."

"I was supposed to die today," Everleigh says, regaining some composure. "Instead my brother, Halfreda and my beloved Archer died. How will I get over it?" As she asks, she answers it in her own head, by killing the man who did it.

Della stands up, straightening her shawl. "I'll fetch some food from mine. Sorry again that Finn isn't here to greet you. He's out and about all the time and I don't know half of what he gets up to. He's only a year older than you, Queen, so younger than me, and he tells me I nag him like a mother, but then I'll be doing the same to you two within a day, so I hope you'll forgive me."

Everleigh laughs. "Thank you, Della. You don't know what it means to me, to us, to have somewhere safe to lay our heads, and someone speaking so kindly to us."

Della nods and leaves the cottage. Ginata smiles at them both. "Isn't she lovely?"

They both nod, and Addyson sits by the fire. "I don't feel so scared with her next door."

"Do you want her to sleep in here with you both tonight? She wouldn't mind, I'm sure."

"Yes, please." Everleigh had been worried about leaving Addyson sleeping alone while she ventured to the castle.

"I'll ask her when she comes back in."

Della comes back and insists she is happy to sleep in the cottage with them. She has food and ale but Ginata declines. "I need to get back to the castle. There is to be a feast, and I dare not miss it. I have to keep on your brother's good side. The sleeping draughts are on the table. If you need them, take them a half hour before you want to sleep, just a few drops – any more will knock you out."

Everleigh and Addyson both nod. Everleigh will make Addyson take it and pretend to take it herself.

After Ginata leaves, the three of them sit and, once again, a wave of peace settles over Everleigh. This is a safe place; Addyson will be safe while she kills Millard.

Della takes the lead, entertaining them with stories of hapless villagers who knock on her door by mistake looking for anything from a love potion to rat poison. Both girls are enjoying the feeling of safety, the warmth of the fire. Addyson's eyes are drooping. "Take this." Everleigh opens the vial and squeezes three drops onto her tongue. It will ensure she sleeps soundly through the night and doesn't wake up to find Everleigh missing.

"I may slip out for fresh air in the night," she whispers to Della, not wanting Addyson to hear.

"Do not venture far, Queen. I have sworn to keep you safe."

"I know. And I thank you for it. And when I can reward you for it, I promise I will."

# Lanorie

SO THERE'S FEW TIMES in my life that I wish I hadn't done something that I had. When I told Everleigh's secret, that was one time. There was a time I pinched a bit of cake off Cook, and she rapped my knuckles so hard, it wasn't worth it.

And now.

Sitting in the tower.

By myself.

Alone.

Cold.

Hungry.

When I think about Everleigh, and I think how pleased she must be with me, then I feel a bit better. A little bit proud of myself, like people would be surprised by me. Impressed with me.

Then I hear the guard outside coughing or spitting on the floor and I'm crying again, thinking no enjoyable feeling is worth the trouble I'm in.

What Everleigh or anyone else might think about me, means nothing, really, because in here by myself I can only pretend what they might think or say and it's nothing compared to what I can see and what I feel.

The only real thing is the cold, bare room. The cold, hard bed, with one threadbare blanket, the cold, tasteless food. Only cold because of the trek from the kitchen to the tower, and only tasteless because I feel so sick, I could suck sugar off my fingers and it would be tasteless.

The little maid who brought me food, a little supper, because Cook felt sorry for Addyson, nearly died when she saw me, and I swore her to secrecy. Let's hope she's better at secrets than I am or what'll become of me?

Well, I know what will become of me. If Millard finds out about me.

I have seen the madness in Millard's eyes. For every bit of handsome he's got; something's gone wrong inside him.

Cook gave me the most beautiful little cake once, it was a honey cake, with frosting on top, and a load of chopped nuts just sprinkled over it. I bit in to it and tasted something wrong with my tongue. When I looked, I fainted dead, and after I woke up, poor Cook was most upset. There was a maggot inside it. Well, it wasn't Cook's fault, so I wasn't cross with her. Long time till I ate another cake, though, I can tell you.

Well, Millard is that cake. He is most beautiful on the outside, tall, broad shouldered, dark haired and dark eyed. But on the inside, he is rotten. He is maggoty.

I feel clever thinking of that by myself.

And then I feel stupid again, because I remember that I have got myself locked in a room, when after all the horrible things that happened today, I was one of the lucky ones. I was safe, I still had my head, but now I have got myself locked up.

The guard didn't even look my way when the little maid came in – that was something. I had been worrying that he would see me and kill me without a word when he realised that Addyson was gone. But he didn't even look at me.

Being alone is not good for me, I think terrible things.

I will have a cold and lonely night and then the guard will look at me tomorrow. He will call for Millard, who will be furious. He won't even just kill me quickly. No, because I was so clever, and let Addyson escape. He will want to know where she is. I've heard about torture, and I can't hold out from him, if he puts a rat anywhere near me, or tries to stretch me on a, who even knows what it's called, I'll just tell him.

And then what good is my outstanding idea then?

When I am dead.

# 7

EVERLEIGH LISTENS TO Addyson's breathing, steady and deep, and then Della's, not as deep, but steady.

She is ready. She cannot wait any longer. She does not want to sleep while Millard is King. She wants him dead.

It is late enough that she is sure the feast will be over, and her brother in bed. If she has mistimed it, she will wait. What else can she do?

Her servant clothes are not as thick as her own, but she puts Della's cloak over hers, so she will be warm enough. She slips two vials of the sleeping draught in her pocket, but keeps the knife in her hand.

She may run into trouble on the way to the castle, and she has to be able to defend herself; nothing can stop this.

Kissing Addyson softly on her forehead, and whispering a thank you to Della, she slips out in to the night.

It's a clear night, the sky cloudless, the stars bright, lighting up the Realm. She hurries quietly, with her head down and the knife ready.

The closer she gets, the faster she goes, until she is running. She forces herself to slow to a walk again. She needs to be quiet and careful, not loud and careless.

As she walks, she whispers the names of the dead, the people Millard has killed. "Macsen, Halfreda, Archer. Macsen, Halfreda, Archer."

All the death is for nothing until she has the crown on her head or at least off his.

The castle looms ahead of her, and tears prick her eyes, she wasn't expecting that, but this has always been her home, a safe and happy place, full of people who love her and care for her, look after her. Now it seems like a hard place, an unforgiving place where hurtful things happen. She looks over at the tower, sending Lanorie a silent message, I'm on my way.

It seems quiet and so she is sure the feast is over. She slips through the courtyard, cloak low on her face, ready to duck into the shadows if she needs to. She knows every twist and turn of the inside and the outside of the castle, and there are plenty of places to tuck herself away if anyone comes, but it is silent. She is sure Millard is exhausted after his busy day and that he's sleeping. She's sure the guards are all happy to see the end of the day as well and maybe off their game a little bit; not paying attention.

She heads to the kitchen first; she wants to catch one of the little maids. She needs just a little bit of help to deliver the sleeping draughts to the two, hopefully just two, guards on his door.

She hunkers down next to a wall and watches. There's light coming from the kitchen and she's sure Cook is busy clearing up after the feast. It takes a while but her patience is rewarded; one of the little maids comes out carrying two ale jugs. She comes to stand near Everleigh and starts pouring the contents away. Everleigh doesn't want to scare her too much, so she slips the dagger into the folds of Della's cloak and moves quietly into her sight, "Hey."

The little maid jumps, but only a bit.

"Princess." She drops into a curtsey, and Everleigh smiles at her.

"Thank you. Can you help me, please? And not tell anyone?"

The little maid nods; she has looked after Everleigh more than a hundred times and would do anything for her.

Everleigh closes her eyes in relief. "I don't even know your name." Suddenly Everleigh feels guilty, so many little maids have looked after her, they had seemed almost interchangeable to her. How awful.

"Molly."

"Well, Molly, I can never thank you enough, but when I am Queen, I will try."

Molly smiles. "I would do anything to serve you, no matter what."

"Can you fetch me two cups of wine?"

Molly nods and takes the jugs back to the kitchen.

She quickly comes back out. "Cook was in the store cupboard. She didn't see me."

"Thank you." Everleigh slips the vials from her pockets and empties one into each cup.

"Can you take them to the guards outside the King's door? With some food, maybe? Say that Cook doesn't want the food to go to waste?"

Little Molly looks at the cups warily, but nods straightaway.

"It won't kill them, only send them to sleep. So I can talk to my brother."

Molly nods again, looking happier. She leaves the wine with Everleigh and slips back to the kitchen. When she comes out, she's holding a tray with a selection of little cakes and some cheeses.

Everleigh puts the wine on the tray and Molly heads towards the castle. "From Cook." Everleigh just wants to remind her. "So it doesn't go to waste."

Molly turns back and nods.

Everleigh hunkers down with her back against the wall, waiting.

Cook throws out some scraps, and another little maid scurries off towards the castle. Watching them Everleigh feels sad. It's her birthday – the worst day of her life – people are dead, but life goes on for others. Nothing has changed for Cook. She will cook for one King or another, or a Queen or anyone who pays her. The little maid would scurry around whether it was Cook giving the orders or someone else.

Everleigh's life is on pause until they crown her Queen, the pain of death a physical sharpness inside her chest, an actual weight on her shoulders. Everyone else is carrying on regardless, but she cannot.

She will sneak inside the castle, make her way to Millard's rooms and put her plan into action; she cannot wait any longer.

She hears footsteps and ducks behind a curtain. She holds her breath as the person passes and then sneaks a look. A page, probably heading to the kitchen. She waits for a moment, then starts slowly and stealthily along the corridor again.

Millard's rooms are close to her own and a bit of her wants to visit them, slip back into the past, pretend this day never started.

It cannot be, and so she keeps going to Millard's rooms.

She stands around the corner. And listens. She cannot hear anyone and usually the guards would chat and laugh.

Taking a deep breath, she risks a look around the corner at Millard's door. The guards are there, slumped on the floor, an empty tray next to them and the two cups of sleeping draught laced wine, laying on the floor, empty.

Everleigh smiles.

This.

This is what she has been waiting for since Millard slashed his sword against Archer's innocent body.

# Ginata

AND THIS DAY IS DONE. I have never been so happy to see the back of a day, the deepening of the dark, and the stars peering through the black above with a soft and reassuring glow; some things remain the same.

I stand in the doorway of my new rooms and give a sigh, a small sigh of contentment. This is the only agreeable thing to have come out of this mess.

When Millard first had a maid show me my new rooms, I felt uneasy. A King had died in these rooms.

But my superstitious nature quickly gave way.

The rooms are beautiful. Three interlocking rooms. All my own. Each one at least three times larger than my entire two-room cottage.

I allow myself a bit of satisfaction as I survey them now: my rooms. Millard has done a wonderful job of making them up for me, all signs of his father gone.

This first room is a receiving room. I have no idea what that even means, but it's a little like a front room, only huge and grand and sumptuous. There are three windows along the side, so they will flood the room with daylight come the morning. Now the drapes are closed, thick drapes, made with better quality fabric than any of my clothes; silver and shimmery. In front of each window is a seat. Each seat is covered in fabric and adorned with cushions. There are three free standing chairs, plump and cushioned, and two sofas that could fit three people sitting side by side.

There are rugs on the floor and hangings on the wall. In my entire life, I would never have lived somewhere so wonderful, were it not for the death of my wonderful friend Halfreda. And though I know it was her plan for me to take over her role here, and that she was at the end of her life regardless of Millard's sword, I feel sad and guilty.

I sit in one of my plump chairs, feet on a footstool, a blanket behind me to drape over my lap should I feel a chill, and I wonder at the change in my circumstances.

Have I made a deal with the devil?

Is that what this is?

I stand up and wander through to my second room, a work room. Shelf after shelf of root, plant, petal, potion, lotion, bottles, jars, vials in every size. The smell is wonderful and smothering at the same time, filling my head and making it ache.

On a table, next to some chairs, is a tottering pile of Halfreda's work books, her 'spell' books, her recipes for this and that. In one of them is the list of ingredients and the steps to make a death draught.

What if I killed Millard myself?

I dismiss that thought with a shake of my head. Despite what Macsen did with the draught Halfreda and I made, I cannot bear even the thought of doing the same thing. Poison is the coward's way out. Maybe what I am doing is the same. Pretending to serve when I don't, but I know I will sleep soundly tonight, regardless.

And in a beautiful bed!

I laugh aloud at my wickedness, but by the gods, these rooms are a delight.

This, I head to the third room, is my private room, a bed and a bath and some chairs, my things from home, for me to place where I choose. My clothes and some new ones.

I have a maid; she has other duties, and I can dress myself at my age, but she will ready me a bath and bring me food if I don't eat in the great hall. I will have fires lit for me and food brought to me, even in the dead of night, if I choose.

I have choices now.

I have never had much of a choice. I could barter a potion for a chicken rather than a piece of lamb if I preferred. I could bathe in the river in the morning and sweep the floors in the afternoon, or if the fancy took me do it the other way around.

But now I have some sway. I have a say in the world. I have someone to wait on me.

Oh, how different Everleigh's life is to my own, and this is only a tiny taste of what she has always had.

I pull back the covers on my bed, a bed that would fit five people, should the need arise, and the fabric is as soft as I imagine a cloud to be, and there is a hot brick just sitting on the sheets, wrapped in silk, warming my bed, but not getting it dirty.

After living through today, and then Millard's request for a coronation just for himself, and the feast which had him grinning, laughing, smiling, joking, drinking, singing. I deserve this.

I have a jug of ale and one of wine on the table beside my bed, should I be thirsty in the night, a plate of food, bread, cheese, cakes, in case I am peckish, a fire roaring and a heavy feeling in my body.

This is payment for all that I have done.

Given the death draught to Macsen, which he used to kill the King.

Stood by while Millard killed his brother and Halfreda.

Offered to crown him when no one else could.

Watched him kill Archer.

Watched him lock Addyson away in the tower.

Watched him drive Everleigh away from her home, her crown, her birthright with threats.

This is my payment.

And for tonight I am too tired to do anything but enjoy it.

# 8

EVERLEIGH STEPS BETWEEN the two guards, their swords slack at their sides, their mouths just as slack, and wet with dribble. She cannot help but smile. Give even the most hardened guards some food and wine and their defences drop to zero.

Sleeping like babies, snoring like fools.

The door to Millard's room isn't locked, it need not be with two burly guards stood outside. She opens it with the slightest of clicks and closes it softly behind her.

His receiving room is empty, though the candles are still lit, and she quickly moves through it. There is no guard outside the door to his bedroom and she knows he sleeps alone.

He had always had a page on a pallet at the bottom of his bed, but several weeks ago, he decided he needed one place where he had peace. It would be his downfall now.

She puts her ear to the door and listens. He could be awake, he could still have company in there.

She hears nothing.

How long can she stay here wondering? She has to make a choice.

She closes her eyes. Pictures her father, her other murderous brother, Halfreda and finally Archer. His shock of red hair, his handsome face. She remembers the prophecy, Halfreda's teacher, who brought it to show her. When she made the river rise. When she saved the deer. All the things that helped her to believe that she could be Queen, that she could live, after her entire life long she had prepared herself to die on her seventeenth birthday, sacrificed as all Kingmakers are and were before her.

And yet here she is, alive.

Ready.

Ready to kill.

She opens the door.

Millard's bed is straight ahead of her, she can see the shape of him under the covers, the slight glow of a candle lighting him up, making him a target.

She closes the door with the softest of clicks, and then moves towards him, stands next to him.

Oh, he's so handsome, this brother of hers. Asleep, he looks like a painting or a statue, perfectly formed with an artist's hand. Every feature pleasing to the eye, every part of him so lovely. He looks like a King; handsome and strong. And he can behave like a King, kind and fair... when he's not killing everyone.

She wipes at the tear slowly slipping down her cheeks. And the next one and the next one. Her crying is silent, she cannot risk waking him up, but she cannot stop either.

All the sadness and pain, hurt and upset, the loneliness, the fear, it all mingles into searing hot tears she is sure must brand her face as they fall.

She has the knife back in her hand before she realises it and she's leaning closer to him, wanting to reach out and touch his lovely face before she ends his life.

She doesn't.

Just holds the dagger above him, moving towards his neck.

Inching closer until the cold, sharp point is against the warm, white skin of his neck. Ready and willing and able to kill her brother. Bring an end to this most evil of days.

"Do it, little sister."

She freezes, the point against his skin but still. Halted.

In the worst way.

"What?" Her voice is shaky, thin, not bold and Queen like. She thought he was asleep; his breathing hasn't changed. Has he been awake the whole time?

"Do it. Kill me. Push the blade all the way in until your hand is bloody."

"I can."

"You can. But the second they find my dead body – which may be in the morning, as I'm assuming my guards are no longer guarding – my men have been told to go to the tower and kill Addyson. If I die, she dies. It's so deliciously simple, Everleigh."

Everleigh snatches the dagger away from his skin, failure and frustration filling her up, disappointment an actual taste in her mouth.

"Not if I go straight to the tower, after I kill you."

"You could try, but there's a guard on the way in and a guard outside her door. If the guard outside sees trouble coming, he knows to open the door, without hesitation, and kill Addyson. I had to be sure, Everleigh. I have to live."

She cannot think of a single thing to say.

"Sorry, sister, you just can't get a break today, can you?"

Everleigh is silent, her mouth tight, her skin itching with impotent fury.

She cannot do it. Even though Addyson is safe, Lanorie is not, and she cannot repay her love and friendship, the way she rescued Addyson, with having her killed. She cannot do it.

And so, her hands are tied again.

She cannot kill him now without having Lanorie killed.

She has failed again.

The knowledge makes her knees buckle, sick come up in her mouth. She swallows it, disgusted at the bitter taste.

"And as I am such a good brother, and a good King, I'll give you a minute's head start before I raise the alarm, but should one of my men, or one of my dogs, find you, they will kill you. They have been ordered by their King to show no mercy, so run fast Everleigh."

"I hate you." Her voice is cold and hard and she wishes things were different, that he wasn't just one step ahead of her. She wishes he was dead.

"And, by the way..."

"What?"

"Happy birthday, sis!"

She turns away from him, the knife heavy in her hand, pure hatred etched on her face, and runs from the room.

She knows that he will carry out his threats. If they find her here tonight, in the castle or the castle grounds, she will die.

On her birthday.

As she was always supposed to.

The Kingmaker, dead on her seventeenth birthday.

No!

Fury and a refusal to lie down and die spur her on; she runs as though the hounds are already at her heels.

She will not die like this.

Not like this.

She flees through the corridors, not caring how loud she is, not caring who sees her or hears her. She falls, sliding to a stop, her ankle turning painfully. She does not rest. She cannot stop.

She can barely breathe as she flings open a door and falls out into the cool night air.

She runs and runs and runs, cloaks flying behind her, boots slipping on the gravel, arms flailing, keeping her upright.

She cannot fall again; she cannot be a target for men with sharp swords or hungry hounds with deadly teeth.

She has to get away; she has to get to safety.

She is crying, her breath ragged, her lungs exploding with pain. She cannot stop.

She runs out of the castle grounds; she runs along the road; she runs and runs and runs and when she sees Ginata's little cottage, her heart is bursting, cold sweat pours off her and she feels as though she will never set foot outside of the safety of Ginata's cottage or Della's sight ever again.

She flies down the path and with her hand on the door, finally safe, she stops. Bent in half, trying to breathe but failing to fill her lungs, tears and sweat stinging her eyes, her knees buckle and she drops to the floor. Cloaks swirled around her. She sobs as quietly as she is able.

Now what?

What now?

She has no idea, no hope.

She balls her hands into fists and pushes them against her eyes, bringing pain of her own making to the pain her life has become.

A clatter to the side of her makes her jump.

"Who's there?" A young man she doesn't recognise is brandishing an axe, eyes slightly wild. "Speak up."

"Please." The end has come. This is one of the King's men it must be. It registers a little late that he's not dressed in livery or armour.

He steps closer to her, axe at his side now. "You're not a thief. Thank the gods." He drops the axe. "What I would have done with my axe if you were, I have no idea. I can barely split a log."

Everleigh looks up at him, and he smiles.

"Sorry, did I scare you?"

"Who are you?"

"Finn. Della's brother. You're the Kingmaker."

Everleigh doesn't reply, just sinks back to the floor, this time the lightness of relief mingling with her tears. She may live through the night.

Confusion on his face, Finn steps closer to the Kingmaker who looks like a peasant girl and slowly wraps his arms around her. He cannot leave her on the doorstep. He stands up, holding her gently, and then the door to Ginata's cottage opens.

Della stares at him. "What's going on?" She shakes her head as she takes in the two of them; she had been unaware that Everleigh had even left the cottage until she heard a disturbance outside.

"Don't ask me," he says, "I just found her on the doorstep, crying. I thought she was a thief. I had my axe ready."

Della laughs and opens the door wider for them to come inside. "What would you have done if she was?"

He shrugs, difficult with Everleigh in his arms. "Why is the Kingmaker here?"

"Not the Kingmaker. Our new Queen," Della says, a smile twitching her lips, as Finn nearly drops her.

# Ceryn

I WANTED TO RIDE ALL day and through the night, so we got there tomorrow, but Pitch's steady galloping is making me drop off. The anger at wasting time and slowing down keeps me going longer, until my head drops again. "Weaver," I call out to him, my voice angrier than I intended. It's not his fault I'm tired. He is slightly ahead of me but slows to ride alongside me.

"I need to stop."

He nods agreeably. He never thought we'd make it through in one ride, anyway. I hate him for being right.

"We'll stop at the next inn," he says, never one to say I told you so.

I would have.

An enjoyable sleep, a substantial breakfast, and then we still might get there tomorrow. It's still a lengthy ride to the next inn and by the time we tether our horses my skin is itchy, I'm so tired. I need to get my mask off; I need to sleep, but I need ale first.

There's one room left at the inn, and so we take it. There's no nonsense from me about not being happy sleeping in with a male. We'll share a bed because there's no point one of us being uncomfortable on the floor, and it'll be fine. I can't stand girls who make a fuss. I'd rather do something I hate than let on and be judged like another useless girl.

Weaver asks for two jugs of ale, he knows me well, and I carry the two cups. We ask if there is any food and the filthy inn keeper grudgingly gives us a hunk of stale bread. Neither of us care. It's a long time since the rabbit and despite wanting to power through all night I am glad we stopped. He passes us a candle, almost down to the wick, and Weaver thanks him. I stay quiet, or else I'll lose my temper with him.

We sit on the bed, and it's surprisingly clean. Not that I would have made a fuss; when you've slept on the floor in the mud, any comfort is welcome. My home is bare, to say the least, I'm not one for pretty curtains or lacy cushions.

Weaver pours the ale for me and some for himself. I take off my mask and put it on the table.

We tear the bread in half and chew. "Do you really think something's wrong?"

I nod as I eat, talking with my mouth full. "Maybe." Do I want to admit my genuine fear, that something is very wrong? "Yes. He was wishy-washy about why he was going and how long he'd be. And telling us he'd call for us if he needed us, I don't know, just felt like he was keeping us away. Besides, a week's long enough." I finish my bread. I could eat the same amount again, easily.

"True. I thought it was strange that he went without us, to be honest. We're always together."

"Exactly."

We are quiet as we drink. I finish the ale and fill up the cup once more, swallowing it down in a few quick gulps. I shuck off my boots and climb under the covers. The very thin covers. It's cold in here and I'm glad we are sharing a bed.

Weaver pulls off his boots and his top; he's a boiler. I'm a freezer.

We leave the candle on, it will gutter out by itself.

I turn away from Weaver and wonder if I have drunk enough to sleep.

"I'm sure he's fine," Weaver says to my back.

I cannot be so optimistic. I have been quietly in love with Archer for three years and something is telling me that something is wrong.

I think Weaver knows. I don't think Archer does.

"I know how much you care," he adds, his voice quiet.

"We both do," I say, admitting nothing.

Weaver laughs. "You're right. We both do."

I wonder for a minute if he loves Archer like I love him, but I dismiss it. Weaver might sew like an old woman, but he is never lonely in his little cottage, and he knows the village girls well enough.

Love takes many forms and I know he loves Archer. Not like I do, but enough to worry and join me on this trek.

I love Weaver too. He is one of only two humans who have anything to do with me.

Villagers are happy enough to take my food and coin, but I see the looks they give me, the weird girl – is she a girl? – who hangs about with the two lads, hunting, riding, with that strange mask on, short hair, boy's clothes.

I try not to care, and when I have had my ale I can sleep without worrying, crying, wordlessly defending myself, while my thoughts, upsets, rejections swarm around me like angry bees.

Weaver and Archer took me on face value. A girl who dresses like a boy and swears like a soldier, cuts her hair short and doesn't care for beauty or fancy things. I fight as well as either of them; I eat well; I sleep well – with ale – and I am happy, mostly.

And the first time after I met them I took my mask off neither of them showed any reaction, not fear or repulsion or even curiosity and then I loved them both.

These boys of mine, they love me and protect me and I do the same for them.

And my love for Archer? A secret I'm happy to keep.

I have lived with rejection all my life. My mother and father both tried to love me for a while and I wish they hadn't because when they eventually threw me out, I was old enough to remember them. I hate them for that.

I will never make Archer say out loud that he doesn't love me too.

Better to stay quiet and always have some part of him, even when he is older and marries and has children; I will know them and love them and keep my broken heart to myself.

And when I am alone forever, I will have my little secret and it will keep me warm. I can pretend that things are different. That I'm not a freak.

## 9

WHILE EVERLEIGH DRIFTS off into a nightmare filled sleep of hounds and guards, Della fills her brother in on their new neighbours, the danger that surrounds them and what their part in it is.

The two of them eventually sleep and they are all woken up abruptly by Addyson's screaming.

Everleigh shoots out of her chair and stumbles, unsure of her surroundings.

"Everleigh!"

Everleigh follows the sound of her little sister's voice and holds her close. "Just a nightmare," she says, smoothing Addyson's clammy forehead and sweaty hair.

Addyson is shaking as she sobs. Will she ever get over all of this upset? Everleigh can't help but wonder at the life the fates have given her sister: Cursed from birth, shunned by her father, put up with by her brothers, loved only by her. People are superstitious and scared of her, and her curse has kept her lonely all her life. Only paid help to play with, no one that really spent time with her because they liked her. And there is so much to like. She's sweet and kind and funny. She's young with all her life ahead of her, but what life? Even with Everleigh to help and protect her, most people can't see past the curse, like it's a physical thing, an actual mark upon her that flags her up as different.

Della comes in with a cup of wine for them both. Everleigh smiles. One person who isn't scared of Addyson. Della takes Addyson's hand. "You'll be fine, lamb."

Addyson sips her drink and smiles at Della. "I keep having nightmares. Sorry."

"Don't be sorry, it was time for us to wake up, anyway. No point lazing around all day, there're jobs to do."

Nightmares that Everleigh has helped give her. After Macsen killed their father, and thought he had killed Everleigh, Everleigh went along with the pretence that she was dead, so she could more easily take the crown, but poor Addyson then thought her sister and her father were dead. Then she had to watch one brother kill the other, before seeing Everleigh come back to life. Then Millard had her locked in a tower, alone and scared, only eleven years old and already so aware of the evil and twisted world she lived in.

She is safe, but her subconscious hasn't realised it yet. "Come and meet my brother," Della says, and the two girls follow her through to the other room.

Now that she isn't half asleep and panicking about why Addyson is screaming, Everleigh is embarrassed, remembering her first meeting with Finn last night.

He bows low to them both and then straightens up, a smile playing over his lips. "Queen." He looks directly at Everleigh, and she covers her face, laughing.

"I'm so sorry about last night. I wasn't very... Queenly."

"Where had you been?" Della asks, the tiniest bit of hurt audible in her voice.

"I went to kill my brother."

All three people in the room, Della, Finn and Addyson, say the same thing at the same time. "What?" Della sounds shocked, Finn amused and Addyson frightened.

"It didn't work. I wanted to. I had the dagger right there."

"Why didn't you?" Addyson's voice is a whisper, filled with dashed hopes.

"He woke up. Told me that the guards in the tower would kill you if I killed him."

"But I'm not there."

"They'd have killed Lanorie instead. I couldn't do it."

"I wish you had..." Addyson whispers.

There is silence in the room and Everleigh is all too aware that she is with strangers. Addyson is too young really to understand it all, and Della and Finn don't know her. What must they think of her, sneaking off in the middle of the night to stick a dagger in her brother's neck?

"He deserves to die." Her voice sounds strange to her own ears, hard, defensive, but also full of sadness. Just one week ago, she would have said nothing remotely like that about either of her brothers. It still feels, sometimes, like a dream, or something that's happening to someone else.

"I was at the coronation..." Finn's voice is quiet. "We both were. We saw what he did to your brother, the wise woman, the young knight."

Everleigh's smile is sad. The prince. The wise woman. The young knight. They sound like characters in a play, and maybe for anyone watching the coronation yesterday, that's all they were. But for her they had been her family, her friend, her first love.

Was it only yesterday?

"I didn't stop him."

"You couldn't have. He would have killed you, too. No question."

"I should have stopped him. I couldn't save the people who meant the most to me. I'll be a terrible Queen."

Della moves from Addyson's side to Everleigh's. "I don't believe that for a minute. Didn't you go last night to kill your brother? Like a man, alone?"

Everleigh nods. A Queen that fights like a man. That's what she will need to be.

"But I didn't. I failed. I failed my friends, and last night I failed Addyson, and for every minute that Millard is King, I fail the Realm, my people."

"You didn't fail me." Addyson's voice is small.

"You didn't fail last night. You tried. And if you are alive, you can try again. You only fail if you stop trying," Finn says.

Della nods. "We'll help you. And your other friends. We'll all help you get to the throne."

"Why? You don't even know me."

Della smiles. "I know Ginny, and Ginny is on your side, so I am too."

"We both are," Finn says.

Everleigh smiles at them both but shakes her head. "Being on my side got Halfreda killed, it's what got Archer killed. I can't ask either of you to do that. It's enough that you're letting us stay here, looking after us."

Finn takes a long drink of his ale. "Do you believe you will be Queen?"

"I'd like to think so, but Millard is always one step ahead of me."

"If you could though, would you? Would you want to rule the Realm?"

"Yes. I believe it's why I lived. Why I was born, even."

"Then you can't stop us serving you as Queen. If it's what we want to do."

Everleigh shakes her head. "And if you die?"

"All who serve a King or Queen put the life of their King or Queen above their own. Nothing you can say will change that. Let us help you."

Everleigh nods, finally. She will agree to it but do her damndest to make sure all her people are safe. And the way to do that is to get rid of Millard.

"Enough talk," Della says, standing up and taking Addyson's hand. "Until Ginata comes back later, we need to get on with our day. We've got jobs to do."

# Lanorie

WELL, I AM ALIVE, AND I guess that's some delightful news. I haven't even been in here a day and I am going mad, that's the terrible news.

Last night, after the sky got black, and the candles went out, I was alone in the dark. Now and then the guard would cough or retch up some phlegm or mutter to himself, and even the company of a smelly pig with a sword was better than being alone in the silence

I don't like silence. I talk to myself when I'm alone, but I couldn't do that here in case he heard me. He might be thick as to not look at me, but he'd know the difference between me and Addyson if I started talking.

Now and then I'd talk or sing or tell myself it would be all right and I had to bite my lip to be quiet. I hate the quiet.

My room is never dark, because it's right by the kitchen and it's always light in there so Cook can cook all night and usually I stay in with Cook talking till late, so really, it's rarely I'm in the dark or the quiet.

By myself.

And the dark in here is thick. There's not a smidge of light. I held my hand in front of my face, and on my life, I couldn't see it.

On my life. Oh, my life is running out, let me tell you. I can feel the end coming.

I might be alive now, but I don't see it lasting. How long till the King wants to come and visit his little sister, whether to frighten her or reassure her?

Oh dear.

Well, I have survived a night, and I have rescued Addyson and I have eaten a wonderful breakfast and so that might be it for me.

I have only kissed one boy.

I have never been in love.

I have never been beyond the castle, never mind the Realm.

I have lived an insignificant life.

And it'll be over soon.

It was the same little maid who brought me food this morning, that saw me last night. I asked her if she'd told anyone and she said she hadn't. I asked her to carefully and quietly – making sure there was no one else in sight – tell Cook. She might wonder where I am, and I wouldn't like her to worry.

And she might send me up some extra special little treats if she knows what I did, how I saved Addyson.

I might get to eat some nice stuff before I die.

Like cheese.

Like a honey cake or a lemon cake.

Or an enormous chunk of pork, with some bread.

I have only just finished my breakfast, but I am starving.

What else is there to do in this horrible little tower room?

Eat and worry. Sleep in the dark and cry.

I have eaten.

I have slept.

And so I cry.

Again.

# 10

MILLARD IS LOUNGING on a chair, his crown on his head, a little maid standing ready to pour wine should he run out and another passing him food when he clicks his fingers.

He is enjoying being King, but he's ridiculously angry with Everleigh. Angry and hurt. After the horribleness of yesterday, he wanted to have a gentle week, while he waited for his new coronation, his proper coronation; he wanted to please himself and relax and enjoy being the King, but now she has forced his hand by trying to kill him.

He frowns, remembering his sister's duplicity. After he let her live, she repays him with a knife to his throat. He shivers, if he wasn't such a light sleeper he would never have heard her close the door to his bedroom, so quietly, but loud enough to wake him. And then he would be dead, and what sort of reign would that have been?

She's wilier than he thought, and more determined to be Queen than he would have imagined. He is her brother, after all, couldn't she just be pleased that he was King, and forget all the nonsense of prophecies?

It's what he would have done if things were the other way around.

It was a worry.

He has waited a long time to be King, and he has plans, splendid plans. It isn't fair of Everleigh to spoil them. Kings get riches, and women, and respect, and the entire world makes sure they are happy. What do dead Kings get?

Nothing.

The hounds and the men had lost her last night, and frustratingly he has no idea where she's gone. He's sure she isn't staying in the castle or its grounds, but he has instructed Wolf and Brett – Wolf's number one, to do a full and final check. He wants every room, every alcove, every cellar checked, inside and outside. There are a million places to hide and he won't rest and enjoy his Kingship until he locks her up with Addyson.

Poor Addyson. Cursed from birth and now locked up. He feels bad, but not bad enough to consider letting her out, or visiting her. He might do that tomorrow. Visit, not let her out. Sadly, she will have to be locked up at least until he finds Everleigh. She's not much of a threat by herself. She is only eleven. Nearly twelve, but still too young to worry him.

Everleigh on the other hand... every time there's a knock at the door he jumps, sure it will be Wolf with the news that they have found her. He has made sure all his men know not to hurt her; if she is to suffer, it will be at his hands.

Last night, he'd been angry and when he set the hounds on her, he truly hadn't cared if they caught her and killed her, but the morning has made him forgiving.

That's what will make him such a good King. If only people could see it. He can defend himself and kill if he needs to, but he can also forgive and be merciful.

Merciful King Millard.

She had held a knife to his throat last night. His own sister. No wonder he was angry enough to send the hounds out. No one could blame him for that.

But today he feels calmer. He will capture her and explain to her he has waited too long for his throne; he will not give it up.

It is his now.

And if she doesn't play the game, then he'll kill her and it will be her own fault.

He calls for a page. He wants to speak to Ginata and Will. They know Everleigh better than he does and one of them must have an idea where she is. She is far too incompetent to be fending for herself.

DELLA USHERS FINN AND Everleigh out of the door. "We need fish for lunch," she says and then adds in a whisper to Finn: "And don't upset her." She shuts the door behind them. She's pleased to have a Queen to look after, but she has a feeling that the little princess is in more need of a kind ear and a friendly face.

Everleigh laughs. "I heard that!"

Finn grins. "My sister is bossy. And a bit of a mother hen. She'll be in her element looking after Addyson. And you, of course."

"I'm glad. I'd hate to feel like we were in the way."

"Not at all. She loves looking after people. She hates that I'm too old for her to boss around anymore."

"She's a fair bit older than you."

"Yes, ten years. Once our parents died, she took over as my mother. I don't have the heart to tell her to stop. It makes her happy."

"Telling you what to do?"

"I don't always do it. But I let her think I'm listening. It's easier than fighting."

"She loves you."

"She does and I'm glad. She could have gone off and left me alone, but she didn't. I think she's missed out, to be fair. Put her own life on hold."

"That's nice, family is so important." She can't stop her voice catching on a sob.

"I think you were really brave yesterday. It was a scary thing to watch."

"Did you know that Macsen, that's the one who got his head chopped clean off, had killed my father, the King?"

Finn is quiet for a moment. "There were some rumours doing the rounds. But I wasn't sure. I don't know what to say."

"There's nothing to say. I'd like you to understand why I want to kill him, Millard, I mean. And why Addyson's so important to me."

"I get both of those things. Even if you didn't want to be Queen, I can understand you wanting to kill your brother for what he did."

"I don't just *want* to be Queen. I'm *meant* to be. Just like they meant me to die. I never questioned that either."

"The Kingmaker thing... I... um." He pauses, a flush spreading over his cheeks.

"What?"

"I used to see you, around the castle grounds, or down by the river when I was younger. I used to watch you and think you were the bravest and most fearless little girl ever, living while knowing that you would die and still being able to smile."

"Why were you in the castle grounds?"

"My father, before he died, was a farmer. He used to bring meat over to the royal kitchen most days. I'd go with him."

"I never felt brave. It was just a fact, like being a princess or a girl. But when Halfreda told me I would live, that I could live, I don't know how I ever thought I could willingly die. Who knows what might have happened, but life to me now, is everything. It's freedom, it's hope, it's..."

He smiles. "We all want to get older, wish away the years, but it's just getting closer to death."

"I've had enough death for now. Well, except for wanting my brother dead."

They are both silent for a while.

"Did you love that young knight very much?"

Everleigh cannot find the air to breathe, to speak the words; her breath catches in her throat and she feels like she will choke on it. She nods.

Finn pats her arm. "Come on, the fish won't catch themselves."

# Ginata

I AM STANDING BEFORE the King, and he is trembling with rage, actually trembling.

I paint a calm smile on my face; I have to look innocent in all this. He cannot know the part I have played in hiding Everleigh. Or Addyson.

"My King." I bow low, take a deep breath and look into his eyes. They are small with rage, small and cold, but I hold them. I do not shy away or let guilt colour my gaze.

"I need your help, your magic, or whatever."

I do not answer, but smile, encouragingly.

"My sister, my dear, darling, sweet, innocent, kind and loving sister, tried to kill me last night." He spits out the words and the shock on my face is genuine enough, which seems to placate him slightly. He turns and reaches for the ever-present wine. I don't get offered any, which tells me his frame of mind. Not the affable host today, but the vengeful King.

"How?" I am shocked. When I left Everleigh, she was settling down to a late supper with her sister and looked as innocent as a lamb. A smile twitches on my lips and it takes all my willpower to straighten out my mouth; she is feisty, this one. Fierce.

"Came at me with a dagger in my bedchamber. She is lucky I was groggy with sleep or she would have been dead at my feet."

"She is lucky." He will take these words one way, though I mean them another. When I see her I will tell her how careful she needs to be. I cannot believe that she has not realised it yet. How close she is to dying at the hands of this madman.

"Wolf has been looking for her all day, but she has vanished. He is extending the search tomorrow out of the castle and into the villages. Someone is hiding her. Someone is helping her. They must be. She can't fend for herself, there's no way. Her handmaiden's disappeared too, there's not much they can do alone together, though. Some traitor is helping them."

I nod along, masking the knowledge of my guilt, though I do not feel guilty for it.

"You say you don't know where she is, then find her. Use your magic. Find her." If he only knew.

My legs go weak at the thought. If he only knew, I would be dead.

"I do not know. I have no loyalty to your sister. Though I helped Halfreda, it was never to aid Everleigh. I have only met her a handful of times. But... it may not be easy to see, if someone is hiding her, that will mask her whereabouts... let me make up a fire... let me try."

"Try... yes. *Try*."

I nod and smile. "I am sure you will find her soon, my King, and then you'll...?"

"Lock her up. Or kill her if she makes a fuss."

I nod again, fear curling around my innards; I can picture it like a furl of black smoke, withering my insides.

"While you *try*." He emphasises the word and I understand the warning, trying is not good enough. Only results will be of any use here. Only results will guarantee my safety. My life. "I will visit my other lovely sister. See how the tower is suiting her."

Panic fills me, a hot and liquid churning, drowning the black smoke.

He cannot go to the tower. He cannot.

"My King. I have had an idea. What if I go to the tower and speak with Addyson? She has always been close to Everleigh and it may help me take in some of that... essence..."

He is silent, watching me with narrowed eyes. "Essence?"

"They are sisters. They have a bond. And she will be happy to see me."

"As opposed to me! True. I cannot argue. I am the terrible brother that killed Macsen and locked her up. I didn't kill our father, though." He nods. "Yes. You go to the tower, give her my love and apologies. See what you can learn about Everleigh and I will see you this evening, at supper."

I nod and bow. "Yes, my King."

If he doesn't expect to see me before then I may have time to go to my old cottage and warn Everleigh. Again. But first I have to see Lanorie.

The guards barely glance at me when I get to the tower and I realise it was probably easy for Lanorie to make the switch with Addyson. Difficult for her to do it or carry it out in the logical or emotional sense, but easy in the physical sense. These guards may be handy with a sword, but they are dim-witted.

I slip inside the door and close it behind me. I put a finger to my lips before Lanorie cries out and I step towards her.

She collapses into my arms and cries, oh so quietly, but she cries.

I pat her and soothe her as best I can, rocking her in my arms. We sit upon the bed and she sobs more.

"It's fine, Millard has no idea."

She wipes her hands over her tearful face and pushes her hair out of the way. She looks up at me, her little face miserable. She is only fourteen, still a baby really.

"Is Everleigh pleased with me?"

All she wants is Everleigh's love and approval. If she only knew that she has always had it. Even after everything.

"She is delighted that Addyson is safe but petrified for you. She wants you out of here."

"I want out of here too. I could hear rats in the night. Whether there are any, I heard them. I imagined them coming to take bites of me, little nibbles."

She's crying again. Did she ever stop? I hold her tight, trying to give her strength and comfort.

"We're not sure how to do it, yet..."

The unspoken truth is, whoever we switch her with will die. As soon as Millard realises the trick, he will kill whoever is in the room out of pure fury.

"I don't want another death on my conscience. I'd rather die myself." The words are brave, but her voice is shaking.

"It won't come to that. We'll sort it out."

"Is she safe, Everleigh?"

"Yes." Do I tell her where they are or is that a foolish thing to do? I do not want to judge her on her past indiscretions, but I need to cultivate my wisdom, the wisdom that came so naturally to Halfreda.

"And Addyson?"

"Both safe, and both so thankful to you. We can't believe how brave you were. All of us."

"I can't believe how brave I am."

We both laugh and then cover our mouths with our hands.

"So, you just wait. And keep being brave."

"I will wait. But I know I'm waiting for Millard. And not for rescue." She sobs so violently that I can barely keep hold of her.

"I came instead of him. He wants to visit his sister. If I can, I will keep him away."

"Thank you."

I rock her again as she cries, more quietly now. I feel so sorry for her. I don't know her well, but I can feel the love she has for Everleigh, the hope in her voice that she will have impressed her Queen. And Everleigh forgives her and loves her and is worried sick about her being in here.

But I cannot think for the life of me what we can do. This King is a clever King, and he is thinking more than one step ahead of us.

The only thing we can think of is a switch and yet it means the death of an innocent. A young innocent too.

Everleigh will not do it and I do not want to either.

I have dabbled in the evil side only once when I helped Halfreda to make a death draught and I don't want to go there again.

We want Everleigh to be Queen, but with as little bloodshed as possible.

Except for Millard's blood.

I'm not sure I care how much of his blood is spilled; it is the only thing that will stop him. Locking him up is too good for him.

# 11

ONE OF MILLARD'S MEN wakes Will from his sleep. They shake him roughly on his shoulder and then shout until he swims reluctantly away from sleep and stares up at them.

"The King wants you."

Will dresses quickly, while the guard waits outside. Last night at the feast, he had tried to be funny, tried not to worry about Everleigh or Lanorie, but it was impossible. Everleigh had been his friend since they were small, two children growing up at the castle, with unique roles, but kindred spirits somehow. And Lanorie, a girl who would never fall in love with him – a fool is not a lovable man – but so beautiful and sweet that he mooned over her, regardless.

He had carried out all the tricks he had learned from his father, with no effort, just acting on instinct, while his thoughts flipped from one girl to the other, pain in his heart but a grin on his face.

Millard had clapped him on the back, beaming, and Will had realised afresh what a maniac he was – like a small child, filled with benevolent bonhomie when the world was going his way, but able to change in a second and have a murderous tantrum. It was scary.

He wonders what he wants this morning, and his tread is heavy as he follows the guard through the castle corridors to Millard.

"Fool." Millard raises a glass to him and Will smiles. Does he want to be entertained or to kill him? Who could guess?

Millard walks towards him, goblet in hand, smile on his face, eyes sharp. Will bows low and raises his head warily, reluctantly.

"Funny little fool. Always lurking around Everleigh. In love with her, are you?"

Will shakes his head rapidly, happy to be telling the truth. "No, my King."

"Where. Is. She?"

Will shakes his head again. "I don't know."

Millard steps even closer, right in Will's face. "I won't kill your father, if I find out you are lying. I will kill you. And her."

"My King..." Will cannot think of anything to say.

Millard steps back and watches him over the rim of his goblet.

Will holds his gaze but then drops his eyes. He knows where his Queen is, but he would never give her up for anything. He would happily die if it kept her safe.

Millard nods at the guard and then at Will. "You may go."

Will bows low and backs away.

Millard smiles at the guard. "Follow him."

Will ambles down the corridor and as he suspects, a guard follows quickly behind, but slows his pace when he sees Will. Will acts as though he hasn't noticed and takes turns skipping and then walking to his room. Once inside, he sinks to the floor.

If Millard suspects that he knows where Everleigh is, maybe he can't see her again until she is Queen. He will not risk her life. But he will speak to Ginata.

He waits a while and then ventures out of his room. The guard is still there, pretending that he's not there for Will.

"Got such a headache," Will says as he passes. "Really need something from Ginata."

He walks to her room and leaves the guard standing outside, just down the corridor, still trying to look nonchalant.

Ginata opens the door and smiles, pulling Will inside.

"We've got a problem."

"I know. Millard still thinks I know where Everleigh is. He just called me in to ask me again."

"Did he tell you what she did?"

"Who? Everleigh?"

"Yes."

"No. What?"

"Came here in the middle of the night and tried to kill him."

"She did what? Why did you let her do something so stupid?"

"I didn't *let* her. I didn't even know. Which is lucky, because when Millard questioned me, I looked like I knew nothing. We need to go to her, tell her she's in more danger than she thinks she is. He's furious. He's got Wolf and Brett out looking for her."

"He's having me followed."

"What?"

"There's a guard in the corridor now, pretending that he's not following me. I came here to get something for my headache, which I really have."

"You can't go to her, we can't risk that."

"I know."

"Did he tell you she tried to kill him?"

"No. But he doesn't trust me."

"Huh, so that means he trusts me..."

"True."

"That's good. I'll go to see her, while the guards follow you. I saw Lanorie."

"Where? In the tower?"

"Yes. She's so scared."

"I don't know how we can get her out."

"Only by leaving someone in her place. He wanted to visit her, but I went instead. We can't let him find her. But..."

"What if we just kill the guards?"

"Just?"

"Well..."

"Will, we can't."

"Why not? Millard will kill her if he finds her in there."

"I don't want to become that person."

"So, let her die?"

"Let me keep Millard away. I will tell him that Addyson's fragile and that I will visit her daily until she's better. If he finds out she's not there, he'll kill me too for lying to him. In the meantime, we try to think of another way. Once Everleigh is Queen, she'll be safe. If I can keep him away that long."

"That might work. And Everleigh? How do we get her on the throne?"

"Millard is having another coronation on Saturday, we can interrupt it properly this time. Make her Queen."

"Plans sound so easy, when you say them just like that. We thought yesterday would be easy."

"It wasn't."

"It wasn't."

They are both silent, remembering the death, the blood, the violence of the coronation. The horror, the shock, how frightened they had all been, unsure if they would live or die.

"Right, you distract the guards, I'll go to my cottage, see if I can talk some sense into our Queen."

They both smile.

"I'll just mooch around outside, turn some cartwheels, juggle some balls, try out a few jokes."

"Sorry you can't come."

"Tell her I love her. Tell her. And it's only because they might follow me that I'm keeping away."

Will leaves Ginata's room with three potions that will clear his head and calm his mind. He drinks one down as he passes the guard, shouting, "Cheers," as he goes.

# Ceryn

WHEN I WAKE UP, I AM snuggled into Weaver, his arm across my chest. We are warm and comfortable and I wish we weren't on this mission. The more the time passes, the surer I am that something is up with Archer. He could be injured or captured; the King's men aren't fans of ours and one of them might have recognised him. His hair makes him pretty recognisable. He mostly covers it with a hat, and when he jousts, he's always in disguise.

I wish we weren't on the way to the castle. I wish Weaver had my heart instead of Archer. I wish I looked normal. How simple would life be?

Weaver rolls over and smiles at me without flinching. "Shall I see what there is to eat before we set off?"

"Yes." He has a much friendlier nature than me, and without arrangement he does most of the talking when we are out and about. Unless we are out and about trying to upset people; in which case I manage perfectly well.

There is a jug of water in the corner, next to the bucket we've used to pee in. I splash some water on my face, cleaning away the fog of sleep and the dust of yesterday's journey.

I am ready to go.

Almost.

I pick up my leather swatch off the table. I love the rough feel of the leather, the dirt, the sweaty smell. It sums me up. Practical. Worn. Smelly.

The door opens without a knock and I look up, expecting Weaver with more stale bread.

Instead, there's a crash of pottery and a high-pitched scream, as someone – all I see is a flash of blonde hair – runs from the room.

I quickly try to do up my mask, but I'm fumbling. Unusual for me.

There's a rush of feet to the door, Weaver's voice calling, "Ceryn. Are you all right?"

The inn keeper bursts in before I can cover my face.

"You!"

I say nothing, just stare defiantly at him, my mark uncovered, my eyes hard.

Weaver comes behind him and pushes past him. "We're leaving." He places a hand on my arm. "It's fine. Let's go."

"How dare you come here? This is a fine establishment. A friendly place. You! You!" He runs out of words and I laugh. I will not cry in front of him.

A group of people join the inn keeper, shouting and jostling.

I tune them all out, but one woman pushes through to stand in front of me. Her voice is loud and rises higher. "The devil's mark!" She spits on the floor, right at my feet, before fainting into her own phlegm, which starts me laughing again.

Weaver recognises that I am hysterical and grabbing our bags, my mask and me, pushes through the angry throng and out into the sunshine.

He whistles for the horses who are already untethered ready for us to go. He helps me onto Pitch and jumps onto his horse, Sweet Mabel.

The crowd hiss and boo and shout at us as we ride away.

We gallop for ten minutes until we are well clear of anyone, and then Weaver slows to a stop. I copy him.

He jumps off Sweet Mabel and pulls me off Pitch.

I sink into his arms, crying and crying and crying.

Only Weaver could see me like this. Weaver or Archer. I feel vulnerable and I hate it.

It is at times like this when I am glad I do not have a mirror. I haven't seen my face since I was about ten or eleven. After they threw me out of my home but before I found my band of brothers.

My parents had told me what was wrong with me before they chucked me out. The fear on their faces made it clear. They tried their best; I suppose. Put up with me for ten years. Fed me, clothed me, ignored me. I cannot remember either of them hugging me or kissing me. I think they were too afraid of me to throw me out but too afraid to love me.

One day they cracked. The strain was too much; I guess. I was ten when they threw me out, old enough to remember them and old enough to hate them.

My life had been no life at all until that point. I had never been out of our house, my parents had been too ashamed of me to let me be seen, and it was only after they threw me out and told me never to come back, that I realised what they had saved me from.

As I walked along, I could see for the first time what was wrong with me reflected in a hundred faces instead of only two.

I stopped hating them and felt sorry for them, for what I had made their lives in to.

People shrank back from me, ran away from me, screamed in fear, clutched their hearts.

Men hit out at me, threw things at me.

Children pointed at me, cried when they saw me, threw stones at me.

Was I really that bad?

Apparently.

The first night of my newfound and unwanted freedom ended up with a beating so severe I don't know how I survived. I have tried to push away all my old memories; they are too painful, but while Weaver rocks me and hot tears scar my face, they all come flooding back.

That night I was aware of being followed, which seemed crazy as I had no clue where I was even going. I was heading away from the life I knew but didn't like where I was going.

How was I going to survive alone with so much open hostility aimed at me?

I almost didn't.

A voice called out to me, and when I turned, three grown men started laying into me. Kicks and punches. Spit and swear words.

I curled up into the smallest ball I could and went limp – something that's worked in fights since then too, though I hold my own better now. *I* can kick and punch and swear now. I try not to spit. Much.

But I couldn't then.

Eventually one of them called a halt. Called the other two off. "I reckon you've killed it."

It. That's what he referred to me as.

I survived. Though I'm not sure how. I crawled to a bush, hid underneath it, and the next morning when I opened my one eye, the other was crusted shut. There was a hunk of bread in front of me. I devoured it and poked my head warily out from under the bush.

Stood a few feet back was a beardy, old, fat man who looked like he smelled.

He did.

But that beardy, old, fat man saved my life.

His name was Carter, and he took me with him. He was only passing through the village, which helped; he took me with him on his travels and eventually when he was too old and ill to travel anymore; we settled in the little cottage that I now call my own.

He also made me my first mask. He showed me my face in a piece of mirror and then he helped me hide it away.

Carter was a hunter; we would travel from village to village. He would hunt rabbits or ducks, or sometimes he'd fish. Then he'd sell his wares, we'd eat the rest and then when he'd had enough, or he'd annoyed some village husband by being too friendly with his wife, we'd move on again.

He was never afraid of me.

I asked him why one day.

"Are you afraid of me?" was his answer. It wasn't much of an answer, and yet in a way it was. I had nothing to fear from him, and I knew it. He had nothing to fear from me, and he knew it.

He reached for the mark on my skin one day, towards the end of his life, and I shrunk back from his touch. "Let me."

I leaned forward, and he smoothed the mark as though he could rub it away. "People are only afraid of things they don't understand. Because they don't understand it, they try to call it a name, to make it something, so they can understand their fear of it. Blame someone else for their lack of understanding, knowledge, empathy. The devil didn't mark you, my sweet child. Why would he? He's got more troubles to cause than colouring in someone's skin. The men who hurt you the night I found you – they were the devil's work. Hurting a little defenceless girl because she has a mark on her skin. Have they never seen a freckle? You are nothing to do with the devil, let me tell you, Ceryn."

He died not long after and I cried the whole night long, holding on to his old, spotted hand. The one person who had loved me.

By then I could fight and hunt and fish and swear and hold my own – he gave me those gifts. I was defiant about my mark, though I still hid it. I wasn't stupid.

After I had known Archer and Weaver for three months, I unveiled myself to them. Neither of them said a word; they would have guessed that I was hiding something. They both kissed me on my marked cheek, one after the other, and nothing was ever said.

# 12

GINATA LEAVES HER ROOMS not long after Will and takes a long meandering walk through the castle and the grounds. She has a basket which she puts flowers in for good measure, but really, she just wants to be sure that no one is following her.

She must risk it. She must see Everleigh and warn her, but also there has to be some communication between the people at the castle and the people at her cottage. If Will is being followed and there's no reason not to think he is – he's not one for being overdramatic – he will have to stay away. Lanorie is locked up. It has fallen on her to be that person.

And it petrifies her.

She wants Everleigh to be Queen, and she wants the end of Millard's insane reign, but she also wants to live. More than anything.

She walks to her cottage, following the familiar paths and waving at familiar people. How many people she has helped over the years she cannot count. Endless love potions, endless charms. She knows the secrets and the foibles of most of the villagers around the castle. She would never tell.

Nobody follows her, and she's glad. She slips into her cottage and finds only Della and Addyson. "Where's Everleigh?" Her voice is sharper than she intended and Della looks up, hurt clear on her face. They have never had cross words in all the years they've been neighbours.

"I swear I didn't know. I would have done my best to talk her out of it."

"Sorry, Dell, I know you didn't know. I just don't think she realises how unsafe things are now."

"She's with Finn. At the river. Shall I fetch them back?"

"Maybe. No. They are probably safe. Millard is searching the castle and the grounds for her. He wants her locked up. Or dead."

Della's face turns white. "He truly is a mad King?"

"Completely. She never should have gone there last night. How he let her get away, I'll never know."

"What can I do?"

"Keep her safe. Keep her here. It's impossible, really. She has her own mind. And if it had worked, if she had killed him, we'd be so pleased with her. Instead, it's reminded him of how unsafe it is having her roaming free. And he's convinced someone is helping her. He's questioned me and the fool. So far, I think I'm safe. But he's not stupid."

"Were you followed?"

"No. I made sure of it. But I'm uneasy now. I thought it was perfect bringing her here, but because she tried to kill him, he won't rest. Once he's searched the castle and grounds again today, he will start searching the villages. He means to find her."

They hear Everleigh laughing before they see her and when she follows Finn into the cottage; her face changes. She is contrite but defiant. "I had to try, Ginny. I'm sorry, but I had to try."

"He wants you dead. He's talking about you joining Addyson in the tower, but it's a lie. He wants you dead. Addyson's no threat to his crown, but you are."

"I know it seems stupid. But everyone is rallying around me, people have died for me, and I just didn't want to be a useless, helpless little princess anymore. I wanted to be in charge, to act. To be a Queen. To show I was worth backing."

"You are. Even without the heroics. We all see that in you."

"If only Lanorie was safe, I'm thinking I'd leave Millard to it. I failed in killing him. He is stronger than me, quicker than me, maybe smarter than me. I don't want anyone else to die."

"And the prophecy?"

"I still have a choice, don't I?"

Ginata shrugs. She could do with the teacher here to help advise them all. With Halfreda gone, there is a chasm where all the wisdom was. "I don't know. But if you choose to rule, if you can even make that choice, Millard will kill you if he finds you."

"He better not find her then," Finn says, plonking himself in the seat next to Addyson.

"We all want to keep her safe. But I know he will start searching the villages tomorrow if he doesn't find her today."

"We cannot hide her if they come here, into the cottage. There is nowhere."

"I will speak to him tonight, see if I can counsel him out of it. I've seen Lanorie."

"How is she? Does she know how proud I am of her?"

"Yes. But she's petrified. How do we get her out?"

"Kill the guards?"

"Everleigh. You are on the verge of choosing the same path your brother would. It's worrying. You cannot kill every person who gets in your way."

"Why not?"

It's Finn who replies to her. "If you kill everyone who disagrees with you or gets in your way, soon everyone would be dead. It's not the answer."

"Maybe not." Everleigh sounds sulky to her own ears. "But I need her to be safe."

"We need everyone to be safe. I just don't know how to achieve it."

"How did you get past the guards last night?" Addyson asks.

"What?"

"When you got into Millard's room last night. You didn't kill the guards then."

"Oh, you're so clever! I drugged them. We can do the same to the guards at the tower. We can do it tonight. Get Lanorie out."

Everleigh grabs Addyson and hugs her.

"Brilliant idea," Ginata says, pacing the floor, trying to work it all out in her head. "I'll make up more sleeping draughts. I've got all the stuff to do it at the castle."

"I'll come and meet you at the island."

"I'll go with you," Finn offers.

Ginata nods. "I'd rather that. I don't think you can underestimate your brother, Everleigh."

"I don't. But maybe he underestimates me. We'll get a little maid to give them the drinks. I'll be happy once she's free."

"Right, let's get your strength up," Della says. "Finn, did you catch any fish?"

"Yes. They're on the table outside."

"Light the fire then, we'll cook and eat outside. While we can."

Addyson helps gather some wood for the fire, glad to be useful. Everleigh hugs Ginata tightly. "Thank you for visiting Lanorie and I'm sorry about last night."

"You need not apologise to me. But I need you safe. I need you alive."

"Well hopefully after tonight, everyone will be safe. And then I promise I'll keep my head down until Saturday."

Ginata grins and hugs her close.

Della fetches bread from her cottage and some ale. Finn cooks the fish and the five of them sit to eat, the silence thick with unspoken fear and apprehension, but also hope.

# Lanorie

SO, I AM GLAD THAT Ginata came to visit me and sad at the same time.

Glad, because she kept Millard away from me. He would have killed me in a heartbeat if he'd walked in here this morning. No doubt in my mind.

Sad, because since she's gone the place seems smaller, colder, scarier, quieter.

I'm not good at being by myself.

I wonder if Millard comes in and I fall at his feet and tell him I only wanted him to be King. How handsome I always thought he was. How much better he was than Macsen, would he take pity on me? Keep me alive?

Or just kill me anyway?

I reckon he'd kill me, anyway.

There is nothing I can say or do now that will save me. I made a big bold gesture by pushing Addyson out of here. But in saving her life I have ended my own.

I feel it in my bones.

I have shown Millard that I am on Everleigh's side. I have made him look stupid.

I feel stupid. Since when do I make big, bold gestures?

Never!

I look after myself. I keep quiet and let others talk. I do as I'm told. I'm a doer, not a thinker.

I don't know what I was thinking. Trying to make amends, I guess. Trying to make myself feel better and look better.

I have too much time to think.

Some of it is nice. Remembering all the years I have looked after Everleigh, bathed her, washed her hair, dressed her in the most beautiful clothes. I remember how she loved me and looked after me. All the clothes and jewels and furs she passed on to me. She was never rude to me. Never anything but polite. Like princesses are. Just perfect.

She made me feel like we were sisters, that we were equal. That I mattered.

I knew it wasn't true, but it didn't matter. I felt it. I felt happy.

Will I ever feel happy again?

Oh, I know I'm a right moaning old misery and maybe everyone would be better off if they left me in here. I won't starve. The guards don't speak to me or look at me. Just open and close the door. Unlock and lock the door. Grunt and spit and cough.

I lay on the hard floor, watching a spider cross the ceiling. How did he get in? How will he get out? If I was tiny I could follow him, crawl through the cracks and escape.

If I was a spider Millard wouldn't kill me, or would he?

I hope he kills me quick. Painless and quick.

Just chops my head clean off. Like he did with Macsen.

# 13

GINATA FINDS WILL TURNING somersaults outside the great hall and falls in with his audience, laughing and clapping at his antics. He sees her and grins, throws himself on the floor and plays dead. The crowd, used to him and his father before him, watch for a second in case some sort of grand finale to his fooling is coming, but when he stays still, they happily wander away.

"She's fine. Della and her brother are looking after her. Addyson is fine too. We had an idea. We'll meet here tonight and give the tower guards a sleeping draught. Get Lanorie out."

Will can't help himself. He gives a whoop and jumps in the air. Anyone who sees him smiles. Being the fool means that no one expects him to behave normally.

"We'll speak after supper."

Ginata goes in to the hall to take her place at the top table, up on the dais where the royal family sit, so everyone can get a splendid view of them.

Millard is sitting on the throne, his crown heavy on his head, deep in conversation with Wolf. Neither man looks merry. The King looks icily furious, while Wolf looks miserable. This time a week ago, the table had the King, Macsen, Millard, Everleigh, Addyson and Halfreda all sitting happily, enjoying their food. Now it holds one angry King who has either killed or isolated everyone who should sit around him, enjoying his new Kingship.

And Wolf.

Ginata feels a shiver every time she sees him, remembering him standing outside her cottage when he pretended his alliances were with the other prince of the Realm. How could Millard trust someone who turned his coat like that? She would never trust him and tried her best not to even look at him, never mind talk to him.

She bows to Millard before taking her place three seats up from him. He calls her over.

"Sit beside me."

She cannot refuse, and so sits. Millard clicks for a little maid who rushes forward and pours wine into a goblet for her. Holding it gives her something to do. It is nice to be waited on, that's one thing she won't mind getting used to, while serving Millard and then Everleigh.

Pages bring forward dishes for the King to try. He chooses what he wants and sends the rest to the other diners. Ginata chooses a few things and fills her plate, but isn't feeling hungry.

The hall is full of people, all still eager to see this crazy new King. Aware of their eyes on him once more, he is smiling and waving, sending out excellent dishes, ignoring Wolf, who stares at his plate.

"Have you had any luck today? Trying to see where Everleigh is?"

Ginata shakes her head. "Sorry, my King. I have tried. I saw Addyson-"

"Ah, how is she?"

"Upset, but understanding of your position, I would say."

"Good. My position... I like that. Shall I see her tomorrow?"

"Let me see her again. Let me see how she feels first."

"I'm happy with that. Little cursed thing. I don't enjoy seeing her much to be honest. When I think of how she killed my mother..."

Ginata says nothing. She cannot argue with this man. Addyson didn't kill the Queen, not really. No baby can be blamed if their mother dies during childbirth, but poor Addyson killed a Queen; hence her curse. Her curse is what we know her for. What marks her out. Identifies her.

"So, you haven't found Everleigh. Wolf hasn't found Everleigh. I am failed by all of my closest allies."

"My King. I am trying. I spoke with Addyson. I made up a fire. I think because she is hidden I cannot see past it."

"She is hidden because someone in the Realm is betraying me. If they have helped her and hidden her, then they work against me. They are traitors. And traitors will hang."

Ginata gulps down some wine so she cannot answer. She is a traitor. Will is a traitor. Lanorie is a traitor. She has even made Della and Finn traitors. Will they all hang for this?

Millard broods as he eats, then remembers the eyes of the crowd on him and smiles, trying to act nonchalant, then he broods again, and so on until his plate is clear. He clicks for a page and whispers something to him. Within minutes a trio of musicians play and he smiles as he listens. He is nothing if not changeable, this new King of the Realm.

Ginata lets the music wash over her and thinks about her predicament. She has to keep Everleigh alive and get her on the throne, get the crown on her head. It's what she promised Halfreda she would do. And if she has to work for somebody in her position as a wise woman, she would much rather work for Everleigh. She knows she is more likely to keep her head that way.

Millard is nodding along to the music. Wolf is miserable and Ginata is watching them both warily. What will Millard do next, if he cannot find Everleigh? Will he let her go, figure that she has escaped for good, or will he keep looking? If he gets Wolf to search the villages as he has warned, then he will find Everleigh and Addyson in her cottage and work out pretty quickly the part she has played in all of it. Her head will roll or her body will hang.

What a choice.

She is determined to keep Everleigh safe and her head too.

EVERLEIGH IS SITTING with her knees tucked up to her chest, back against the fence, watching the flames die down. Addyson is inside the cottage with Della. Everleigh wanted her to take a sleeping draught to help her sleep a dreamless sleep, but she refused. She wants to know what happens with the rescue. Everleigh hopes she will fall asleep before they get back, but she knows that she will be safe with Della either way.

Finn smiles down at her. "Ready?"

She jumps up, straightening her skirt and her cloak. "Yes."

She will feel better when Lanorie is safe.

The walk to the castle is different tonight from last night. Last night she had been filled with anger and hatred towards her brother. Tonight, she is calm. They will rescue Lanorie, and then on Saturday she will take her brother's crown. In the five days between then and now she will lie low and wait. Keep herself and everyone else safe.

If only she had done the same for Halfreda and Archer.

She cannot think of him; as soon as she does she feels a helpless ache inside and wants to drop to the floor in a hopeless puddle of tears. That won't help, though, not yet.

"I used to think you were brave, when I was a boy. But now I know it," Finn says after a few minutes of silence.

Everleigh shoots him a sharp look. "You know nothing."

"I do. I was there yesterday."

"I wasn't brave yesterday. I was useless."

Finn shakes his head. "What could you have done?"

Everleigh stops and spins, facing him, hands on her hips. "Watch this."

She mutters under her breath, loud enough that he can hear her, but too fast for him to make out the words. She calls louder. "Rain. Rain. Rain. Now."

He looks up at the clear sky, shaking his head.

"Rain." She repeats the word firmly, and closing her eyes, she holds out her hands.

Finn watches the sky, his eyes widening in amazement. Light fluffy clouds change before his eyes, filling the sky, deepening to grey and then black, filling the air with the damp heat you get before a storm.

"Rain." She says it one more time and the clouds burst. Within a second they are both drenched and Everleigh stares at him defiantly. "*I* did that. But I let everyone I love die."

Finn wipes a hand across his mouth, pushes his wet hair off his face. "That was amazing. I have never seen anything like it. Magic?"

Everleigh nods. "That and being Queen. Almost Queen."

"But that wouldn't have saved anyone."

Everleigh shakes her head. He's not getting it. She searches the floor, finds a rock, passes it to him. "Throw it."

"What?"

"Throw it at me." She backs away from him, stopping after ten feet. "Throw it at me."

"I can't." His hands remain at his sides.

"Do it," she calls.

Finn shrugs and lifts his hand. He hesitates for a second but then throws the rock. He flinches as it hurtles towards her and he runs forwards as though he could catch up with it.

When it's a foot from her face, she twitches her head to one side and the rock follows suit, hitting a tree and dropping to the floor. Finn stops dead in his tracks, silent.

"I'm magic," she says. "But when Millard stabbed Archer through the heart, I did nothing to stop it. I should have stopped it." She's crying before she realises it. And Finn is holding her before he realises it.

"Everleigh. What you just did was amazing. Have you always been able to do it?"

"No. Just a week."

He throws up his hands. "So, is it any wonder you couldn't help them?"

"I should have."

"Maybe." He shrugs. "But I don't think anyone would blame you for not being able to. It was madness at the castle yesterday. You wouldn't have been thinking straight. Millard was quick and vicious."

"I will never forgive myself for not stopping him."

"You probably won't, but you should."

They walk along in silence. Everleigh lifts her face up to the rain, washing away her tears. Then she calls it off.

When they get closer to the castle Everleigh lifts her cloak over her face, and Finn does the same. They head to the island and sit on the bench, quietly waiting for Ginata.

# Ginata

WHEN I ARRIVE AT THE island, I can see Everleigh has been crying and they're both soaking wet. "Everything all right?" I ask and they both nod. I don't even push it. We have a job to do, and I want to do it quickly.

I feel anxious after spending time with Millard. He's in a strange frame of mind, swinging between moods like the child he is. He told Wolf to come to his rooms tomorrow at first light and then dismissed him. I kept my eyes down and kept out of it. He poured my wine and tried to be a friendly host, the affable King, but I cannot help but be wary of him.

As soon as I was able, I excused myself. I told him I wanted to raise a fire, to look for clues of Everleigh's whereabouts once more and he was happy to let me go. If he saw me now, it would be the end of my life, I know.

I am wearing one of Halfreda's old cloaks, and I have two sleeping draughts in my pocket. "Let's go."

Everleigh will hide by the wall again, like she did last night. She will wait for a little maid, like she did last night, and she will ask for help, like she did last night. Any of the little maids will help her, probably hoping to be promoted from little maid to handmaiden or kitchen assistant. Little maids are the lowest on the work totem pole, charged with doing anything that anyone asks, anywhere in the castle.

Once the guards have been given their drug-laced drinks, we will wait five minutes before storming the tower. Well, not quite storming, as we don't want anyone to hear us and we have no weapons and no army and just Everleigh and Finn, hoping for the best.

I won't hang around; I cannot risk being caught.

Everleigh and Finn will steal the keys, head up to the top of the tower and free Lanorie. By the time morning comes, the guards will have awoken and believe they have lost Addyson. No one will ever know about the switch and we can all rest until Saturday.

So simple. And yet I feel a twist in my guts; is it going to work? We can only try.

I will be glad when it is all over.

There is room for the three of us by the wall and we silently wait, watching the kitchen for signs of life. It's not as late as when Everleigh came last night, but it is dark enough to aid our adventure.

"I hope this works," I say, more for something to say than any belief that it won't. It's a good idea. The guards are always boozing on wine and ale and will be happy to be brought a drink. The sleeping draught is undetectable; it has no smell and no taste.

Once the guards are asleep Everleigh will easily be able to get the keys and with Finn's help she can shift the guards one way or another if she needs to get them out of the way. Lanorie has no injuries and will walk out of the tower and down to my cottage before the night is even half over.

I will slip off to my bed soon and prepare to look shocked in the morning. I know how furious this will make Millard and I do not relish having to face him. But I am good at hiding my true thoughts and my genuine feelings, just as easily, really, as I can see them in others. Most of the time.

We sit in silence, the three of us, squashed in a row, waiting for some help. The moon is covered in cloud and the air feels damp and just as my leg cramps, a little maid comes past us whistling for the dogs. She has a bowl of meat scraps. I shrink back as Everleigh steps forwards. "Hey."

The little maid turns and smiles. "You again. Did you speak to the King yesterday?"

Everleigh smiles at her. "Yes. I did thank you. Can you help me again? I want to see my sister in the tower."

The little maid shakes her head, fear passing across her features. "I don't know."

"Please." Everleigh's voice is soft, and when Everleigh reaches for the little maid's hand, I see her face change. She will not refuse her princess or her Kingmaker. Even if she wants to.

"I just need two mugs of ale for the tower guards. They won't get hurt, just fall asleep."

The little maid nods and darts back to the kitchen.

"I'm going to move back a bit." I tell them both once she's out of sight. I pass Everleigh the sleeping draughts and back away from the wall. I cannot be seen here and I cannot help. I am sure nothing will go wrong and yet...

I try to concentrate my mind on Lanorie, on her freedom, on her happiness and I cannot. Maybe the walls of the tower are too thick for me to penetrate. I don't see death, but I sense danger.

But then this situation *is* dangerous. Everleigh being out of hiding is dangerous. Me being near her is dangerous. Lanorie swapping places with Addyson is dangerous.

Yes, there is danger in the air. It smells like a fire that's just gone out, sharp and acrid, but not unpleasant to me.

I close my eyes. Everleigh will not die tonight. Lanorie will not die tonight. Finn will not die tonight. Neither will I. That may be the best I can do.

The little maid comes back and now I cannot hear what she says, but she has two mugs of ale. Finn helps Everleigh to undo the bottles and pour them in.

The little maid nods and walks carefully across to the tower, a mug in each hand. I can just make out the shadowy figure of the first guard as he leans against the tower door.

He will be glad of a drink, I am sure. Pleased with the diversion. It must be a boring job.

The little maid stops in front of him and I can see her hold out a mug. Then I hear her scream.

And all hell breaks loose. The guard is yelling, though I don't understand what he's saying. He has hold of the little maid and I can see her struggling. I hear dogs barking and the sound of people running, men shouting. Everleigh and Finn have both shot up from their hiding place and I can see Finn's hand on her arm. I run forward. Whatever is happening here, she cannot help.

"Finn, take her back to the cottage."

"No!" Her voice is fierce.

"This may be a trap of some sort. We can't risk your capture or death. I'll go to help her."

The fight goes out of Everleigh, and her shoulders drop. Finn takes her hand and leads her away.

I run over to the guard. "What is going on here?" My voice is sharp and hard, but I am scared.

He has hold of the little maid, tightly and roughly, his arm across her neck. Her face is red, and tears stain her cheeks. She looks petrified. "Unhand her."

"I hold her on the King's orders."

"I will be responsible if you let her go. She will promise not to run. Where would she run to?"

He loosens his hold but doesn't let go. This is one of the castle maids, probably ten years old. From one of the neighbouring villages, she has more than likely worked here since she was six, her duties changing as she has grown up. She is hardly an equal opponent for a man of his size and strength and were she to run home she would get a clip around the ear off her father for abandoning her duties.

He lets go of her, coming to the same conclusion that I have. She is not a flight risk.

The hounds and the King's men come running into the courtyard and surround us, and the little maid sinks on to the floor sobbing.

Wolf steps forward, taking charge and grins at me. "Ha! I never trusted you. Wait till I tell the King."

Molten fear loosens my insides, and then I smile at him. "I just got here. I was walking through the grounds when I heard this little maid screaming." I stoop down and gather her into my arms, pull her to her feet, keeping her next to me. I feel so guilty that we put her in this position, but so glad that I kept myself hidden. "I have no clue what's going on. But it's good to know where *we* stand." He glowers at me and asks the guard if what I say is true. The guard nods, and I scowl at Wolf.

"I may be a new advisor to the King but I know he thinks highly of me. I cannot imagine what he'll say about you accusing me like this."

Wolf kicks at the stones on the path. "Apologies. I saw her with the drink and I saw you and I thought..."

"What drink?" I am missing something here, a feeling I'm not used to, a feeling I don't like.

Everyone snaps to attention and even the hounds are quiet.

Our King has arrived.

# 14

MILLARD MARCHES TOWARDS the gathering of guards, King's men and Ginata with an icy glare etched on his handsome face.

The crowd bows low, and he cannot help but smile despite his clear fury.

"You?" He raises a hand and points at Ginata, but Wolf jumps in.

"My King, I thought the same. I was wrong. The guard agrees with her version. She was passing by when she heard the maid scream."

"Truly?" His eyes soften and he smiles at his new wise woman. He'd like to believe she serves only him.

Ginata steps towards him and takes his hand in hers. "My King. These are early days for us two. You, a newly crowned King, crowned by me. Me, a newly appointed wise woman. I understand that you might not trust me fully, but I assure you with an open and true heart, I serve only you."

Millard's eyes mist with tears, and he hugs her to him. Ginata smiles and lowers her gaze from his.

"I hope I am right to trust you, Ginata. I feel like I am, but I wish I could be sure."

"Be sure. And tell me why this brute was hurting this poor little maid?"

The guard has the grace to look embarrassed and Millard nods at the little maid.

"What's your name?"

She blushes when he looks at her and stammers out the word: "Molly."

Millard gestures to the two mugs of ale, placed on the floor next to the tower door. "Who gave you these mugs, Molly?"

"I got them from the kitchen."

"On whose say so?"

She stutters and mumbles and shrugs helplessly at him. She does not want to tell him, but it petrifies her not to. Little maids only ever follow orders; there is no such thing as initiative at the castle, and she cannot lay the blame anywhere other than at Everleigh's door.

"The Kingmaker. Everleigh."

Millard all but hisses and grabs hold of her wrists. "She was here? Where is she?"

Molly cries out and Ginata reaches out for her, covers Millard's hand with her own. It loosens his grip and as he looks at her; she wonders if she has overstepped the mark, but he smiles at her, head to one side, as though he's contemplating something about her.

He lets go of Molly, who is still crying, too scared to wipe at her tears, just standing as still as she can, hoping the King will turn away from her.

"Last night when my lovely sister tried to kill me, she drugged my guards. I thought she might stoop so low as to try it again and I was ready."

"A sleeping draught? I suppose Halfreda had so many options it would be all but impossible to know if any were missing..." Ginata says, and it's true, it's not just to distance herself from Everleigh.

"Ha! She is so sneaky. So, after she drugged my guards, it got me thinking. Aside from having me killed, what matters most to Everleigh?"

Ginata shakes her head, though she knows the answer: Addyson.

"Our little cursed sister, Addyson. So I thought to myself that if she could drug my guards once, she could do it again. I warned the guards here that if anyone offered them a drink, outside of their normal meal times, they should keep hold of them and call out for my men."

He looks so proud of himself for thinking of this, for making such a plan, for guessing what his sister had planned.

Ginata is nodding along with him, trying to keep a smile on her face when she realises that they have walked right into his trap. He *is* one step ahead of them.

"My King, let her go." Ginata gestures to Molly.

"Molly, do you know where she is or where she went?"

Molly shakes her head no, fear silencing her.

Millard gestures for her to leave and as she runs back to the kitchen, he turns to Wolf and whispers so that nobody but Wolf can hear him: "Kill her. When you get the chance. Just kill her."

He turns to Ginata. "I'll move Addyson. I have to. I can't risk Everleigh getting hold of her. She will stop at nothing to ruin my reign."

Ginata keeps her voice as calm as she is able. "Leave her, my King. Surely Everleigh will not try again tonight. She must have seen what happened to little Molly. She must have fled. She wouldn't try again."

"I can't trust her, Ginata. Men, take the hounds out, see if you can find Everleigh. You, Sir," he claps the guard on his back, "did an outstanding job. Now I need you to drink this, just to see if I was right."

Millard picks up the mug and passes it to the guard. "Brett will watch the door if it knocks you out."

The guard smiles and takes the drink. Whatever he asks him to, he will do it. He lifts the mug in a cheers motion and downs it.

If she wasn't as on edge as she was, Ginata would probably laugh; within seconds he falls on the floor like a sack of spuds and is snoring in less than a minute.

Millard curses. "My sister will be the death of me."

Ginata gives an almost, she hopes, unperceivable nod of her head, let's hope so.

"Brett, guard the door until he wakes up."

Brett nods, and Millard turns away, upset marring his features. "Wolf, join the others, see if she's anywhere close around. She can't have gone far. Maybe I'll be lucky."

Ginata falls into step with him, happy to be moving away from the tower.

"Lock your door, Ginata. If she is stealing potions, she may try it again."

"I will, though I have to say I have not seen her."

"I believe you." He reaches out and strokes her arm, just for a second.

"I would feel happier if I locked away her. If she was safe," Ginata says, hoping to sway him away from the idea that he has to kill Everleigh.

"I hate to say it but I don't think locking her away will be enough."

"My King?"

"She wants me dead. She wants my crown. She came here tonight to steal Addyson from under my nose. I cannot bear her. I cannot let her live and make a fool out of me at every turn."

"My King. I agree that she has done some things which would make you question keeping her alive. But to lock her up would be to take away her freedoms, her ability to usurp you. And the people would thank you. You know she is beloved, don't you?"

"I do. And you are right. Maybe the tower would work..."

He stops still, looking back at the tower, before turning and walking away from it.

Ginata almost collapses to the floor, relieved that her treachery will go unnoticed for at least another night.

# Ceryn

WE HAVE RIDDEN HARD and the fury over what happened at the inn has pushed me on. I will not stop again until we reach Archer. I will sleep tonight in his care, at the castle; I will not put myself in danger or in an awkward position again. My boys will keep me safe.

Weaver pretends he isn't, but I know he's watching me as we ride. "What?" I shout at him after the twentieth time I catch him looking.

"Nothing."

I don't even answer that; just glare at him, pull Pitch to a stop, forcing him to do the same.

"What?"

"We love you. Archer and me. We love you. Regardless... That's all."

I huff and snort at the same time, the sort of unfeminine noise I often make. Weaver laughs and I ride on again, ignoring him. We are almost at the castle, following the river now, letting the horses drink as we go.

I spot the castle and spur Pitch to go faster for the last leg of the journey.

We ride to the gates and call up to the guard that we are here to visit the wise woman. I don't know Halfreda personally, but the guards will. They might not know Archer by name, though they will surely know his shock of red hair. There will be fewer explanations wanted and waiting around in the cold and dark, if we ask for her instead.

He shows us where the stables are and tells us the pages will help us from there.

I jump off Pitch's back and walk along with her, rubbing her side as we go. Weaver calls out to a page. "Can you help us, please? We are here to see Halfreda and her kin, Archer."

The page turns white, upset changing his face. "Halfreda's dead. The wise woman's dead. The King killed her."

"Who can help us, boy?" My voice is harsh, and he scoots away. I have a feeling in my stomach like a thousand angry wasps have woken up in there, they are writhing around, stinging me with sharp little snaps. If Halfreda is dead, is Archer all right?

A woman is walking towards us, young-ish, pretty, worried looking. "Miss, can you help us? We've ridden to see Halfreda and her kin, Archer. The young lad told us she's dead. That the King killed her, but the guard let us in when we asked for the wise woman..."

I trail off, watching her face. "Archer?" She closes her eyes, like we might have disappeared when she opens them again, but we won't. I need answers and I don't think I will like them.

She looks at us both and the sorrow on her face confirms it. Halfreda is dead, and so is Archer. I drop to the floor crying.

I hear her talking to Weaver, but I don't know what she's saying. It just sounds like a mess of noise.

In my life, my friendship with Archer and Weaver, after my love and protection from Carter, has been the most important thing, the only thing. It has become part of me. When my feelings changed for Archer, I kept my secret locked inside, a tight, hot, emotionally charged ball; that ball has burst open now, killing me from the inside.

How can he be gone?

He was the most perfect man. He made me want to be a girl.

I can hear myself howling and the voice is not my own; something's changed forever.

Archer is dead.

Weaver drops to his knees and gathers me up. Back on my feet, but unsteady like a baby animal, not a fighter, I stare at this woman like it's her fault. Maybe it is.

"Archer is dead?"

She nods. And I am crying again. I knew something was wrong. It seems to take a year to find my voice. It's choked and dying from the pain. The grief. "What happened?"

This can't be right. It's not fair. He can't just be gone.

"It's a long story." She says it like that's that. As if I'd just say, ah, thanks for your time, and stroll away. It might be late, but I don't care. I have to know what's happened in the week Archer has been gone.

I have to know everything about him, fill my head and my heart and my ears with him.

For the last time.

Just a week. He's only been away from us for a week. If I had known when he left that we would never see him again, would I have let him go? Could I have changed his mind? Would I have told him what's in my heart? I would have taken hold of him and never let him go.

"I've got all night," I say to her, and she turns her head to the side, green eyes boring into mine. I feel uncomfortable, but stare back at her.

"Interesting." She appraises me like I'm a thing, something for her to assess and I realise that I don't like her. Whoever this woman is.

"Who are you?"

"My name is Ginata and I'm the new wise woman of the castle, since the old one died."

"Well Ginata, let's you and me find a place to park our backsides and you can tell me everything you know."

Weaver places a hand on my arm; he knows I'm narked off with this woman and he knows that sometimes I need him to temper me. Sometimes he needs my charmless personality, and he's happy to let me loose. But I know he's right tonight. Our friend is dead and we both want to know why.

She leads the way and we follow, Weaver still holding on to me, to my hand now. I feel hot and sweaty under my mask, where my tears have puddled.

We go into the castle and it is so ridiculously beautiful and swanky that I feel dead out of place. I keep pulling at my mask and yanking at my clothes. I look like a smelly old farmer next to this wise woman and I couldn't look more out of place if I tried.

If Archer wasn't dead, and I didn't need something off this woman, I would probably punch her in the eye, just to make myself feel better. That's just who I am.

# 15

GINATA LEADS THE WAY through the castle corridors to her rooms. Her heart aches for this abrasive woman and her quiet companion and if there was a way of saving them the hurt they are feeling she would.

"Come on in." She opens the door to her rooms and gestures for them to go through.

They stand awkwardly, the pair of them, gawking at the splendour that she isn't even used to yet. "Take a seat."

She sits on a chair and smiles at them, using all her skills to convey to them several things: that she is a good person, that she means them no harm, that she is so sorry for their loss, that Archer was a good person, that he died doing something he had chosen to do, that he had fallen in love with Everleigh and was happy to protect and serve her.

"Archer was a wonderful man. I only knew him for the shortest of times, but I know you would be proud of him."

"Why was he here?" Ceryn is blunt to the point of rudeness, and Ginata is taken aback. Her skills obviously didn't convey much of anything to this woman.

"Didn't you know?"

"He told us he was visiting his kin, but I never bought it."

"You were right."

Ceryn leans forward on her chair, ready to drink in everything she can hear about Archer, tears pouring unbidden from her eyes. Maybe they will never stop. "Halfreda asked Archer to come here. She knew what a magnificent fighter he was. She needed his help."

"With what?" Weaver leans forward too, just as eager to hear the story of Archer's last week, his own tears silent but plentiful.

"Halfreda knew of a prophecy, it's the reason she was at the castle, it's the reason she oversaw the Kingmakers. One Kingmaker would live. She found out it was Everleigh and she wanted Archer to help protect her."

"So, it's *her* fault? The Kingmaker?" Ceryn's voice is filled with bitterness and hatred.

"I don't even know your names," Ginata says, changing the focus.

Weaver answers for them both. "My name's Weaver and this is Ceryn. We were Archer's best friends."

"Weaver, Ceryn, I'm so sorry, I can see that you're shocked by this."

Ceryn snorts. Weaver pats her arm again. "What happened?"

"Well, Halfreda was worried that Everleigh would be in danger if people realised that she would live, and rule as Queen."

"Queen?" Ceryn interrupts, a look of disbelief on her face. "We have never had a Queen in the Realm. He died for this nonsense?"

"He didn't think it was nonsense. He wanted to help Halfreda and after he met Everleigh, he was more than happy to call himself her knight. He wanted to protect her. They fell in love."

Ceryn snorts again and then sobs, a mixture of the two sounds. She leaps out of her chair and huffs over to the window where she stands with her hands on her hips, sobs shaking her shoulders.

Weaver ignores her for a minute. "He was in love?"

"Very much so. Young love. Who knows now what it would have grown into, but they were both infatuated with each other."

"Really?"

"Yes. He was a lovely man. Strong, fearless, sensible, fun, all agreeable things. I know this must be hard for you."

"It's hard. I loved him like a brother. We both did."

"Just like a brother?" Ginata nods her head to the window where Ceryn has slumped onto the floor, her head on the window seat, small mewling sounds coming from her, sounding just like the injured animal that she is.

"Maybe a little more. You could see why?"

"Yes. He was very handsome and perfectly lovely. Everleigh fell hard for him. She's pretty devastated too."

"So, is she Queen now? The stable boy said that the King had killed Halfreda?"

"It's all complicated here. She should be Queen, but her brothers were both as mad as each other. One of them killed their father, determined to get on the throne before being killed by the other one. He also killed Halfreda and Archer. Now he wears the crown that should be on Everleigh's head."

"A Queen. Really?"

"It's written in a prophecy. I've seen it."

"Does that make it so?" Weaver sounds genuinely interested.

Ginata shrugs. "If you had seen her brothers yesterday at the coronation, you'd back anyone to rule instead of them. Millard is King, but he is unstable, violent, dangerous. I think Everleigh will be Queen. Archer believed so. He died for her. He fought for her."

"He'd talked about serving a Queen. Some funny idea he'd got in his head. I wish I could see him." Weaver drops his head to cry in silence.

Ginata pats his arm and walks over to Ceryn, sits on the floor beside her. "Archer was brave to the end."

Ceryn doesn't answer, just cries louder.

"Did he know that you were in love with him?"

Ceryn shakes her head, no.

Ginata rubs her back, soothing her as best she can, this awkward, grouchy, masked stranger.

After a while Ceryn sits up, wipes her hands over her wet face, straightens her mask and looks at Ginata, whose eyes focus on the mask but look away quickly; she knows it's not the time to ask.

"Did he really love her?"

Ginata nods. "I think so. He was happy to fight for her, die for her."

"Is she that special?"

"She is special. I think so, Archer thought so..."

"And she will be Queen?"

"I hope so. We're working on it."

"Working on it?"

"Well, her brother is King now, but we would like her to rule. There's a prophecy. It's what she was born to do. But her brother's more than a bit mad. We're worried that he'll kill her. He won't give up his crown easily, if at all."

"And that's why Archer was here?"

"Yes."

"I want to meet her."

Weaver looks over at them. "Not a good idea, Ceryn."

"She's the reason he died. I want to see her."

Weaver comes to her side, takes her hand, looks at Ginata for some backup.

But Ginata nods her head. "I think it's a good idea. Sleep here tonight, there's plenty of room. I will have the little maids bring in extra bedding and pallets. I'll get a bath drawn up for you both. Some food."

"Are you sure, Cer?" Weaver's voice is low and soft. "Shall we just go home, remember Archer together, grieve for him..."

"Not yet," she says, and her voice is as firm as the set of her mouth.

Ginata leaves them talking at the window seat, crying and hugging, remembering their friend, and goes to fetch a little maid.

She asks for food and drink, clean sleep clothes – boy's ones – for them both; she can tell already that Ceryn will not be happy in a nightdress, and for a fragranced bath to be filled. She asks for the fire to be lit, and extra beds to be made up.

She is ready to sleep herself, but at least the arrival of these two has taken her mind off the fear that Millard would go to the tower and find Lanorie instead of his sister. If he did that she would die for her part in it all, and she didn't want that to happen.

A little maid comes in with mugs and wine, followed by a steady stream of others sorting out all the little details that Ginata has asked to be done. She enjoys this part of living in the castle. One of the little maids brings a goblet to her, one she recognises from Millard's rooms. "From the King. He says thank you for your good counsel."

Ginata takes it and sniffs at it, suspicious since Macsen killed the old King with a death draught. But then Millard has no reason to kill her and every reason to be happy with her. She is doing everything to make him happy.

"Here." She pours wine for the two grieving friends and sips at the drink Millard has sent her. It tastes fine, and she doesn't drop dead.

Ceryn and Weaver are silent, in shock, in fury, in helpless misery, and Ginata feels sorry for them and for Everleigh facing the wrath of this woman in the morning.

# Lanorie

I HAVE SLEPT TWO NIGHTS in this tower of evil and I'm ready to die. If I heard Millard now, I would call him in. Ask him to end it.

Oh, it is a sorry state I'm in. I am smelly and cold and hungry, even though I am eating three meals a day and doing no work.

My mind is running with thoughts and ideas and I have bitten my lips bloody trying to keep quiet.

I hear the key in the lock and turn away from the door. I know these guards are thicker than me, but still I won't let them catch me here. I won't make it easy for them. I lay with my head facing the wall and ignore the door swinging open, as I did all day yesterday too.

There's silence until the door shuts again, the key turned in the lock. I shift to look at the little maid, whichever one has brought me food, and I cry out, before covering my mouth with my hand.

Cook!

I jump up and fling my arms around her neck.

"Shh, you silly girl." Her voice is low and I know she's not cross with me, just pretending, like she does.

I don't answer, just cry and cling to her.

"You've got yourself in a right pickle, haven't you?"

I nod and draw back from her, looking at her kind old face. Cook is the person I'm closest to except Everleigh. She always looks after me, answers my questions, is kind to me. I love her.

"Why are you here?"

"To see you, you sausage. To make sure you're all right. To tell you off for trying to be brave."

"I had to. You don't understand..."

"Oh, I understand it all." She takes a seat on my bed. "Ooh, this isn't very comfy, is it?"

I shrug. I don't suppose Millard wants his prisoners to be comfy when he throws them in here.

"Lanny, love, I see and I know more than you think I do, stood in my kitchen. You think I don't see you all rushing past, this way and that, making your little plans? You and the Kingmaker, and the fool who's half in love with you."

"What?" I know she's wrong now. Will's never in love with me.

"Ah, shh, poor fool. And that boy you were sweet on? I see it all and I know it all. I know you're stuck in here now, because you switched places with poor little Addyson. Not so clever, Lanny, love."

I nod miserably. Oh, I thought I was clever.

"How will you get out, then?"

I shrug. This visit is making me feel awful. I reckon Cook meant to cheer me up, not just tell me off, but I feel terrible.

"Ginata came to see me, they are working on getting me out."

"He'll kill you if he finds you here... Broke my heart yesterday seeing that darling boy turn like that, killing everyone, easy as anything. I fed him from a baby. How often he'd sneak in the kitchen looking for freshly cooked bread or hot cakes, icing dripping off the sides. He was so handsome. Not sure what went wrong..."

We'll never know. I lie on the bed and snuggle up to her back. She feels warm and smells of food. I can smell the food she's brought too. I shut my eyes, pretend that I'm back in the kitchen, late at night, chatting and laughing. Putting the Realm to rights, she'd say.

"Poor love..." Cook smooths my hair, whispering sweet words. I might die soon, but I am happy right now. Ready to eat and then sleep another night in this awful tower, with spiders scuttling over my face and rats trying to nibble me.

# 16

WILL IS SOMERSAULTING through the corridor on the way to
Ginata's rooms. He is still being followed and quite enjoying being
ridiculously foolish for the sake of the guard following him. He has
already eaten the dog's scraps for his breakfast and juggled with full
water jugs, soaking himself and a few people that were passing, and
now he is flipping his way to Ginata.

"I need a potion, a love potion," he tells the guard who pretends
to be uninterested, though he could not be more obvious about
following him. Will is sure by now that he is far less foolish than
most of Millard's guards.

He knocks on the door but doesn't wait for Ginata to call for
him; he is fed up of being watched and slips inside. Ginata is sitting
at the window seat, two people Will doesn't know standing in front
of her, hugging each other.

He shakes off his fool's self, and straightens up, taking the silly
look off his face; really, he's a superb actor. He acts the fool, but he's
sure he's not. Not really.

"Good morning."

Ginata turns to him, relief palpable. "Will!"

She beckons him over and he joins her. "Will, these are Archer's
friends."

Will's face drops, sadness and empathy taking the place of his
normal open and friendly expression. "I'm so sorry."

"Thank you." It's Weaver that speaks; the woman, a mask
covering most of her face, is sullenly silent.

"He was a fine fellow. You must be heartbroken."

"That's an understatement." Weaver says, wiping at fresh tears.
Will he ever stop crying?

Ceryn glares at Will but doesn't speak.

"I'll leave you two to eat," Ginata says and draws Will away from them to the other end of the room.

"Poor things," Will says, looking back at them. Neither of them is eating, just talking, their voices low, hands wiping at tears.

"Indeed. She wants to meet Everleigh."

"Why?"

Ginata shrugs. "I think she was in love with Archer. I think she blames Everleigh. I think she's furious. And pretty spiky anyway."

"What's with the mask?"

"I'm not sure. I feel like she's had a rough life. There's a lot of unhappiness inside her. And anger. And defensiveness. Maybe the devil's mark? Hard to say, but it must be bad to keep it covered. Maybe pox scars?"

"Nasty. Is it a good idea to let her see Everleigh? She looks like she can take care of herself."

"Oh, she's a fighter all right. But I'll be there, and Della and Finn. I think her friend, Weaver, will keep her calm. He's got a lovely energy."

"Unlike her."

Ginata smiles. "How are you bearing up? With Lanorie locked up and not being able to see Everleigh?"

"I'm fine. I'm enjoying messing around for my guard's sake though. That's fun."

"I bet. It will be over soon. Just a few more days. We tried to rescue Lanorie last night, but Millard was expecting it. We won't stop trying, though. Everleigh won't let her die."

"Do you think?"

"I know."

"Can you see anything?"

"My visions are slow, sludgy now. I see fragments of things, symbolism more than anything else. I think I'm too worried to make sense of it all. I need peace."

"There's not much of that going around."

"Not at all. What will you do today?"

"Be foolish. I'll see you at lunch though. Will our visitors be gone by then, d'you think?"

"I think so. There's nothing here for them."

"I'll have some breakfast before I go."

Will's presence seems to calm Weaver and Ceryn slightly; they both eat and drink, and Weaver even smiles once or twice.

"You would have been proud of Archer," Will says. "He was so brave and so capable. He won the joust."

"He always wins the joust," Ceryn says shortly. "Won."

Everyone is silent. Will and Ginata both wishing Millard was here so they could strangle him with their bare hands.

EVERLEIGH IS SIPPING ale, nibbling on cheese and watching Della with her sister. It makes her happier than anything, to see Addyson so taken with someone and someone being so kind to her; and not because they have to, because they want to. She is blossoming under Della's watchful eye and care. Della loves playing mother, and Addyson has never had one. They are finding genuine joy with each other. Everleigh is happy to watch from the side-lines and Finn is pleased that Della is off his back.

"I can go to the inn and have an ale now without her worrying where I am," he whispers to Everleigh, taking a seat beside her. Everleigh grins. "She's wonderful, your sister."

"Thank you. I like her. I just don't like her nagging."

"I'm sure. Addyson loves her."

"All Della wants is a load of family around her, and with only me, she's been left short."

"Do you think she's sad?"

"She would never tell me. But I think so."

They are both quiet, watching Della show Addyson how to lay the fire properly.

"She's good for her," Everleigh says.

"She's good for *her*," Finn says, and they smile.

"If I survive this week and I get my crown, do you think your sister would be happy to keep spending time with my sister?"

"Do you think we could stop her?"

"Hopefully not. My poor sister, she's been lonely her whole life. There's only so much I've been able to do... you know about her curse?"

"Yes, of course. Everyone around here knows everything about you lot. Royal watching is a big hobby."

Everleigh laughs. "Really?"

"Absolutely. My sister has been obsessed with your brothers for years. If she'd only known..."

"That's madness. I miss my brothers. Who they were before, I mean."

"I can't imagine. Your family has always been happy and close."

"And all the villagers watch us?"

"The whole of the Realm." Finn is quiet for a second. "I'm glad you didn't die. I've never seen a Kingmaker killed before."

"I can't imagine it's pretty."

"I can't imagine it, full stop."

"I know you thought I was brave."

"I did. I'd be carrying some dead animal, helping my dad, and I just thought you were amazing."

"Is that what you still do? Farm?"

"Yes, and hunt. I help down the road. I do a bit of everything, but hunting and fishing are the primary things I'm good at."

"I'm not good at anything."

"What do you mean? You will be Queen."

"Being Queen isn't being good at anything. I was born to die as the Kingmaker, now a prophecy says I'm born to live, to rule, but that doesn't mean a thing."

"What about your magic stuff?"

"That helped save the people I love; you mean?"

"Well, maybe you'll get better at it? Work at it? I know I would, if I was magic. I'd be magicking all day long."

"Magicking?"

"Doing magic, I don't know. But you can't say you're not good at anything."

"Maybe..."

"We'll try it later, when everyone's together. We'll help you. Then you'll get better."

Everleigh smiles. "Deal."

# Ginata

THE WALK TO MY LOVELY little cottage is full of awkward silences and tension. No matter how hard I try to chat and smile and engage these two, I can't.

I understand why, of course, but I am struggling with everything these last few days.

Everleigh has had her meltdown, Will is stuck in the confines of the castle and I feel like I am shouldering it all.

Weaver is lovely, though sad and quiet. Ceryn is hard work. Her anger doesn't just stem from Archer and that's why she's so difficult. Her life has been full of anger and sadness, disappointment, hurt, shame.

Even with the fear of Millard finding out I'm involved in helping Everleigh I don't feel the way this woman feels. It fills her with stresses, with darkness. I imagine peace is a feeling she has never once felt. I know Weaver brings her happiness and I am sure Archer did the same, but the demons inside her fill her with blackness.

Archer. So, she was in love with him too. I wonder what these two girls will think of each other. They are both so young, and they've both had tough times. I am sure they will clash; Ceryn looks ready for a fight, more than ready.

As we approach my cottage, I warn her.

"Ceryn, I don't know you but I can see that you are angry and unhappy. I will not allow you to physically harm Everleigh. She is ready to be the Queen of this Realm – the place you call home. By Saturday, if all goes to plan, she will be your ruler. Do nothing rash."

"*Physically* harm? So, what? I'm allowed to call her names?"

Weaver swats her arm, and she gives him an innocent look.

"I don't know why you're so sure that you *will* hate her."

"Because I have nothing in common with her. And she killed Archer."

"You are similar enough that you both loved the same man. And she didn't kill Archer, her brother did."

Ceryn stands up a little straighter. "You're right. I should just kill the King."

"Ceryn!" Weaver pulls at her arm this time, turning her to face him. "Ceryn. You sound mad now. You cannot kill a King; it's treason. His guards would kill you as soon as you tried."

"I wouldn't try. I would succeed."

"And then you'd be dead."

Ceryn shrugs and I am sure she has imagined ending it all before now.

Weaver's voice is quiet, hurt. "You'd leave me all alone?"

Ceryn looks at him and shakes her head. "I won't leave you. But I could kill him."

"Something else you and Everleigh have in common. She wants to see her brother dead. She wants his crown."

I lead the way down the path to my cottage. The door is open, Della and Addyson are looking at the fresh flowers that grow along the pathway. Della is teaching her everything she knows.

They both look happy and I smile. I had a feeling Della would enjoy looking after Addyson. She has spoken to me so many times about her fear that she has left her own love life too late, because she's been looking after her brother. I know she worries that she may never be a mother.

Everleigh and Finn come out of the cottage and Everleigh waves when she spots me, frowning, only slightly, when she sees Ceryn and Weaver.

I take a deep breath; this may be unpleasant, and I feel bad for surprising her in this way.

I go ahead so I can tell her who they are and why they are here, but Ceryn pushes past me and runs down the path. She stops in front of Everleigh, her eyes flashing above her mask; she looks mad and I imagine it is taking every ounce of willpower she has to stop herself knocking Everleigh out.

She contains herself, like I asked her to, and she doesn't hurt Everleigh, but she screams in her face. "I HATE YOU!"

Everleigh stumbles backwards slightly, and Finn puts a hand on her back to steady her. Her face turns white and tears spring to her eyes. We are all living under such tension and stress now, it only takes those three words for her to fall apart. She stifles a sob with her hand, but then she shakes her head. Instead of crumbling into sorrow like she did the day after the coronation, she quickly works herself into a fury.

# 17

THROUGH A HAZE OF TEARS, Everleigh shouts at the masked woman. "Who are you? What have I ever done to you? How dare you come here and shout at me?"

"You killed Archer."

"What? I loved Archer. I would never have hurt him."

"But you did. He died for you."

"That was his choice."

"You shouldn't have *let* him."

"I couldn't have *stopped* him."

"You weren't worth it. He's dead because of you."

"How do you know I'm not worth it? Who are you? Who are you to tell me anything?"

"His friend." Ceryn points at herself.

"His Queen." Everleigh points at herself.

"I loved him."

"So did I. And I would never have asked him to die. I would ask no one. I don't ask for subjects. I don't ask to be Queen. Or Kingmaker. I was ready to die before all of this."

"I wish you had!"

"I wish I had too!"

The two girls stand opposite each other, faces angry, fists curled, tears coursing down their cheeks, breathing laboured.

"Everleigh!" Addyson has moved from Della and the flowers to her sister's side, a pained look on her face. "You're all I've got left. You can't wish for death. Never."

"I just can't stand being blamed for this." She faces Ceryn again. "I would never have hurt Archer. I didn't know him anywhere near as long as you, but I loved him."

"I miss him."

"I miss him, too." Everleigh reaches out a hand towards her.

"I... can't-" Ceryn spins and runs away from them all. She reaches the end of the pathway and turns towards the river. Weaver puts his hands up, an apology, and turns to follow her.

"Wait!" It's Addyson. "Let me talk to her, please?"

Weaver hesitates, but then nods slowly. He looks at Everleigh, "I'm sorry. When you are Queen, please don't punish her. She's just hot headed. She was in love with Archer. Not that he ever knew it. And we rode this entire way to see him; we didn't know he was dead."

"I'm so sorry. It must have been an awful shock. I won't punish her; I'd never do that."

"You're too nice."

"Maybe."

"I'll get some ale," Della says, smoothing her hands on her apron, rubbing away the awkward atmosphere. "Maybe you'll join us for a cup?"

Weaver nods, and they troop inside the cottage.

CERYN RUNS UNTIL IT hurts and then stops, dropping to her knees and then onto her side, curled up like a baby. She's crying again. Will she ever stop? Will she ever get over this hurt? She can feel Archer's absence and it's a physical split, a rip, a tear through her heart.

Maybe she doesn't want it to stop. Maybe she can wallow in this hurt, this pain. Maybe she can make it worse, make it more, add to it.

Maybe she will just slit her wrists right here and let the blood and the upset drain from her body.

Someone walks softly towards her; she hopes it's not Everleigh. She cannot bear to see her face.

"Hey."

Ceryn looks up. It's not Everleigh, it's her sister, Addyson.

"Hey."

"I'm sorry about Archer."

"Me too." They are silent and Ceryn cries.

"What's your name?"

She sniffs. "Ceryn."

"That's pretty."

"Thanks."

"What's up with the mask?"

Ceryn sits up, looks at Addyson and shakes her head. "Why would you ask? No one ever asks."

"I'm young. Adults are polite. Children aren't."

"You're a curious one."

"I am. They have stared me at my entire life. People whisper about me. Talk about me. Draw back from me. You can't see my curse, though."

"Well, you can see mine."

"It's covered, though. Show me?"

Ceryn laughs, shaking her head. Why is she even having a conversation with this princess? Why isn't she far away on her horse, crying over Archer's death with Weaver?

"I'm not scared of you."

"You would be if you saw it."

"Why?"

"You just would. My whole life people have been afraid of me because of it. Hurt me. Ridiculed me. Hated me. You might think you want to see, but you would hate it. Hate me for showing you."

"My entire life – not that I'm as old as you – people have done the same to me. And I have no visible mark to speak of. They hate me because someone else told them to. They are frightened because of stories and rumours. Please."

Ceryn shakes her head and sits with her knees pulled up to her chest. She ignores Addyson and cries quietly.

Addyson touches her arm. "Please."

Ceryn looks at her. Just a little princess with no fear on her face, just curiosity. She reaches up and touches the leather swatch. She closes her eyes. Then she pulls at the ties and slips it off.

Addyson takes care not to gasp. She hasn't ever seen anyone with a mark like it. It's like someone has spilled blood all over the left side of Ceryn's face, across her forehead, her cheek, her nose and down her neck. It looks angry and sore. "Does it hurt?"

Ceryn shakes her head and opens her eyes.

Addyson reaches out a hand, but Ceryn takes hold of her wrist. "Don't."

"Why not?"

"You've nothing to prove."

"I've everything to prove. People hate me because of my curse. People hate you because of this... mark."

"The devil's mark. That's what they call it."

"It's just colour. Like you've been painted."

Ceryn snorts. "Badly."

Addyson reaches out and runs her fingers across the mark before Ceryn can stop her. "I'm not scared. I don't hate it or hate you."

Ceryn can't help but sob. She sniffs it back. "Really?"

Addyson nods.

"Thank you."

"Come back to the cottage?"

Ceryn nods and stands up slowly, pulling Addyson up with her. She ties her mask back on and they walk back together in a strange, companionable sort of silence and when they come through the cottage door Everleigh jumps up and offers Ceryn her seat.

"You're too nice." She takes the seat though, and the ale that she's offered. "I can't kill the King, but I can do something. Let me help your cause before we head home."

"There's no need. I know you need to grieve."

"Stay tonight," Della says. "Then go home tomorrow."

"Thank you. But only if you give me something to do. Weaver and I are handy with swords. Let us help. For Archer."

Addyson sits on the floor at Ceryn's feet, smiling at Della and smiling at Everleigh. "I've got an idea..."

# Ceryn

THE CURSED PRINCESS has a cheeky look on her face, and I grin back at her. When I heard that Archer was dead I was sure I'd never smile again. She's got to me. Quickly.

So like me, but so different. People might hate her, but they'd never hurt her. Never beat her. She's been lucky. And yet I like her.

She's got fight in her.

Like me.

I feel like fighting now. I can't kill a King, even I'm not that reckless, but I can do something. Hurt someone.

There's a stubborn bit of me that wants to storm away again, make them all pay, sulk and whinge for longer, but I can't do it. I could, but I look at this little group and I don't want to. I want to be good.

"They could rescue Lanorie."

"Who's Lanorie?" Weaver butts in, nodding at me, quietly checking that I'm all right. It surprised me that he let the princess come after me, instead of coming himself, but now I am sitting here grinning and I realise why. He knows me best.

"My handmaiden. She swapped places with Addyson when she took her food. She rescued her."

"But now she's stuck in the tower," Ginata says.

"If we swap someone else with her and my brother finds out, he'll kill them"

"Who guards her?" I ask. My brain, always battle-ready, trying to figure something out.

"A guard at the bottom, outside, and one outside her room."

"Do you mind if they die?" I don't mind a bit of bloodshed, but if this girl will be Queen, maybe she won't like it.

Everyone is silent, but Everleigh looks up at me. "We tried to do it peacefully, but Millard was expecting it. I can't see any other way."

"There's probably not," Weaver says. "If she's locked up and you can't swap her with anyone, we'll have to kill them."

"But Millard told me that if the guard upstairs hears any problem downstairs he will kill Addyson, well, Lanorie."

I am trying to think this through, my eyes closed. One girl rescued from the tower, on the sly, another one left in her place. A mad King who will kill whoever is in the room if he goes there and it's not his sister. Two guards.

What would Archer do? The question comes unbidden. He was my moral compass, both him and Weaver, really. I choke back a sob. Am I grief stricken? Should we go home while we can? Back to our village, to the people who need our help?

I look around the room: my little friend, cursed like me, marked like me; an older woman who seems motherly to Addyson. The wise woman, Ginata. I like her better now, but not massively. Weaver. And another man. No one has introduced us, but he looks about our age, handsome and friendly, but quiet.

And Everleigh. I should want to hurt her, cause her harm, rally against her for getting Archer killed, but I can't.

I don't like a lot of women. Or many people. Most people don't like me. But I like this woman and I like her sister.

I think she could be Queen. She has a way about her, something about her that makes me like her, trust her, want to help her.

Is that what Archer saw in her? Why he wanted to help her?

She's not helpless or damsel in distress-ish, but she is vulnerable somehow. But strong. I wanted to hate her. But I warm to her. I want to be on her team.

We will do something here, something to help, like a legacy to Archer, and then we'll go home.

And if she gets her crown and her throne, we'll raise a cup of ale, me and Weaver, and remember how we helped her get there.

I speak up. I feel sick at what I'm about to suggest, but I do it anyway.

"I've got an idea. What if I dress up as a handmaiden and take her some food? Once inside, I'll be able to kill or injure the door guard and, on the way out, I'll be able to kill or injure the outside guard. Lanorie can follow me out. She's not lame or anything?"

Everleigh is smiling down at me as though I am the most wonderfully clever woman she has ever seen. I think she likes my idea.

"Would you really do that for me? For Lanorie?"

I nod. "Weaver can lurk around outside and step in if I need him to."

Weaver is nodding along. I know he'll do what I want him to.

There is one problem though. I reach up to my mask, Weaver puts a hand out to me as though he'd stop me, but I shake my head at him.

"I'll need some help, though. To cover this."

I let my mask fall and close my eyes so I cannot see the looks on the faces of the group that sit and stand around me. Addyson's hand slips into mine and I give it a squeeze.

There is silence, but I don't mind that. No one screams or shouts or tries to shoo me out of the door.

I give it a few seconds, and then I open my eyes.

Instead of disgust and fear, I see sympathy and kindness on these faces and I feel glad that Archer came here, glad that we came here too and glad that we can help.

# 18

GINATA IS THE FIRST to speak. "I know what they call your mark, but that's not what it is."

Della nods and steps towards Ceryn, leaning down to hug her, enveloping her in the same non-judgemental love she's been showing to Addyson. "There're no devils in this world," Della says, rubbing at the mark like she would smooth it away, happy to show Ceryn she's not scared.

"People fear me." Ceryn shrugs.

"We don't," Finn says, smiling at her. "I'm Finn, by the way."

Ceryn smiles at him, blushing a bit. "You're not scared? Really?"

Everybody nods. Everleigh pulls Ceryn to her feet and hugs her. "I know you can't like me. I know what it's like to love Archer, to lose him, but if you would help me, despite how cross you are with me, that shows who you are in your heart."

Weaver jumps up and claps Ceryn on the back. "See?" He is grinning like an idiot, pleased for his friend.

Ceryn wipes at her tears, not able to look anyone in the eye. "My heart is angry. Always," she says to Everleigh. "But I am happy to help. It's what Archer would have done."

"What about the mark?" Addyson asks. "Can we cover it?"

Ginata nods. "I think a paste would do it, a chalky, floury paste. It doesn't have to last long."

"What if Millard is watching the kitchen, after the last time?"

Finn explains for the benefit of Ceryn and Weaver: "Last night we asked one of the little maids to give the tower guards some ale, laced with a sleeping draught. We wanted to rescue Lanorie. But Millard was watching because the night before that, Everleigh tried to kill him, after drugging his guards with a sleeping draught."

Ceryn looks at Everleigh, respect and admiration in her eyes. "You tried to kill him?"

"I had a knife to his throat. But he told me that if anyone found him dead, they'd kill Addyson. He didn't know that Addyson was out of the tower and Lanorie was in, but I couldn't let him kill Lanorie either. She's looked after me since she was seven and I was nine."

"But he's on alert. He's also sent men out trying to find her. He's desperate to lock her up or kill her. He cannot stand her being out of his reach, plotting to take his crown."

"My crown," Everleigh butts in.

Finn laughs. "Sorry. *Her* crown."

Ceryn is nodding, as is Weaver. Their minds already trying to work this out. They love a fight, a battle, a war. "So, the little maids get Lanorie's food from the kitchen and take it up to her?"

Everyone but Weaver nods.

"So, if the little maids have been in the tower, they know Addyson is gone?"

Everyone but Ceryn nods.

"Then the cook must know that Addyson is gone and Lanorie has taken her place."

Again, everyone nods.

"So, if we can get Ceryn into the kitchen, we can get the cook to help us, and then we can send Ceryn into the tower, dressed as a little maid with the food and her sword hidden in her skirts."

"Easy." Ceryn sounds as though she means it.

"I can't be seen with you," Ginata says. "Now, the King trusts me and thinks I'm on his side. We need that connection."

"What about Will?" Finn asks. "Will could take Ceryn into the kitchen. Millard's men are watching him, but if we dress her a little differently before she goes back to the castle, no one will look twice at her."

"Splendid idea. I'll start making a paste, Addyson, and Della can help me. Della, have you got flour? Any chalk?" They talk amongst themselves, pondering the best way to cover Ceryn's mark.

Everleigh takes a seat and Ceryn sits next to her. Weaver and Finn wander outside, chatting about hunting and fishing.

"I'm sorry about the way I spoke to you when I got here. I needed to attack someone."

"I understand. I was so angry at first, then heart broken, in a fog, you know. I can't say anything to make it better, I'm sorry."

"Did you love him very much?"

Everleigh nods, looking directly into Ceryn's eyes. "He was easy to love. Did he know you loved him?"

"No. I couldn't tell him. I couldn't risk the rejection."

"I feel selfish, but I'm glad. I'm sorry, but if he had known about you, maybe he wouldn't have had the space in his heart for me."

"I understand selfish. That's why I wished you dead. Because you got to love him and have him love you too. You got what I wanted and I couldn't stand to look at you, but..."

"What?"

"I haven't had a simple life, with my mark, I've had to be hard-faced, hard-hearted. I can feel an actual pain that Archer's dead, but I have spent years hiding my feelings, determined to be strong. I can't crumble like a little girl. I can't faint or die. I just have to keep on fighting. Archer loved me as a friend, at least, and that's one thing he loved about me. I'm not a soppy girl, I'm a fierce one."

"You are. I can't believe you've offered to rescue Lanorie. You don't even know her. That's so brave."

"You trying to kill your brother was brave."

"Or stupid."

"Not stupid. Brave. I'm seeing why Archer liked you."

"I can see why he liked you. You are a bit scary, but you have a good heart. It's good for my sister to see."

"I know about her curse. Is it really that bad though? No one can see it..."

"True. And I can't imagine what your life's been like, having to hide your face away, your lovely face. But Addyson has a different kind of mark on her. It's not visible, but it's always there. Everyone knows. I don't know how she'll thrive in this Realm, but I love that she's got a role model like you now."

"I don't think I'm a role model, not really."

"Well, you are. I can see the way she looks at you. She's so impressed. You are what she wishes to be. Bold and bad despite her curse."

"Bold and bad!"

"You know what I mean. You don't take any messing off anyone; you can stick up for yourself, defend yourself."

"True. But I wish I didn't have to."

They are both silent and then Addyson comes in, grinning and waving her arm at them. "Look, look at this." There is a smear of white, chalky paste on her arm, covering the fine hairs and tiny freckles.

Ceryn grins and touches her mark. She's excited and follows Addyson into Della's cottage.

Everleigh is about to follow her when Finn pulls her back. "Are you all right? She was pretty nasty to you there for a bit."

"I am. I wasn't. But I am. I... I know how she feels. We both lost someone we love, and..."

She trails off, feeling strangely awkward talking about the love she had for Archer in front of Finn. He looks as awkward as she feels and suggests they go next door.

Della has fetched clothes for Ceryn to change in to. They are a little big but better than the boyish clothing she is wearing. Her face is unrecognisable. Without the mask, you can see she is a girl; a pretty one. She has lovely eyes, which don't look so fierce, and her skin is smooth. They have blended the paste in. Up close it is obvious, but the guards are not likely to notice if she keeps her head down. They will also be able to approach Cook, with Will's help, without her losing her mind over Ceryn's face.

Ceryn gives Everleigh a hug, and then a longer one to Addyson. "Thank you for coming after me."

"Thank you for coming back."

"Good luck. And thank you. Lanorie means so much to me. I need her to be safe."

"She will be."

# Lanorie

SO, COOK HAS GONE AND my mind has gone and I am happy to wait for my life to be gone.

I might sound dramatic, but I am waiting for my death, so I think it's fair enough.

I think Everleigh has forgotten me. I have slept here two nights now, and I am done.

The spider is my only friend.

Tears silently slip from my eyes, and I don't even bother to wipe them away.

I ate my breakfast, but only because Cook had sent up my favourite. I didn't want to be rude.

I lie on my back on the hard bed and watch the spider.

The tears drip down my face and pool into my ears, tickling them.

I don't even wipe them away.

# 19

THE WALK BACK TO THE castle is far more pleasant for all three of them than the walk down. It took a while for Ginata to convince Everleigh to stay at the cottage, but she listened eventually, with the promise that Lanorie would be with her by nightfall. Sooner.

Ceryn and Weaver are armed, but they don't look like they are. Ginata keeps sneaking looks at Ceryn; without her mask and dressed like a girl, even with her short hair, she looks completely different; free and happy.

Weaver looks happy too; he strides along, filled with purpose.

When they reach the castle, Ginata explains where to find Will. If he's not in his room, they should listen for a laughing crowd, or ask a page. If anyone asks, they are friends of Halfreda's, and are grieving after finding out about her death. Though the castle is often full of strangers, Ginata knows that Millard is on high alert.

Ginata leaves them and goes to her rooms to wait. Whatever happens next, Millard will be alerted very quickly. If Ceryn and Weaver rescue Lanorie and injure or kill a few guards, she will know about it. If they fail, and get caught, she will know about it. The only absolute is that in the next hour Millard will be furious about something. And she knows, just in this brief time of knowing him, that he likes other people to share in his misery. She will find something to do in her rooms so when he comes he will find her innocent and unaware.

WILL IS SKIPPING THROUGH the grounds, trying to shake off the guard who is still watching him when he spots Ceryn and Weaver heading towards him. He grins at them and somersaults towards them.

"Impressive." Ceryn's voice is laced with warmth despite the sarcastic comment.

"I am impressive," he says with a laugh. "You look different."

"I took my mask off."

"That was brave."

"You think?"

Will nods, steps closer to her and inspects her face and the white paste. "Do you ever take it off?"

"Not in public, no."

"Very brave, then."

Ceryn grins, and Weaver laughs, patting her on the back. "Can we talk about how brave she is later? We've got a rescue to carry out."

"A rescue?"

"Yup. Ceryn is going into the tower to rescue Lanorie."

Will hoots and somersaults again. "Woo-hoo. Thank you."

"You like her?"

"I love her. But she doesn't like me. Not like that."

"I know how that feels. I was in love with Archer. Quietly."

Will smiles. "We're losers in love, both of us."

"We must be losers together. Maybe after we rescue her, she'll realise how much she's missed you?"

"Maybe. So what's the plan?"

"We need to get Ceryn into the kitchen, we figure the castle cook must know that Lanorie is locked up instead of Addyson. We'll enlist her help, send Ceryn up the tower."

"It's probably best if I attack the guard upstairs and you get the one downstairs."

Weaver nods. "I'll try to disarm him, knock him out maybe. I'd rather not kill them..."

"But we can if we need to..."

"Excuse her, she's pretty blood thirsty."

Will stares at her, her face free of the mask, her eyes sparkling instead of being cloudy with anger, a grin tugging at the corners of her mouth. "I kind of like it."

Ceryn smiles at him, a blush colouring her cheeks. "Let's go."

Cook is busy icing a cake when they slip into the kitchen. Will gives her a tap on the shoulder. "Cook. We want to rescue Lanorie."

"Oh, thank the gods. I thought she would be in there forever. Who are these two?"

Will introduces them. "We need to send Ceryn up to the tower with food. How long till her meal usually goes up?"

"Just about a half hour. What's on her face?"

Ceryn steps closer, holding out her cheek for inspection. "I have a mark. It's nothing to do with the devil."

"Course it's bloody not. What nonsense. Are people scared of you?"

"Usually."

"Poor thing. Well, I'm not and I'll be happy to help you. That poor girl is falling apart in there by herself."

"Thanks Cook."

"As if I wouldn't have helped. You must keep your head down, though; we need to make sure the guard doesn't notice your face."

"I know. Thank you for not being frightened."

Cook snorts. "There's some nasty people in this world, happy to blame others for their own evil, I'm not one of those. That mark is nothing to do with the devil or anyone else. Ridiculous. Now what have I got for you three..." She moves around the kitchen finding little scraps of deliciousness for them: little cakes, nutty bread, pastries, tarts. By the time they are ready for Ceryn to head to the tower, disguised as a little maid, they are all stuffed.

"Are you nervous?" Will asks them both. "Our rescue plans haven't worked so far."

"I'm not nervous at all," Weaver says, checking his sword is ready at his side, hidden but there.

"I love a good fight." Ceryn's eyes are gleaming and Will knows she's telling the truth. She's got spirit, this one.

"Ready?" Cook hands Ceryn the tray and Will can see her hands aren't shaking at all. Weaver kisses her forehead. "Be safe."

She walks alone to the tower, head down, tray steady.

Will stays in the kitchen with Cook, but Weaver makes his way slowly across the courtyard.

The guard barely glances at Ceryn but knocks on the tower door before unlocking it. He moves so she can walk past.

She walks up the stairs, breathing steady, hands steady, imagining how this will go down. What she'll say, what she'll do. If this handmaiden is even worth all of this trouble. She supposes if Everleigh likes her, that's enough. It's what Archer would have done, and that is her new benchmark, her gauge of what's right or wrong.

The second guard is as conscientious as the first, namely not at all. He unlocks the prisoner's door without looking up and Ceryn slips inside the door. She puts the tray down and looks the girl up and down. She's plain looking. Thin and miserable looking, actually, but that could be because of where she is. "I'm Ceryn. A friend of Archer's. I'm here to get you out."

Lanorie rushes towards her and wraps her arms around her, shaking and crying, whispering: "Thank you. Thank you. Thank you. Really?"

Ceryn stands stock still, not returning the hug; she doesn't like strangers touching her. In fact, they never do.

Lanorie pulls back. "Ooh, what's wrong with your face?"

Ceryn grimaces, thinking how charmless this girl is. Why Will is in love with her, she can't imagine. He seems such a lovely chap.

"They call it the devil's mark."

Lanorie shrinks back, and Ceryn loses her temper. "Listen, girl, everyone is worried about you, for some reason. Everleigh can't wait for you to be safe, for some reason. I'm your only hope. If you think I'm too scary and I might eat you while you're looking the other way, I'm happy to leave you here."

Lanorie shakes her head. "I'm sorry. I've just seen nothing like it before."

"Forget about it. Are you ready?"

"I think so. I'm scared."

"Well, don't be. I'll sort out the guard, you just run."

"Where do I go?"

"Just out. I'm here with my friend Weaver. We'll take you somewhere safe. Ready?"

Lanorie shakes her head, but Ceryn knocks on the door, anyway. The second the guard swings it open, she leaps forward, lifting her arm up and smashing his nose. He screams and reaches for his sword, quick despite the shock attack, but she's quicker than he is, ready for a fight. She slashes his sword arm, just a surface wound but enough to make him shriek and drop his sword. In all fairness, none of Millard's guards are used to real fighting and he would never have been expecting a little kitchen maid to slash around with a sword.

She pushes Lanorie past him and tells her to run.

The guard closes his eyes, and she grins. She hasn't hurt him very much, but he has decided that it's not worth his life to keep fighting.

She barrels down the stairs, catching up with Lanorie. Outside of the door, the other guard is flat on his back, an egg-shaped bump on his forehead, but no bloodshed. Weaver is standing there grinning, bouncing on his feet. "Let's go."

Lanorie stands stock still, but they each grab an arm and start running.

# Ginata

I HAVE PACED MY ROOM until I fear I will wear a groove into the floor. I cannot stay here. I am just waiting for Millard and Wolf. Either furious that Everleigh's got one over on him or gleeful that she's failed somehow. I cannot bear either of those men tonight and so after checking I am not being followed, I flee to the cottages.

Everyone there is as anxious as I am, but there is something good in sharing those anxieties together. Upsets are always worse when we are alone.

Della is fussing over us all, but mostly Addyson. Finn is pacing. Everleigh is sitting with her knees drawn up, watching the door obsessively. I bite my nails – a recent habit, a grubby one. We all have our ways of dealing with stress.

I feel good about this rescue attempt, though. Ceryn is an angry young woman, but a fighter through and through. Weaver is one of the easiest going souls I've ever encountered, but I can tell he's a fighter too. I think they'll do it.

We hear Lanorie before we see her; loud protests that her feet hurt, her arms hurt from them pulling her, she's too tired to go one more step, she's too hungry to move.

Everleigh jumps up, laughing with delight at the grumpy moaning from her handmaiden. She opens the door and runs along the path, catching Lanorie as she collapses into her arms, both crying. "Oh, Everleigh. Thank you, thank you, thank you."

I wipe a little tear away too. It feels better with all of us being safe. Though I know the fury, this will awaken in our new King. I'm not looking forward to seeing him later.

"Thank them. Not me."

Lanorie doesn't move from Everleigh's side though, her tears soaking her dress. Ceryn rolls her eyes and strides over to Addyson, ruffling her hair. Weaver collapses onto the grass, a groan rushing out of him.

"Was it awful?" Addyson asks them both.

"The worst bit," Ceryn says, gesturing at Lanorie, "was getting this moany lump away from the castle before Millard's hounds came looking for us."

I cannot help the burst of laughter that rushes out of my mouth and I laugh harder when Lanorie shoots me a furious look, a look full of anger and then a split second later pitiful misery. She is crying again, and I stifle my laugh when Everleigh looks at me, a reproachful look on her lovely face. She knows this girl's flaws well enough but loves her, regardless.

I feel almost lightheaded; the fear that Millard would find Addyson gone and take my life because of my part in it, is over. While Lanorie was locked away, I knew that Millard could find his sister missing any second and I would get the blame and the punishment. Now Lanorie is safe, so are we all, to an extent.

The silliness spreads through me and I scoop Lanorie into a big cuddle, kissing her hair and then making a face at the smell of her.

"A clean up?" Della asks, ever the mother.

I nod and am laughing again. Everleigh taps my arm. "Are you all right?"

I sober up as Della tucks her arm around Lanorie and takes her through to her cottage with Addyson tagging along behind them. Della will heat some water and clean her up, dress her in clean clothes; she is wearing Addyson's beautiful dress now, and it's scruffy and dirty. Her hair needs washing and brushing out; it's full of knots.

"I'm good. I just don't think I realised how scared I've been of your brother finding Addyson missing and killing me. I think it just hit me."

Everleigh nods and I think about Saturday. Making her Queen, betraying my King; a sudden and unbidden jolt of guilt hits me and I shake my head, literally shaking it off. I am happy and ready to do it, and I'm not doing anything wrong, not really. Only a few more days of pretending that I admire and serve him and then we'll all be free.

I smile as I think about how giddy I'll feel then. How much lighter we will all feel when this is over.

Ceryn and Weaver give us a rundown of the great rescue, and it hits me again how furious Millard will be when I see him later.

I stay as long as I can, enjoying the talking, the laughing, the moaning – off Lanorie – and the camaraderie of it all. I will put off meeting my King for as long as I can.

# 20

GINATA EVENTUALLY LEAVES the warm friendliness of her cottage and heads back to the castle. She is nervous and dawdles, wondering how Millard will be, will he be sad and hard done by or will he be icily furious or maybe unhinged, axe swinging?

She has no way of knowing and the closer she gets to the castle, her current home, the bigger her urge is to run away. Why did she have to get caught up in all this drama? Damn Macsen, Everleigh's dead brother. He was the one who got her roped into this when he came to her door looking for a death draught.

She keeps her head down as she walks to her rooms. Maybe she will have some peace, maybe she won't see Millard until later, at supper. Maybe he doesn't even know yet.

Turning the handle and pushing her door open, she feels her knees buckle and the blood drain from her face; Millard is standing there and she can feel the icy fury from across the room. She steadies her legs, hidden under her long skirt, and smiles widely at him before bowing low. She closes her eyes and in that brief second instils calmness into her mind.

"My King." She is pleased not to hear even a slight tremble to her words.

"Addyson's gone." His voice is harsh, but not accusing, which can only be a good thing.

"Gone where?" Feigning innocence is the only answer.

"My two guards were attacked and left for dead. She's gone."

Ginata closes her eyes. "She is alive," she says, trying to sound mystical.

"I don't care if she's alive or dead. I just need to know where she is and who took her. Who helped her? Who helped my sister? Who is in cahoots with her?"

She shrugs and makes her face show concern and finds that she feels a tiny bit sorry for him. In his head, he's a good King, who only killed his brother to stop himself being killed, only killed Halfreda because she defended his sister, only killed Archer because he fought him. In his head, he is hard done by and she can see all that from his expression; he doesn't hide his emotions very well. A little bit of her wants to pat his cheek, tell him it will all be fine, if only everyone would stop being so mean to him.

"My King, if I knew, I would absolutely help you. You know I would."

"No one is helping me. Wolf is useless; he has searched the castle and beyond but cannot find her. Brett has been gone all morning. Everleigh's handmaiden's still missing. I am watching the stupid fool but all he does is prance around the castle looking like a bigger idiot than he is. You are no help. You see nothing. You know nothing. And now Addyson is gone. I am King. Why won't anybody help me!"

"My King, I would if I could. I promise."

She keeps her face contrite, focussing on his eyes, full of unshed tears, a tremble to his full lips.

He slams his hand on the table and she flinches and then turns away from him when she hears high-pitched screaming from the corridor.

Wolf is marching ahead of Cook, who is being man-handled by two of Millard's men. She is crying and struggling to get their hands off her. "Please, please, please." Her voice is pitiful as she pleads with her new King, who has a nasty smile playing on his lips.

Ginata roots her feet to the floor but comments, as sarcastically as she dares: "That's a lot of force for one old lady."

"True, too true, my wise woman." Millard's voice is dripping with sarcasm; he need not hide his genuine feelings, really; as King, he can say and do as he pleases. "But this old woman is a deceitful bint who has been helping my sister."

"What?" Ginata's voice is full of shock, but then she realises their mistake; they disguised Ceryn as a handmaiden and she took food up for 'Addyson' and so Millard knows that Cook was in on the escape plan. Nothing would get out of her kitchen without her having full knowledge.

And it was Will who took Ceryn and Weaver to the kitchen. And as she looks at Cook, Ginata can see that it won't take too much for the poor old woman to spill her secrets; she looks ready to faint or have a heart attack. Ginata's eyes fill with tears but she cannot show sympathy for her no matter how much she feels it.

The two guards roughly let go of Cook; pushing her towards Millard. He scoffs at her tears. "Cook. I cannot understand why you, who have known me since I was a babe in arms, would do this to me."

"Please. I have done nothing. Nothing."

"You liar." He steps towards her and raises his arm to hit her.

"My King." Ginata cannot hold her tongue but bows her head to show respect to this crazy man. "She is old. You don't have to hit her to get her to speak. She will speak."

Ginata knows there is no way to save Will now. Cook will speak his name to save her own skin. No one would expect anything more from her. She isn't one of them; she isn't part of the group of individuals who have helped Everleigh. But she has helped and Ginata wishes she could help her, save her this indignity, despite not knowing her at all.

Millard nods, but steps closer to Cook. "I won't hurt you. But I am so disappointed in you. Who took Addyson from the tower?"

Ginata closes her eyes, the swooping in her stomach making bile rise in her throat.

Cook knows that it's Lanorie who was rescued today and not Addyson. If she says so, it will not only drop Will into trouble; it will drop Ginata in it too. She has visited the tower and spoken to Lanorie and not Addyson, and told the King lies.

Ginata holds her breath.

"My King." Cook's voice is firm. She doesn't sound like her life is in peril and Ginata finds herself impressed with her mettle, even while worrying what she will say and do here. "I have always loved and looked after you. A little maid came to the kitchen, and she was an unfamiliar face. I asked her where she came from and she said she was a new maid appointed by the King. Appointed by you. I had no reason to question her further. I asked if she was busy attending to you or if she could go up to the tower. She seemed pleased at my suggestion, but I didn't feel suspicious at the timing of her coming to my kitchen. I had no reason to. I sent her up to see Addyson with a tray of food and the next thing I know, your guards and Wolf here were dragging me away from my cooking. I honestly serve only you. And your mother and father before you." Cook drops to her knees and Millard pulls her to her feet, a contrite look on his face now.

"Ah Cook, I am heart sorry. What have I done to you? I am so full of upset and suspicions I see snakes everywhere I look."

Ginata wants to breathe a sigh of relief but knows better. This man who has changed his tune so suddenly could very well change it back again. She watches with interest, beyond impressed with, and grateful to, Cook for keeping her head and keeping her mouth closed.

Cook pats Millard on the head, a loving gesture despite what has just happened to her, and Ginata allows herself a smile. This woman is far shrewder than any of them would have thought.

"Forgive me?"

Cook nods her assent and Millard turns to Ginata. "Please take Cook back to the kitchen. I'll see you at supper and we will make a plan. I need to get both of my sisters back and I need help. Wise woman."

Ginata recognises her dismissal and feels a little bit aggrieved; she could offer help and advice here, help to cheer him up, but no, he dismisses her. She takes Cook's arm. She makes sure not to rush away or run – which is what her instincts are telling her to do – and takes them both to safety.

For now.

# Ceryn

I AM FEELING A FEELING THAT I have never felt before. I don't enjoy dwelling on feelings or talking about them, but it's niggling at me.

I'm sitting in Della's cottage in front of the fire, chewing on a twig – Weaver hates it when I do it, reckons I look like a bloody beaver or a squirrel or something, but I like it. It gives me something to do. And without my mask on, it helps cover my face a bit. I have washed the paste off, and my mark is there for anyone to see it. Not that there are many of us, only six. Ginata's gone back to the castle. And I have to admit I like her more and more. I like all of them more and more and I think that's what this feeling is.

Friendship. Contentment. Peace. Self-acceptance.

Yesterday when I found out that Archer had died I thought I would never smile again; that me and Weaver would ride home and grieve for him, talk about him, laugh about him, and maybe carry on with what we've always done, but then drift apart, because being together would remind us of him.

But we didn't ride home. We stayed here. We helped. And now I want to stay longer.

Everleigh's just told us the story of when she made the river rise and Finn's told us about when she made it rain and then threw a rock off course.

"Show us something," I say, spitting a bit of chewed up twig into my hand. Della's trying not to look disgusted and smiles as she points at the fire. I throw it in, though it's too damp to burn straight away. I chew more, watching this Kingmaker, this princess who will be Queen. Will I bow to her?

I think I will.

Yesterday I wanted to hurt her; to kill her.

Today I want to fight for her.

Funny how things change. I spit more wood into my hand and throw it on the fire. "Come on."

Everleigh smiles at my words but shakes her head. "I'm not very good. I'm just learning."

"Well learn more," I say.

I cannot believe I am speaking up, having my say, with all these people and my mask off and no one is scared or disgusted or ill with it.

She nods slightly and looks around the room. Her gaze rests on the fire, and I see her lips move. I can't hear her whisper and my eyes flip between her and the fire and then I see it.

The flames are growing higher, and then they are burning blue, and then they are spitting and Weaver shouts out, shuffling back out of the way. She calls the fire down, and it obeys her.

I look around the room and we are all suitably impressed. "Do more! Do more!" I am like a child at a street show. Well, I think I am – I never went to any of them. If I had they might have tried to recruit me, freak that I am.

I shake my head at my silent words to myself. I am not a freak here today. I am amongst friends. New friends and old. I reach for Weaver's hand.

The girl we rescued is a bit dim, a bit wishy-washy, but I can see that Everleigh likes her. I cannot see why Will is in love with her, but then what do I know about love?

Everleigh stands up and we are all watching her.

"I'll throw you this twig," I say, remembering what Finn said about her moving the stone with her mind.

She nods, and I fling it at her, hard. I don't want to make it too easy for her.

She watches it intently and then flicks her head to one side ever so slightly, then as the twig goes off course she turns her head the other way and my jaw drops. It really does, because the twig flips in mid-air and then with another shake of her head it is flying back towards me and I have to duck my head, so it doesn't poke me in the eye.

Everyone laughs and I join in. Normally something like that would have narked me right off and I would have hit her or something, but she is smiling at me so sweetly that I cannot be cross.

"All right. Enough showing off," I say, but my tone is light, and no one looks twice at me. Everleigh laughs and comes over to me, giving me a tight squeeze.

Later, when Weaver goes out for fresh air, I follow him and slip my arms around his waist. I love hugging him. Not that I'd tell him that, though.

He hugs me back. "What do you think about staying for a bit?" He asks what I was going to ask and I love him for asking it instead of me. Saving me from feeling weak or foolish.

"Could do," I say and I hug him harder. He laughs and I punch him.

Some things never change.

# 21

GINATA FINDS HERSELF next to Wolf, waiting to go into supper. Millard is taking his time, a queue of people shaking his hand and bowing low to him and asking for favours as they make their way along, which he just loves.

"Hope you're proud of yourself." She whispers the words so no one can hear her.

He looks down at her, a frown on his grisly face. "What?"

"The way you treated Cook."

"I just do as I'm told, me."

"Would you ever say no to him?"

He shakes his head then, his expression hard.

"What about his brother? Didn't you work for him first?"

"Only because Millard told me to."

Ginata shakes her head and frowns at him. "You make me sick."

Wolf looks down at his feet but doesn't answer. What can he say? He works for the King and will do as he's told, whatever he's told, however awful it is. If Millard had told him to kill Cook there and then, he would have.

"You work for him too." Defending himself.

Ginata shrugs.

"And if he tells you to do something you better."

"I would, of course I would." She lies easily.

"People always do as they're told. By whoever has the power. Or by whoever they love."

Ginata looks at him sharply, surprised by something so profound coming out of his mouth.

Eventually they take their seats; Wolf on one side of his King, Ginata on the other. There is no one else to join them.

Even though he is smiling so that his people can see how affable and easy going he is, Millard is still furious about his sister being taken from the tower.

"Who. Is. Helping. Her?" His words are stark and angry and Ginata is wishing herself back in her cottage.

Neither she nor Wolf volunteer an answer.

"Please help me. I am King, and yet one of my subjects is betraying me. Maybe more than one. Someone is being traitorous to me. It's just not fair."

Ginata hides her smile by taking a bite of bread. He swings from mood to mood like a spider on the thread of his own web. First, he is furious, then he is hurt; baffled by how unkind life is being to him, then he is murderous again, in the space of minutes. Who could please this man? This King?

"My King," Wolf says, wiping the sweat off his brow. "I have searched the castle and the grounds and beyond. I cannot find her anywhere."

"So tomorrow you will start sweeping the villages. She must be somewhere. And now Addyson is with her. And whoever is helping them must die."

Ginata swallows thickly. The tension is too much for her. If she is found out, she will die. The knowledge of that is making her insides loosen, her hands sweat.

"Take this," Millard says, passing her a drink. "You look thirsty."

"I am." Ginata downs the drink in one go, glad to have something to do.

"What about," Wolf says, brow crumpled, thinking making his head hurt. "Instead of looking for her in all the villages, we draw her out?"

Ginata rolls her eyes; now Wolf becomes a tactical genius. It's a great idea, but Ginata doesn't want Everleigh lured out of hiding.

"With Addyson gone, there's nothing to tempt her out of hiding with," Ginata says, a sorrowful look on her face. "It would have been a good idea, if we still had her."

Millard is nodding his head. "Wolf. You are brilliant. Lure her out of hiding. She's somewhere in the Realm, we just need to get her in to the open."

"But how?" Ginata's tries to convey the hopelessness of the situation in her tone, but Millard is beaming, and she is struck again by how handsome he is, when he's not killing people.

"We don't have Addyson anymore, but we have someone she cares about."

A sick feeling bubbles in Ginata's stomach, mixing with the stress she is already feeling. She knows what's coming, and she knows it will work, and she knows it's the worst thing that could happen. Damn Wolf. And damn Millard.

Millard grins at Wolf. "Bring me the fool."

# Lanorie

I AM FREE. I AM FREE. I am free.

And I have decided to never be brave again.

I will keep my head down. I will do as I'm told and I will serve my Queen.

I have changed from Addyson's dress into one of Della's. I am clean, and I've brushed my hair. I don't feel like rats and spiders are running over my skin anymore.

But I don't feel happy. I don't like this marked girl – Ceryn – who rescued me. Not one bit. Her friend is handsome and very kind, but she is nasty looking and mean.

She might have saved me from the tower, and death, but she isn't very friendly.

And everyone is acting like they don't care about that thing on her face, but they do. They must. It's scary. She looks like she's been burned or something. It's so red and angry looking. She washed all the paste off and it's so bright. So horrible looking. I reckon it's catching, so I make sure not to touch anything she's touched or sit anywhere near her.

Everleigh keeps smiling at me and patting me, like she can't believe I'm alive. I know what she means. I thought I was dead for sure.

But her and Addyson are so happy to see me and so grateful that I helped them, I feel all warm inside.

Once Della has fed us all and Everleigh has done some magic tricks – which I saw her do ages before anyone else – we all decide it's time for bed.

Ceryn will sleep in Ginata's cottage with Addyson and Everleigh and me, but Della, Finn and Weaver will sleep next door.

I don't want to sleep anywhere near Ceryn, but I won't leave Everleigh either. I know her better than any of these, maybe even better than Addyson. I spend the most time with her. But I can't even pretend to be nice to Ceryn.

I keep looking at her and she catches me, and I look away because I can't even smile at her. I don't know who she thinks she is.

Everleigh is talking with her and laughing so I interrupt, making sure not to stand too close to Ceryn, or the nasty stain on her face.

"I'm going to go for a walk," I say, hoping Everleigh will stop me, make a fuss of me.

"Really? It's getting dark."

"I've been locked up for days. I need fresh air."

"I think you should stay here," Ceryn says, trying to look concerned about me, though I'm sure she's not. "It might not be safe out."

"No one's looking for me. Only her and Addyson."

"True..." Everleigh smiles at me.

"Still." Ceryn folds her arms, staring at me.

"I think I'll be fine. I'll just take a walk for five minutes. Enjoy not being locked up, you know."

"Let me come with you." This marked girl is a nag.

I'd love Everleigh to come with me instead and leave Ceryn, but I reckon she'd just follow along to annoy me, so I shake my head. "I won't be long."

Everleigh says, "Just be careful, stay close to the cottage."

As I walk out of the door, they are laughing about something and I decide I'll be longer than five minutes. Make them worry about me.

They seem to have forgotten that I've been locked up and all alone for days.

It is nice to be outside. I wish I could go to the castle and see Cook, but I'm not that stupid. I'm sure no one is looking for me or even remembers me, what with Everleigh missing, but I won't go to the madman's castle.

The river will be nice though. It will take me ages to get there and back and then they'll all be worrying about me.

Good.

I sit by the river and think maybe I am being a bit silly. Everleigh is so happy I'm free I shouldn't try to spoil it. And that marked girl will leave soon and then we can go back to being like we were before.

I head back along the path and see one of the King's men riding along. I keep my head down; sure he won't look at me. I don't look like I work at the castle in Della's clothes.

"You!"

I turn away and walk faster, but he gallops to my side, jumps off his horse. "I know you."

"No," I say wishing I was still at the cottage, even with that horrible woman there.

"You're the Kingmaker's maid. The King is looking for you."

"No." I say it again, hoping he'll listen, but he doesn't.

He lifts me off my feet and even as I struggle he throws me over the horse so I'm facing the floor with my backside in the air. He sits behind me and once he's holding the reins, I can't move much at all, and tears are stinging my eyes but I kick off one of my shoes.

Maybe Everleigh will see it and realise something's wrong.

As he rides away from the river and takes me back to the castle, I'm crying.

What have I done now?

# 22

"I'M WORRIED ABOUT HER; she's been gone ages."

"She's probably just sulking," Addyson says, going to Della's side; she spends a lot of time by Della's side and she's blooming with the love and attention of a mother figure. It means Everleigh can be a sister again.

"Do you think?" Everleigh is biting her lip. "We've only just got her back."

"She loves a sulk," Addyson says.

Ceryn shakes her head. "She's a pest, but we'll look for her. I'll fetch the boys and see you soon."

"Don't be too cross with her."

"I won't." Ceryn grins at Everleigh but she's got a nasty glint in her eye; she's gone before Everleigh can say any more and Everleigh sinks into the chair, groaning.

"She will be fine." Della rubs Everleigh's arm and then pours her a drink.

"I've got a nasty feeling. I told her to be careful." Everleigh cries and Della moves to her side, pats her shoulder. Everleigh looks up at her. "Why can't everything be simple? And everyone be safe?"

"Ah lovely. It doesn't seem like it, but if life were simple, it would be boring. Trouble and strife strengthen us. Lanorie will be just fine, probably got caught up in her freedom, or fell asleep with nothing to worry about anymore."

"I hope so."

"I'm sure so."

THEY PULL WILL FROM the floor, where he was showing off a headstand, and drag him to the great hall. Will knows this isn't a good sign. Millard is cross again – maybe ready to question him about where Everleigh is again. Well, Millard can ask, and he won't say, same as last time.

As they approach the doors, the guards let go of him, and allow him to straighten his clothes. "No funny business, fool," Wolf says and the guards laugh.

Will isn't as foolish as everyone believes. He walks quietly to the dais and bows low to Millard, whose smile is icy.

"Will. I have to apologise for what's about to happen, but I need to find my sister and I-"

"My King, I don't know where she is."

"I believe you. I really do. But I know how much Everleigh loves you. You've been her friend all her life. If you're in trouble, then she'll come."

"But I'm not-" The truth dawns on Will because he isn't a fool. "I *am* in trouble?"

Millard smiles at him, nodding his head slowly, a strange glint in his eye.

Will lowers his head; bows low. "My King. I have loved Everleigh all her life and you are right, if I am in trouble, she'll come. I understand."

Ginata works hard at keeping her face a mask. She cannot allow Millard to see that her heart is breaking. Everleigh *will* come out of hiding to help Will, and Millard *will* lock her up or kill her. But she cannot think of anything to say or do to alter what's about to happen.

"Let me go!" The voice is recognisable to both Will and Ginata who look towards the heavy doors of the great hall.

Lanorie.

Millard looks over at the furore and gets to his feet, a nervous look on his face. He sees three of his men holding on to a screaming, fighting, shouting woman and shakes his head for them to move away from the great hall and the crowds of people and out to the corridor again.

They follow his silent orders and he nods and smiles at his fellow diners as he threads through the tables to see what's going on. He nods for the men holding Will to come with him. Wolf and Ginata follow without being asked and Will tags along too.

Millard's face is etched in fury as he stares at his guards. "Why would you bring this screaming, shouting bint into the hall? With all my subjects there? With every eye on me?"

The men bow their heads and don't even try to give excuses.

"Who is she?"

By now they have stood Lanorie back on her feet, a guard holding on to each elbow and one behind her. She's no longer screaming or struggling; instead she is crying and wailing.

Ginata stands next to Millard; she wants Lanorie to see her face when she finally stops performing; to see the silent warning she's trying to give, *if* she ever stops performing.

She knows what this girl is like, how her mouth runs away with her, the problems she has already caused for Everleigh. She sneaks a glance at Will and can read on his face he has the same fears. If Lanorie mentions that she has been in the tower, then they are both dead.

"This is Everleigh's handmaiden." A guard speaks up, though his voice is trembling. "We thought you'd want to see her straight away."

"I would." Millard's face has changed again, his moods always changing, too fast to keep up with. "I just wish you hadn't brought her into the hall."

He steps towards her and Lanorie's legs are shaking as he puts a finger under her chin and gently lifts her face to meet his.

"What's your name?" His voice is soft and deep, dangerous. "I recognise you..."

Lanorie looks at him, this handsome prince that she has been half in love with all her life and chokes out another sob. "Please don't kill me. My prince. My King."

She bows her head low, tears dripping onto the stone floor, and Ginata and Will exchange looks. Will has been in love with Lanorie as long as she has been in love with Millard, as long as they have both been in Everleigh's life. But he's watching her now, a look of abject fear on his face. Ginata is just about masking her feelings in case Millard turns to her, but her insides are a mass of liquid snakes.

What is this foolish girl about to say or do and what can she or Will do to salvage things?

Millard touches Lanorie again; this time a palm against her wet cheek. She lifts her eyes up to meet his, keeping her head bowed low. She is trembling.

"What's your name?" His voice is lower, laced with danger, and both Ginata and Will take a step closer to Lanorie. "Stand up properly. Look at me."

Lanorie does as she's told, tears, snot and dribble trailing over her face and clothes. Despite having been in the tower, she made a choice to be there and was never in immediate danger. This is different; she knows this, she can feel the tension and the threat. She looks at Ginata, who widens her eyes and slowly shakes her head.

"My name is Lanorie."

"And you look after my sister?"

Lanorie nods.

"And you know where she is?"

Lanorie nods, and Ginata and Will both close their eyes. Neither one of them can step in here to stop her talking without implicating themselves. If they implicate themselves Millard will kill them and then they will be even less use to Everleigh than they already are.

"And you'll tell me?"

Lanorie nods again, her eyes locked on Millard's refusing to look at either Ginata or Will, knowing what she will see in their faces and wanting no part of it. She has been captured, and now she has to do what she has to do.

# Ginata

MY HEART HURTS. SHE will tell Millard where Everleigh is and then it will all be over. Our Queen will be dead and our King will rule without opposition and then what?

If I had a weapon, I would kill her myself. And that is so unlike me I understand why my heart hurts. I stay silent and I keep my face impassive, but I am crying inside.

Why wasn't she safe inside with Everleigh? How have they captured her and still not know where Everleigh is?

I close my eyes and concentrate. Since Halfreda's death, my visions and inklings and feelings have been all over the place. I know no more than any other person around me and I don't like that lack of intuition, that loss of insight. I feel empty except for the inner turmoil I have felt since the coronation, moving into the dead King's bedroom and living on a knife edge with the new King and I know that is why my natural gift is muted.

Looking at Lanorie I try to see past the slightly too big clothes, the dull blonde hair, the plain but pleasant face. I try to see her heart, what she's thinking.

I know she loves Everleigh; there's no doubt about that. And she's loyal to her, despite her big mouth. She's simple and yet brave. The way she switched places with Addyson was something none of us would have imagined of her.

So, she has hidden depths... and yet the young boy she fell in love with just last week had her spilling her own secrets and other people's. She cannot be trusted because she doesn't see the big picture. She wants to be happy, now. She wants to be safe, now. She wants to be kissed now, or fed now, or whatever now. She's like a puppy. She doesn't understand that getting Everleigh to the throne isn't as simple as wanting it or hoping for it; we all have to work together.

And yet she's done it once. She freed Addyson.

But now she has the King's guard's hands on her, the King looking at her with soft but insane eyes. She blushes as she looks at him through her tears.

He is handsome. More than handsome. Tall, dark haired, dark eyed, gorgeous. Powerful. I can see why she thinks what she thinks. Although he is changeable and frightening, he is also powerful, good looking... he's the King. The most important man in the Realm.

I can see Will looking at Lanorie, his eyes pleading with the girl he loves to keep quiet. But like me, he cannot speak up. If either of us says anything, if she says too much, more than Everleigh's head will roll. We will all be dead.

"Where have you been, you and my sister?"

His voice is so pleasant, this dangerous King, chatting happily with his sister's handmaiden, lulling her into a false sense of security with every word. Like Will is, I know, I am silently pleading with her to please keep our secrets.

"We've been hiding."

She hasn't mentioned the tower yet and I feel ridiculously grateful but hateful at the same time. She will have to give Everleigh up. Or die.

What a choice.

What would I do? I told Will I wouldn't die for Everleigh. Does that still stand? I cannot think straight. With Lanorie in front of me, flanked by guards and looking pathetically sad, and Will, Millard, Wolf and I forming a semi-circle around her I feel like we are all too close to the truth coming out. One misstep, one word out of line and we could die.

I don't want to die, when I feel like the truth may come out I feel sick to my stomach. I do not want Millard to know I am false to him, for him to end my life. I like my life. I like my new home. I like the castle and my suite of rooms. I also like him liking me, and I can't imagine why. The need to survive is strong and I know that if he likes me I am more likely to live than if he does not.

But then I also like Everleigh. The prophecy says she must live, and she must rule. Halfreda thought so, her teacher thought so. I won't argue with that. I'll do my best to get her on the throne, but not at my expense.

And yet if Lanorie drops Everleigh in it now, which she has to, to save her own neck, what can I say or do?

If I step in or speak up, I will die.

So, is that my answer, I'll help her reach her throne, serve her brother in the meantime and do everything I can to secure my life?

I have become a selfish witch indeed, in a short space of time. I wonder what difference there would be to my thoughts if Halfreda was still alive. She was a better witch than me, a wiser woman than me, I know. Was she less selfish too? Probably. She never had a love of her own, a life of her own. She was here only to serve the King. As am I now, I suppose.

Still trying to see Lanorie's intention, I focus on her face, her eyes, her tears, her heart. I feel despair and tension in the air, but I suppose that is coming from me, Will and Lanorie.

There is glee and excitement. A building of anticipation; probably Millard and maybe Wolf.

There is a mixture of revulsion and the rush of power that I guess maybe the guards are feeling. Power over someone is a heady thing, and yet when a young girl crumples against you, sobbing and wretched there must be a part of any good man, any good heart, that feels pity for her and despair of themselves.

The mix of emotions is making me feel dizzy. Or is that the fear?

"I'll take you to her." Lanorie's voice is small but steady and I can see Will is ready to fall over. With all attention on Lanorie, I move from Millard's side to Will's and I take his arm. He cannot show loyalty to Everleigh at this moment; now is not the time to admit fealty.

Millard laughs, and the sound curls my toes. Just not in an enjoyable way. My head is spinning and spinning and spinning trying to think of anything to do or say that will help buy us time, anything.

"Can you trust her?" I ask, my voice surprisingly steady. "Where's she been all this time? Where was she found? What if this is a trap or something?"

"She was found by the river, my King," one of the guards speaks up. "I recognised her straight away. I knew you were looking for her. Needed a bit of help to bring her in. She's feisty."

Millard smiles at Lanorie. "Feisty... I like it. Take me now. Wolf, gather more men, in case she won't come quietly and we'll see. Will Everleigh live or die? I'll see what mood I'm in when we get there."

He has totally ignored my words, my questions, and I sink into a gloom of upset and a bit of indignant fury. I thought I was supposed to be the wise woman here, isn't he supposed to accept my counsel?

I hold on to Will even tighter, for myself now as much as him.

"What can we do?" My voice is less than a whisper, and his reply is the same. "I have no idea."

We are watching Lanorie and she meets our eyes and gives us the tiniest of nods. If we hadn't been desperately searching her face for an answer why she's doing this would we even have seen it?

A nod. What does it mean?

I'm sorry.

I have no choice.

We may never know.

As Millard pulls Wolf along the corridor and calls for his hounds and his horses, we stand together, not invited to the party.

Not wanting to go, either.

## 23

CERYN PULLS HER HORSE up at the river. There's no sign of Lanorie, and though she might be hiding, Ceryn doubts it. She has a feeling that Lanorie would want everyone to see her and whatever misery she imagines she's feeling. She might have wandered off; she seems a bit mindless to Ceryn.

Finn and Weaver are rushing around, looking in ridiculous places no one would ever hide, under a tiny hedge row, behind a particularly large rock. Ceryn shakes her head, stifling her laughter.

She walks around, eyes scanning the ground, the trees, the entire area. What happened and where is she?

"No sign here," Finn calls out, head tucked behind a bush.

"Or here," Weaver says, backing out from a thatch of trees.

Ceryn laughs. "She's not playing hide and seek, boys. I think something happened."

Weaver comes to her side. She has a good instinct for things like this, and he knows it. "Trouble?"

Ceryn nods.

"Here." Finn is holding up a single shoe.

Ceryn takes it off him. "Was she captured? Did she kick this off?"

"Let's take it back to Everleigh. She'll know if it's hers."

"It has to be hers. Why did she go out wandering; stupid girl."

"It's not her fault."

"That she got captured? Of course it's her fault. Going off in a huff. Come on, let's head back."

The three of them run back to the cottages, Finn bringing up the rear, Ceryn and Weaver evenly paced; all of them filled with a fresh sense of urgency.

Ceryn pushes through the cottage door. "We can't find her, but we found a shoe." She holds it up for Everleigh to see, who promptly lets out a cry.

"So, it's hers?"

Everleigh nods.

"Damn her!" Ceryn kicks the chair and gets a shocked look from Della. "Sorry."

"What's happened to her?"

"We think one of your brother's men has captured her. I can't see who else would carry her off on a horse, well we presume a horse. There's no sign of a struggle, just the shoe."

"So, she kicked it off, so we'd see it?"

"I think so. Listen, you lot stay here, Weaver and I will go out on our horses. We can travel further afield, see if there's any sign of her. We're quick and no one from the castle will recognise us if they see us."

"What will Millard do if he's got her?" This from Addyson, her little face white and eyes filled with unshed tears.

Everleigh hugs her. "I've no idea."

Ceryn clears her throat. "Will she give you up? If it's him, that's got her. Will she give you up?"

Addyson shrugs, but Everleigh shakes her head. "I know she wouldn't."

"Let's go. Let's see what we can see. If there's anything we can do."

Ceryn turns back to face them all. "Stay out of sight. Is there anywhere you could hide, in case?"

Della shakes her head. "Both cottages are tiny. There's nowhere to hide. You don't think-"

"I don't know her like Everleigh does. But she's only young. And she'll be frightened. If she has been captured, and she tells Millard everything, then he'll come here looking for you. Just close the door and Finn, keep a lookout."

Finn nods and puts a hand on Everleigh's shoulder.

Ceryn and Weaver leave them behind, jumping up on their horses, who were enjoying their grassy dinner outside the cottages. "What do you think?" Weaver's voice is quiet as always, measured.

"If they have captured her, I reckon she'll squeal like a pig."

"Really?"

"She'll be petrified."

"Have we missed something? Is she lost or... I don't know, fallen in the river."

"She won't be lost. There's nowhere around that river to *be* lost. If she fell in the river, she'd have climbed back out. It's not deep there. The shoe means they have taken her."

"Right, so who else would take her?"

"If not, the King's men? I have no idea. She's a harmless young girl alone by the river. Any men with unpleasant thoughts would have attacked her there and then and left her behind. We'd have found her. They have taken her. She's got nothing worth stealing."

"So, someone's seen her and recognised her from the castle?"

"Any of the King's men would know her. If she's been with Everleigh since they were both little. All his men would be on the lookout for Everleigh and Addyson. It's got to be killing him that they've gotten away."

"So, what do we do? We can't ask for her back."

"We'll ride around, see if we hear anything, see if we see anything. We'll go back to the river and take the path to the castle. It's all we can do."

"Do you wish we'd just gone home? After we found out about Archer?"

"No. I'm enjoying myself. I never thought I'd say that, with Archer gone. But I think he'd want us to help her. If he loved her like they say."

"He would have wanted us to help, even if he didn't love her."

"True. So, let's help."

WILL AND GINATA ARE standing in the middle of her room, white faced and silent. They have no idea what to do or what to say or what will happen next.

No one is guarding Will because all the King's men have gone with Millard, and yet he has no idea what to do with his freedom.

"Shall we go to the cottage?"

"We can't. If Lanorie leads them there, then they'll find us too."

"He's baying for blood."

"He is." They are both silent, remembering the rush of men and hounds that left the castle in a swarm of promised violence. The dogs were literally salivating, probably left hungry. The men were laughing, calling out and whooping. Millard was silent, as was Wolf, but the menace was tangible.

Lanorie, thrown on a horse, with Wolf riding behind her, looked like a prisoner in some sick war game. She hadn't said a word to either of them before they took away her, and Will and Ginata had trooped straight to Ginata's rooms.

Ginata holds her stomach. "I feel sick."

"We need to think."

"I can't. All I can see is Everleigh being captured and killed."

"He will kill her, won't he?"

Ginata nods. She is sure, if Millard gets his hands on his sister, she will die.

"We cannot do anything. Even with horses we won't catch them up."

"I hate not being able to help her. I hate that I haven't seen her. If Lanorie tells Millard where she is, I will kill her. I will."

"Will. If Lanorie tells Millard where Everleigh is, he will probably kill her himself."

Will wipes away furious tears. Ginata is right. They have no way of helping and no way of knowing what's happening. All they can do is sit and wait and wonder.

# Ceryn

WHAT I SAID TO WEAVER is right. I am enjoying myself. I enjoy being useful. I enjoy being useful. I hate being idle. I hate being girly, helpless and waiting for things to happen. Riding through the woods now, heading for the castle, I feel happy.

Though if I see Lanorie and she's not dead, I'll happily wring her neck.

Why she had to fuss and sulk off to the river, I'll never know. I hate girls like her. Pathetic and whiny and looking for attention all the time.

Weaver whistles a low note and I fall in beside him. We both stop. With our horses quiet, we can both hear the thundering of hooves, the calls of men. We pull the horses back into the trees. They are near, but I can't see anything yet.

"Can you see anything?"

Weaver shakes his head. I jump down off Pitch, patting her flank as I do. She snorts softly and I pat her again.

I look for a tree I can climb and see one straight away. If we are down low and the other riders are down low, we'll sit here all day not knowing anything about them. It might be nothing to do with Lanorie, just the King's men hunting deer.

I'm a quick climber. I am surefooted and fast, up a tree or otherwise. I pride myself on being good at physical things. It has always made up for my face.

I am pretty high up when I see them, a snake of hounds and horses threading through the trees. The men are wearing the King's livery and two of them hold banners, like they are heading off to a grand battle. The King's banners mean the King is riding out, and, right enough, one of the horse riders is wearing a crown. And next to him is another horse with Lanorie on, being ridden by a right scary looking man.

Lanorie looks miserable – though she always has since I rescued her – and she's not trussed up. Does this mean she's helping the King willingly? Though how many people would refuse the King? He'll kill anyone who won't help him.

So, she's helping him.

But the direction they are going is not the direction of the cottages.

Is she leading them the wrong way? If she is, then he'll kill her.

I bound back down the tree, easily hopping from branch to branch.

"It's the King and his men. About thirty of them on horseback, about thirty hounds running ahead. Lanorie's on a horse with some enormous fellow holding onto her."

"Tied up?"

"No."

"So willingly helping?"

"Probably not. In fairness, she'll have no choice."

"What shall we do? We need to warn Everleigh."

"That's the thing. She's leading them the wrong way."

"But he'll kill her."

"I know. But with thirty men, I don't know what we can do."

"Let's follow, anyway. See what happens."

It's exactly what I would say and as we quietly ride along in the same direction, but far enough away that they won't see us, I try to think of how we can help.

Thirty men, all on horseback and me and Weaver the same. I have my bow and arrows, my dagger, Weaver has his dagger. What can we do against all those armed men, hell bent on protecting their King?

Will he kill her? All I know of this King is what I've been told. I've seen him from a distance a few times but never been in his company. We've been told he's mad. And he wants his sister, dead or alive.

If Lanorie has told him, she'll help him find Everleigh, and I can't think of another reason they'd all be out in the woods together, then he'll be furious when he realises she's not.

He will want her dead.

"Any thoughts?" I whisper to Weaver. I don't think we'll be heard but I'm not stupid. We are well outnumbered here.

"He'll kill her, if she doesn't take him to Everleigh. And she's obviously not, given the direction we're going in. Good on her, though."

"Yes, I suppose." I agree grudgingly. I think little of this handmaiden of Everleigh's. I think she's sulky and whingy, helpless and stupid. She might have been brave when she swapped places with Addyson, but I reckon she was just too dumb to think through what she was doing.

If she is leading the King the wrong way though, I suppose she is brave.

But she'll die for it.

"There's too many of them." Weaver's voice is strained. "I don't see what we can do."

"Try?"

"Yes, we'll try."

"What if we get hurt? Or killed?"

Weaver shrugs. "We said we'd help. If we serve the Queen, we do so at our own risk."

"I think so."

We are moving quickly and start closing the gap between them and us, riding forwards and slightly to the left as we go. We don't want them to see us, but we need to see them.

They ride into a huge clearing, the woods behind them, and flat land ahead. The King calls out, and they all come to a halt.

Lanorie raises her head and says something. It's so frustrating not being able to hear.

The King bellows something at her. Again we cannot hear the words, but he doesn't look happy.

He jumps off his horse, and the man behind her does the same. He pulls her down, and she drops to her knees. The King pulls her up by her arm and she staggers.

We both ride forward; I don't feel good about this.

We are still too far away to be helpful. We cannot make out what is being said or done. The dogs are sniffing around the grass, some of them peeing, some of them laying down and resting. The men stay on their horses, where they are harmless enough for now.

Lanorie is gesturing as she talks to the King. I wish we knew what she was saying.

Is she begging for her life? Apologising for duping him? Crumpling with fear and telling him the truth?

I canter forwards a little, Weaver beside me, and cry out when I see Millard reach for his sword.

In less time than I take to squeeze my thighs against Pitch's sides, ready to spur her forwards, he has sliced Lanorie's head clean off.

He just kills her.

Despite what I thought about her, I am sobbing, and sliding off Pitch. Weaver has come off his horse and catches me, turning my head to the side to hold me.

I pull at my mask, ripping it off in time to vomit all over the grass.

Spent, I wipe my mouth on my sleeve and stand up, pulling an arrow from my quiver.

"Ceryn." Weaver's voice holds a warning and I know he is right and I know I cannot inflict anything like what the man deserves but

I cannot let Lanorie die without at least answering his violence with some of my own.

I am one hell of a shot, but I jump back up on Pitch so my arrow can fly higher and farther.

Weaver is on his horse. "One shot then we ride away."

I nod.

"Don't even stop to check if it hits him."

"I won't need to check."

I trust my skill, aim and fire and seconds later as we hammer in the other direction I hear a cry and I know I have hit the King.

I vow, not for Lanorie, or Everleigh, really, but for Archer, that it won't be the last time he feels pain because of me.

# 24

MILLARD IS SCREAMING. An arrow, flying out of thin air, has hit him right in the top of his arm and there is blood, swearing and threats as Wolf rushes to help him. He rips the bottom half of his shirt off and wraps it around the King's arm.

"Get me back to Ginata." Millard's voice is rough, and he has already forgotten that he just killed someone, in the sadness he is feeling for himself and the pretty minor injury he's received. "Men, find out who did that. Search the woods."

The men take their order, but Wolf stays with Millard. After helping his King on to his horse, he holds the two sets of reins and leads them back to the castle.

Neither of them looks back at Lanorie's body on the floor.

"Who did that to me?"

Wolf shakes his head. "No idea, my King. You have no enemies other than your sister."

"She can shoot an arrow. I've seen her."

"She wouldn't have known we were here, my King."

"I hate this. Why won't she just let me reign in peace?"

They are silent the rest of the way, Millard brooding about his injury – the murder he just carried out completely forgotten and Wolf waiting to do as he's told.

CERYN AND WEAVER RIDE faster than they ever have and when they get near to the cottages, they walk the two horses to a copse of trees and tether them. They don't want them visible if any of the King's men ride by.

They are both crying by the time they get to the front door. Weaver wipes his eyes. "I'll go first?"

"Let me."

She pushes open the door and four faces look up at them, hope and worry etched on soft skin. Everleigh shakes her head when she sees Ceryn's face, how her eyes flood over with tears, her mouth tries to speak, her shoulders shake.

"No!"

Ceryn is nodding now, Weaver standing behind her with his arms around her. "I'm so sorry. We found her, but we were too far away."

"Your brother killed her."

Everleigh drops to her knees, crying and muttering the word no, over and over.

Addyson buries her head in Della's clothes and cries quietly.

Finn looks at them. "What happened?"

Della sits Addyson in front of the fire and eases Ceryn into a seat. Weaver sits on the arm. Everleigh stays on the floor, and Finn sits next to her, patting her back and trying to think of any way he can be helpful.

Everleigh raises her head as Ceryn talks, tears streaming, though she does not wipe them or stem them.

"We rode through the woods from the river to the castle. Weaver heard a noise, so we stopped. We could hear horses, men, dogs... but we couldn't see anything. I climbed a tree. I could see them. About thirty of the King's men on horses and about the same number of dogs. Lanorie was on one horse with a man and the King was riding next to them."

Weaver rubs her arm and takes over. Ceryn is crying too much to talk. "We kept up with them, narrowing the gap between us and them."

"Was she bringing them here?" Addyson's tone is accusing and Weaver is quick to shake his head. "No, they were going in the wrong direction. When they got through the woods and there was only empty land ahead, I suppose the King realised it. He called the horses to a stop, and we got a bit closer."

Everleigh sobs louder and Addyson drops next to her, holding onto her, crying with her.

"Millard got off his horse, then the other man did as well – he pulled Lanorie off."

"It happened too quickly, we couldn't help."

"What did he do to her?" Everleigh's voice is so quiet they all strain to hear her.

"He..." Ceryn can't make herself say it.

"Within a second he got his sword and he-"

"Beheaded her?"

Weaver and Ceryn nod, and Everleigh screams. "I hate him. I hate him. I want to kill him!"

"You will," Ceryn says, her voice steely. "I'll help you."

"We were too far away, it happened so fast. We were ready to try..."

Everleigh's smile is faint. "Really?"

"Yes. We agreed we would try. For you. Die for you."

"I shot an arrow at him, though."

"She hit him too if his scream was anything to go by."

Everleigh's laugh turns to a cry and they are all crying, too shocked by the turn of events to speak.

GINATA HEARS THE FUSS from the corridor before Will. Will is sitting on the window seat in a daze, knees drawn up to his chest, cheeks wet with tears.

As the door slams open, Ginata is already on her feet, eager to know what's happened. Will jumps up too.

Wolf is holding on to Millard, who is injured, and leaning on Wolf heavily. Blood is dripping from a wound in his arm and on to the floor.

"He needs help. They shot him."

Ginata takes Millard's hand and leads him towards her workroom, an instinct to help and heal taking over. "What happened?"

Millard is groggy from the pain and comes quietly.

"Someone shot him." Wolf's voice is tinged with anger.

"Did you find Everleigh?"

"No. That little witch was lying to us. She had no intention of taking us to Everleigh."

"Where is she?" Ginata keeps her voice light, like she's not too bothered. She can see Will behind Wolf and quickly shuts the door on him. Whatever has happened to Lanorie – and it is likely she is dead – Wolf need not see Will's reaction. She knows he will listen at the door, but she cannot stop that.

"I need to lay him up here."

Wolf helps her get Millard on the table where he passes out from the pain and shock.

"She's dead." Wolf sounds pleased.

Ginata turns away from him, reaches to the back of a shelf for some cloth to tie around Millard's arm. She is glad that Wolf cannot see her. She hopes that she looks briskly efficient and not at all upset. She turns back to face him. "Did you do his dirty work for him again?"

Wolf shakes his head. "No, he was that furious, he did it himself. Sliced her head right off."

Ginata bites the inside of her cheek, hard, tasting blood. "Leave me alone. I need to help the King."

"I'll be out there." Wolf opens the door and Ginata is glad to see no sign of Will. He hasn't fainted on to the floor with the news of his sweetheart's death. She doesn't know where he is, but she cannot be seen to care.

She must do her job now, with Wolf outside. She must help the King.

# Ginata

WOLF IS PACING IN THE other room, worrying about his King.

I am standing stock still in front of Millard, worrying about Will. Everleigh. Myself. How simple was life just a few short weeks ago? I wish with all my heart that Halfreda was here, to hold my hand, and help me out.

Looking down at the King, unconscious and vulnerable, a wicked thought passes through my head. Wolf is in the other room; he isn't watching me.

Millard is laying in front of me, the cause of all our problems.

How simple would it be to kill him?

My eyes spill over with tears. What has happened to me? Heal not harm, help not hinder. Until the damn death draught I have only ever used my powers for good. Where have I gone wrong? My moral compass is so skewed that I am standing in front of a King and wishing him dead, actively plotting in my head how I could hurt him.

Shame on me.

I close my eyes, tears staining my face, branding me. I am changing from myself to someone I don't recognise and don't like. I reach over to the shelf and take a swig from the flagon of ale. I never need to look for food or drink since I have moved into the castle and I like it. But the enjoyable things are being outweighed by the bad; like my brain thinking wicked things, like wondering if I should kill Kings.

I stand closer to him. Look at his face. This man may be a cruel and slightly mad King, but he is a man, a person. I have no right to end his life; I have no claim to his life. I can help Everleigh in any way possible, but I cannot go down this road. It will only end badly for me.

I touch his skin. What happened to his soul to rot it? How is he so evil at such a young age? I close my eyes, my hand on his cheek and I tell myself, silently but firmly, this man was just like me once, innocent of wrongdoing but considering it. He stepped over that line.

I will not.

I concentrate on my skin touching his and will some of my goodness (just about) to leech through and heal him.

I will never know why this young prince turned out to be a crazed King with murder on his mind. I will not know his thoughts or secrets. And I do not need to.

I need only serve.

Him.

Everleigh.

Whoever holds the crown must hold my loyalty, if only to stop me doing something terrible that I would never recover from.

I let my hand wander to his heart. I feel the beat of his life and I focus on him feeling well and being good. Is it too late to save him, whoever rules? If he was repentant, Everleigh could lock him up, let him live.

When did his heart change? He would have been a beautiful baby, an innocent boy, with all the privileges and riches any child could desire.

He is a handsome man. With his eyes closed and the hate they glow with covered up, he looks even better. He is handsome and I know some revulsion I felt for him has dissipated, despite what he's done to Lanorie. After all, I just thought myself about crossing that line. Whatever stopped me didn't stop him. That's the only difference.

We have both had dark thoughts. I was strong enough to deflect them.

Or too cowardly to follow them through. I shake my head at that thought.

The bleeding has stopped, but I need to tend to his wound. I need to wake him too. I go to a shelf of potions and find one that will slowly revive him.

I lift his head awkwardly and let a few drops wet his lips. He stirs and I drip a few more into his now open mouth.

He opens his eyes and closes them again.

Wolf pokes his head through the door. "He awake yet?"

I shake my head. "Help me get the clothes off his top half. I need to get at his wound."

Wolf lifts Millard under one arm into a sitting position and I step around him, pulling at his clothes, ripping one bit of his shirt, struggling to get it up and over his head, with little help from Wolf, who seems to enjoy my discomfort.

Pig.

Wolf-Pig.

I shake my head to clear it again; I need to focus.

Millard opens his eyes, and this time they stay open. He winces when I touch the skin around his cut, trying to figure out how bad it is. Wolf ripped the arrow out before he got here, so the skin is ragged and sorer than it would have been had the arrow been removed carefully.

I gather all the things I need to clean and sew the wound closed.

Wolf looks a little queasy and leaves me alone with the King again.

"Sorry my King, but it will hurt."

"I can take it." He says the words with a clear voice, but the way his eyes fill with tears as I clean the cut show me how much it hurts.

I pull a stool over so I can sit close to him, stitching him up, mending him and I wish I could mend his heart, his soul, his lust for murder and violence, his manic desire for power.

His body is fit, and I can smell the manly smell of him. I have never sat this close to an undressed man before and it unnerves me. What a different feeling this would be if I wasn't the wise woman of the castle and he wasn't the lunatic King.

But I am the wise woman and so I bend my head, avoid his gaze and stitch him, slowly, carefully and neatly back together. I am pleased with my work and when I straighten up to look at his arm; it looks good.

"Thank you," he says, taking my hand, the needle dropping to the floor, spots of his blood dripping onto my hand, my skirt, the ground.

I freeze as he leans over and puts his face close to mine. I freeze when he kisses my cheek. And I am still frozen when he puts his lips against mine.

# 25

WOLF COMING INTO THE room breaks apart their kiss and he scowls at them before turning on his heel and walking straight back out.

Ginata is silent, her fingers touching her mouth where the King's lips had been only seconds before. In that instant, she had forgotten he was mad and evil and awful and murderous and traitorous and horrendous and only felt warm lips on her own, only felt a tingle of sweetness she had never felt before, only felt time stop and the world disappear.

"Forgive me," Millard's voice is smooth and deep. "It's been a gruelling day."

He slips off the table and strides out of the room without looking back.

Ginata's arms drop to her sides, and she cries. What is wrong with her? She takes another sip of ale from the flagon, washing away the taste of her first kiss.

She hears footsteps and then Will is holding onto her and crying against her shoulder and she is crying too and holding him but for different reasons.

"I can't believe she's dead."

"I know."

They cry together for who knows how long.

"I have to see Everleigh."

"We'll sneak out tonight. We'll go after supper."

Will nods, too upset to speak.

EVERLEIGH STANDS UP, breaking the inertia that has set over the entire group. "Where is she? I need to see her."

Della is shaking her head. "No, Everleigh, that's not a good idea."

"I have to."

"Everleigh-"

"I can't leave her alone. I can't. The animals will eat her."

The silence says that she is right.

"I'll take you," Ceryn says. "Weaver you stay. Just in case."

Weaver nods, and Everleigh holds out a hand to Ceryn. "Now."

Ceryn nods and takes her hand. "It won't be very nice."

"I know, but I can't leave her. She's looked after me for so long. She died for me."

The truth of the words hit her anew and the tears sting afresh.

"Let's go."

"What will you do with her?" Finn asks.

Everleigh stops; they usually wrap people up and let them go off the island. Or they're burnt at the Ashes. Neither of these will work because of where she is.

"We could make our own fire for her..." Ceryn's voice trails off as she remembers how much she disliked Lanorie and feels ashamed of herself for being so mean spirited earlier.

"Fire is good," Della says, nodding at Everleigh who looks unsure. "It's not in the Ashes with any old body. It's nicer than that."

Everleigh nods. What else could they do?

"We'll take the horses."

Everleigh gives Addyson a hard hug before following Ceryn out of the cottage. They untie the horses and Ceryn helps Everleigh onto Weaver's horse. "What's her name?"

"Sweet Mabel."

"Nice. What's yours called?"

"Pitch."

"Pitch. It suits her. It suits you."

Ceryn smiles and takes the reins. "Just squeeze your thighs and she'll canter along."

"I can ride." She's used to riding horses and finds Sweet Mabel easy to manage. She wipes tears away. "She was my best friend. Apart from Will. Have you met Will?"

"Yes. We saw him at the castle. He seems nice."

"Ah, he's more than nice. He's the most wonderful person in the world. He was in love with Lanorie."

"Yes, he said."

"He mooned after her all the time. She wasn't interested."

"Why not? If he's so great?"

"He's the fool's son. A fool in waiting..."

"And?"

"Most people can't see past the title. But he's no fool. Not really." She's crying again.

"Are you all right?"

"Not at all. How am I going to do this? Stand this?"

"You just will. We surprise ourselves with what we can do, what we can stand. When we have to."

"Your mark?"

"Yes. It's hard for me to talk about it."

"I bet. We don't have to."

"Thank you. Until this week only my parents, the man who looked after me after they threw me out, and Archer and Weaver had seen my mark. I still can't believe I showed you all."

"I'm glad you did. It's helped Addyson no end."

"I'm glad something good's come out of it. I hate it, it's why I'm so defensive, I guess."

"Defensive? No!"

They both laugh and then fall silent. "How far?"

"Not very. Everleigh. Let me take the reins, close your eyes. Just till we get there."

Everleigh shakes her head. "No. she died for me. I owe her this. I should look. I should see. I have to."

Ceryn nods. She understands. "Through this last lot of trees, but stop a sec, let me check it's clear." Ceryn is sure that the King won't give a second thought to this girl he killed with no regard at all, without a second of hesitation, but she wants to be sure. She will not lead Everleigh in to danger.

As quickly as she had earlier, even though it's a different tree, Ceryn climbs to the top in seconds. The way forward is clear. She cannot hear anyone or see anyone. Except Lanorie. In two parts.

Satisfied, but sad again, she shimmies down and jumps back onto Pitch, stroking her behind her ears. "It's clear."

"But she's still there?"

Ceryn nods. "Are you sure you want to do this?"

"I have to."

They ride along, horses close together. "Thank you." Everleigh's voice is quivering. "I can see why Archer was friends with you. Both of you."

"Thank you. That means everything."

Everleigh stops the horse when she sees Lanorie ahead of them and takes a deep breath. She jumps off Sweet Mabel's back and takes a second to steady herself, face against the horse's mane, breathing in the scent of her.

Ceryn follows suit, leaving Pitch and Sweet Mabel to stand together and graze. She takes Everleigh's hand.

Together they walk towards Lanorie. The two parts of her so cruelly separated. Everleigh stops and looks between Lanorie's head and the rest of her, sobs wracking her entire body. Ceryn lets her drop to the ground and then moves over to Lanorie.

The girl she took an instant dislike to, for no good reason really.

She closes her eyes and then, checking that Everleigh's not looking, carefully picks up Lanorie's head, touching her soft hair, almost forgetting that it's separate from her body and that she's dead. She takes it over and lays it on the floor, right atop of her body, so that with a quick glance, she might still be alive, just sleeping.

She drapes some of Lanorie's hair in front of her, disguising the break between the two body parts; she's not even sure why. Trying to make amends for being such a witch to her when she was alive, maybe.

"Everleigh," Ceryn calls her again and this time when she looks up relief clouds her face, seeing what Ceryn has done.

"Thank you," she whispers the words and Ceryn smiles. Everleigh gets up and walks over to her friend. Her dead friend. Her face crumples, and she kneels beside her, tears spilling freely.

# Ceryn

I LEAVE HER KNEELING by Lanorie's side and tramp through the grass looking for flowers, thinking that might make her look less dead. Not something I normally do, pick flowers, but then life has changed these last few days.

And flowers will make burning her less grisly, I guess.

I sit on the grass, feeling my backside get damp and start making a pile of flowers. I don't know the difference between a flower or a weed really, so I just pick all of them.

I watch Everleigh crying over her friend and I think about Archer.

I was so in love with him. He was everything.

I miss him.

I am glad we came looking for him. I like this unknown group of people. Finn is quiet, but easy on the eye. Like all good men should be. I laugh at myself then – like I know anything about men.

Men have been worse than women about my mark. Those three men that beat me and left me for dead didn't make allowances for my gender. Not that I'm very feminine. But the fact that they were three enormous men attacking a little girl never crossed their minds, I bet.

I hate girly things. They make me feel weak. Boyish things feel like a shell around me, an armour. I wear my mask, and I wear boy's clothes like another disguise. I have a pretty boyish shape; I go straight up and down and I'm often mistaken for a boy. I correct no one.

So what would a boy or a man ever see in me?

I shake my head. I don't want to think about love and how I probably won't ever find it. I think about Finn's older sister instead.

Della. She makes me feel happy. She's a hostess. She's a mother. Even though she's not. She wants everyone to be happy.

And she loves fussing over us all. It's strange for me to let myself be fussed, but she does that to me.

Addyson. I feel proud to have connected with her. Another thing I don't do. Weaver calls me prickly. Archer used to call me a little cow. I don't like many people. I don't even feel bad for that. What have people ever done for me? Most people? Abandoned me, hurt me, attacked me, judged me.

But then what do I do now? Attack people, judge people. I guess I have become what I hate in other people. Strange.

I sneak another glance at Everleigh and Lanorie. Everleigh is sitting up, holding Lanorie's dead hand. I wipe away a tear. I think about Everleigh. I wanted to hate her so much. She had taken Archer from us. Actually, more than hate her, I wanted to hurt her. Pull her hair, scratch her face, gouge at her skin.

But there's something about her. She instils something in me. I want to help her, love her, serve her. Be great for her. I want to get her on her throne, help her seize the crown from her mad brother.

I picture him murdering Lanorie again. The way he shouted, his temper rising. The way he whipped out his sword. The way he killed her so casually, like she didn't matter.

But then she didn't matter to him.

If you're in charge, you can do as you please. And he obviously does.

And yet I know Everleigh will be a good Queen, a kind Queen.

She will have the entire Realm vying to please her through love, not fear. Her brother is already ruling through fear and not love. I'm glad I hit him. I'm a bloody outstanding shot. And that's me, a bit rusty.

I will pledge my allegiance to this Queen and tell her that if she cannot kill her brother herself, I will happily do it for her.

I gather my pile of flowers. Weeds.

I head back over to Everleigh, making plenty of noise to snap her out of her reverie.

She smiles up at me and I know I'm right. I will fight for this Queen. Help her win her throne. I don't even know why, really. It's nothing I can put my finger on.

"Oh." Suddenly she's crying again. "I brought nothing to light a fire."

I sit beside her, keeping my gaze away from Lanorie. "Your magic."

"I've never made fire."

"I bet you can."

I lay the flowers all around Lanorie and then sit back, giving Everleigh the time and space to do what she needs to. She closes her eyes, and she's still crying, tears slowly trailing along her cheek.

When she opens them she stares at the flower in Lanorie's hand. She stares and stares, muttering under her breath.

I watch, fascinated.

After a minute or two, not long really, I see a hiss of smoke rise from a flower, just a wisp at first, then a little more, then a spark and then a tiny flame.

She watches the flames and they grow. She mutters and nods, turning her head this way and that and the flames spread. Once several flowers in a row are ablaze, she kisses Lanorie's forehead and whispers goodbye.

# 26

THE MOOD IN THE COTTAGES is worse than sombre.
Everleigh is sitting, holding hands with Addyson, and they are both
crying. Weaver has gone out for a walk and taken Finn with him.
They are patrolling really, making sure there's no sign of any more
trouble. They are all confident that Lanorie kept Everleigh's location
a secret, but they don't want to relax and become complacent.

Della and Ceryn are sitting in the two chairs, silently watching
the two sisters grieve. There's not anything that anyone can say to
help, so they don't even try.

Now they are all quietly waiting for what happens next.

GINATA IS PACING THE length of her rooms, repeating
Millard's evil crimes to herself. "He sat by while his brother killed
their father, while his brother tried to kill his sister. He killed his
brother. He killed Halfreda. He killed Archer. He killed Lanorie."

It's not that she needs convincing so much as reminding.
Millard's kiss came completely out of the blue; it wasn't something
she was expecting or hoping for.

She knows he is handsome, but she also knows he's a murderer.
There has never been a second where she contemplated anything
happening with him and she isn't about to start now. It was
disconcerting, though, feeling warm, soft lips on hers and having to
remind herself whose lips they were; an evil, murdering madman.

She leaves her rooms in a rush. She'll find Will, make a plan
for tonight. They need to see Everleigh. They need to tell her what's
happened to Lanorie. They need to all be together, taking strength

from each other; reminding each other why they are even fighting this battle.

She wonders briefly whether, despite the prophecy, it's all worth it.

Making Everleigh Queen, living through all this upset and drama.

And yet within a few days it will all be over. Everleigh will be Queen. Millard will be locked away. Dead. It won't be her call to make.

Will is lying on his bed and when he sees her he shifts over to make room for her. They lay next to each other, looking at the ceiling, crying.

How many times have they cried this last week?

"Do you know, she never looked twice at me. I don't know if she even knew I liked her. Loved her. She was so perfect. So lovely. Funny. Kind. The way her hair fell so prettily. Her eyes, her smile. She had a lovely smile."

Ginata lets him talk.

"I didn't think she'd ever love me. Even if she knew I loved her. I'm just a fool."

"You're not though. You are one of the wisest people I know. One day someone will see past the fool thing."

"Maybe. Probably not."

"What made you love her? How did you know?"

"I just loved her. She didn't say or do anything except be herself. I just fell in love. She's perfect. She was perfect."

"She did the bravest thing. She saved Everleigh and Addyson. She did two wonderful things."

"She was wonderful. I know she wasn't perfect, really. She told Everleigh's secret. She could be selfish and silly and ditsy. But that's love. You can't help who you fall in love with. And maybe when two people are in love, if she had loved me, we would have made each other better. Like I wouldn't have been so foolish and she wouldn't have been so selfish, like we would have smoothed each other's edges out."

Ginata's mind flashes briefly onto Millard. Could she smooth out his edges? Why was she even thinking about him?

Will squeezes her hand. "I miss Everleigh."

"I know. We'll go tonight. It's almost time for supper. Let's eat, then when it's night time proper, we'll sneak off. Are you still being followed?"

"I don't think so."

"There was no one outside when I got here."

They are silent then, each thinking their own thoughts, neither knowing what the other is thinking.

The door slams open, making them both jump. Wolf and Brett barge in.

"Get up, fool!" Brett says, grinning nastily.

Will stands up, heart sinking, stomach twisting. Before Lanorie's earlier capture, they had hauled him up in front of Millard to use as bait to bring Everleigh out of hiding. He hoped that had been forgotten.

"The King wants you."

"I can walk," Will says as Wolf tries to take his arms. "I won't run away."

Ginata goes to Will's side. "Will does whatever the King wants. You know what that's like, Wolf."

Wolf doesn't answer, but doesn't make a move to manhandle Will.

Ginata holds Will's hand but stays silent, and they head to the King's rooms.

"Will!" Millard's voice is loud and full of bonhomie; it hits both Will and Ginata that he has forgotten all about killing Lanorie. Or just doesn't care.

It also hits Ginata that he has forgotten all about their kiss. Or just doesn't care.

Either is as likely.

"I apologise again, my fool, but without the handmaiden I need to draw Everleigh out. I need you."

Will nods and bows low. "My King. I am happy to assist, but I fear..." He cannot finish his sentence; he doesn't want to give Millard any ideas, though he has plenty of despicable ones of his own.

"You fear what? Me?" Millard moves closer to Will, just inches between their noses. His voice has that dangerously nonchalant, high pitched, innocent edge to it and Will feels his toes curl under, helping to balance him, making sure he doesn't sway or fall.

"My King. I understand your position and you must do what you must do."

Millard grins and steps backwards. "Not so foolish after all. Wolf. Brett. Take him to the tower and we'll put word out tomorrow to all the villages in the Realm; I will hang the fool unless my sister comes forward."

The two rush forward and take an arm each, carting Will away.

Millard nods as he watches them go. He smiles at Ginata. "Do you think I'm terrible? A monster?"

"My King. You're *King*. How can I judge?"

Millard walks towards her, a sweet smile on his face; the way he changes personality so often and so completely are baffling. He is so dangerous.

"I have to say, Ginata, I had my doubts about you, you helped Halfreda and Halfreda helped my sister, and so I thought... but I can see that you serve only me. You're good for me and the castle."

"Thank you, my King." Ginata takes a tiny step backwards, more of a shuffle than a step; she doesn't want him to see her move. But as she squirms away from him, keeping a comely smile on her face, he leans in to her and she knows that while he is King, she will never get away, if she even wants to.

He swoops then, one arm around her waist, hand on her back, pulling her towards him. Her knees buckle, but not from desire or from fear, but a strange and potent mixture of the two.

His kiss is as warm and sweet as before. His body pressed against her is not unpleasant, but the feeling in her heart is. Shame.

Will is in the tower, Lanorie is dead and she is kissing the King.

# Ginata

SHAME ON ME. BECAUSE as he kisses me, I don't stop him and while I am afraid of him, I also kind of like it. I tell myself it is just the fear of upsetting someone who will kill me if I make him unhappy and my female brain being taken in by a handsome face, a pleasant kiss and the power he wields.

But the shame is real all the same; whatever I tell myself.

And yet I can't help but feel a little bit smug that I handle him so well. Like earlier, when I told him I couldn't judge him because he's King. It was the right thing to say and I always know the right thing to say to him. I know what makes him tick, know what will make him happy.

If he would rule or even live past the weekend, it would be worth me cultivating that knowledge. Make him think I am in love with him, make him think my devotion goes further than King and wise woman, that I feel genuine affection for him. It would be a handy game to play.

But there are mere days left. And I am glad. Once Everleigh is Queen, I won't have to acknowledge what Millard and I have done.

I'll go to Everleigh tonight, tell her about Lanorie. Her heart will break. And I hate to be the bearer of dreadful news. She will hope that she's just missing, or lost, but to know that Millard has captured her and killed her will devastate her. So soon after Archer's death as well. And now with Will being held prisoner, there's two lots of terrible news.

We need to work out a plan to rescue Will. We've rescued Addyson and Lanorie so far, despite Lanorie's additional capture and murder; we should be able to rescue Will, with Weaver and Ceryn around to help.

I also must convince her to stay hidden. Millard's hope is that she will come out of hiding to rescue Will. We cannot let her do that. The risk is too great.

It's all too much for me and I close my eyes and turn my vision inwards, focussing on myself. My lips feel warm, like Millard's kiss has left an actual mark. My stomach though is in a twist of knots; how is murder suddenly so common place, the rescue of prisoners so regular?

The change in my simple little life is dizzying.

I wish I was at home, in my little cottage, sipping a brew with my lovely neighbours and waiting for my next customer. Instead, I'm holed up in a castle full of intrigue, risks and death, like it's the most normal thing in the world.

I like my life when I feel at peace with myself. I don't feel peaceful anymore.

My eyes are still shut and yet the tears sneak out from behind my closed eyelids.

We cannot undo the past; how many customers have I had who wished it could be done. I would help and counsel them, give them some potion or other, but ultimately: what's done is done.

The old King is dead.

Macsen is dead.

Halfreda is dead.

Archer is dead.

Lanorie is dead.

Will can't be next.

I will sit through supper with the King and his horrific henchman, Wolf, and when I go to Everleigh, after dark, I will take some potions – some tonics – to lift spirits and calm worried hearts.

Everleigh will be beside herself; they all will.

I feel bad again. And yet, they know I am showing fealty to Millard now. It can hardly be my fault if that fealty involves a little kissing. It wasn't my tactic.

I busy myself in my work room, finding potions, some herbs to throw on the fire, a lotion to massage into the temples before sleep.

I cannot believe Lanorie is dead and yet this world I find myself in now holds no time for grieving, no let up. We are in the middle of a war against this mad King and we must stay alert, ready for the next battle.

And now this new battle. We cannot save Lanorie, but we must save Will.

And I must save myself.

# 27

GINATA MAKES IT THROUGH supper, smiling at Millard and ignoring Wolf. She excuses herself from the dancing and the singers and goes to her rooms. She paces, sits, paces, sits, paces and sits. She is worrying about Will, alone in the tower, and she is worried about herself.

Eventually she lights a fire, kneels in front of it and stares in to the flames. Can she read anything there? Any help? Will Everleigh rule after Saturday? Will Millard die?

She is a principled person; she helps people. She is only in this mess because she wanted to help Halfreda, who wanted to help Everleigh.

What does she want?

The flames lick higher and her vision blurs, the heat makes her woozy as she tries to see Everleigh with the crown, tries to see what will happen next. She didn't see Lanorie's death; why can't she see anything?

She knows why. Her mind is in such turmoil that she cannot harness her powers, her sight. She needs peace and calm, and she does not have it. She may never have it again.

The flames reveal nothing.

And she knew they wouldn't.

Maybe they never will again.

Maybe she will help to crown Everleigh and then run away where her shame cannot reach her.

Or maybe she will spend the whole of Everleigh's reign making it up to her. Helping her, guiding her, steering her right.

Maybe she will run away with Millard and save everyone the bother of killing him.

She buries her head in her hands and groans.

WILL IS SITTING ON the floor and wondering if he is in the same prison cell as Lanorie was. She must have been so frightened. He is frightened. He doesn't want to admit it, but really it doesn't matter if he does; there is no one here to tell. He is alone.

He doesn't enjoy being alone.

He thinks back over his life. It hasn't been very long, and he was hoping it would go on for many more years, but now he has to accept the possibility of his death. Not a simple thing for anyone to do.

So many people have died in the last week. Will he be next?

There are only three people that he will miss and one of them is already dead. He chokes back a sob as he thinks the word.

Dead.

It's so final, so harsh.

Lanorie is dead. He will never hear her singing in the kitchen again and howling with indignation when Cook clips her around the ear. He won't see her in the great hall, carrying platters of food and jugs of ale with an ease that she didn't have outside of her work. She wasn't graceful, not really. She was simple and so, so lovely.

Missing her hurts like a physical pain. Not *like*. It *is* a physical pain. A physical manifestation of his emotional turmoil.

He lies on the bed. Had her head laid on this same bed, her warm body? Her poor dead body.

He has to take his thoughts elsewhere and thinks about his father.

Not his actual father. He has never met his proper parents, and he has no idea who they were. He was abandoned and found by the man he now considers his real father. The man who loved and raised him alone, because who would ever love a fool?

Well, he loves his father, and his father loves him. He remembers how they had talked and laughed and hugged after Millard had threatened his father. "Son, I love you and you must do what is right by that girl, the girl who will be Queen. If you will believe in her and serve her, so will I. Even if it means my life is over." That was a father. Will is crying again. He has lived an insignificant life really, compared to some, but he has lived an honest and happy life.

Now all he can do is wait.

And hope that Everleigh doesn't risk her life for his, that Ginata convinces her to stay safe, that she is crowned and then as Queen comes and opens the door to his tower and he is free.

Or Millard comes with a sword and kills him.

ONCE THE LAST FLAME in her fireplace fizzles away to nothing Ginata pulls on a cloak, picks up her filled basket and heads out of the castle. She knows Millard and all his hangers on will be too busy enjoying the evening's entertainment to miss her and she wants to get to the cottage before everyone beds down for the night.

She is quick getting there and is relieved to see the lamps still on inside both cottages. She goes to her own cottage first and gently knocks while pushing the door open, taking a deep breath to steady herself for the awful news she has to deliver.

But there is already sadness in the room, it's palpable. Weaver and Finn aren't there, but the four females are. Della is brushing and plaiting Addyson's hair. Ceryn is chewing on a twig, and Everleigh is blotchy from crying. They must be worried sick just wondering where Lanorie is and now Ginata has to deliver the worst news.

Everleigh rushes to Ginata's side and they hold each other tightly. "I have some news about Lanorie," Ginata says.

Everleigh pulls back. "We know. Ceryn and Weaver were there. They saw it."

Ginata puffs out an enormous sigh of air. What a terrible mess all of their lives are at the moment. "How? I didn't think you'd know..."

"She went for a walk, but never came back," Della volunteers the information because Everleigh is crying again.

"She was captured by one of the King's men. He recognised her."

"Poor Lanorie..."

"Me and Weaver went looking for her on our horses and we saw the King kill her. He's bloody evil."

Ginata nods, thinking of his lips on hers. "He is. I'm so sorry, Everleigh."

"We went back. Everleigh made a fire for her."

"Oh, poor things."

Ginata hugs Everleigh again and reaches over and touches Ceryn's hair. She sinks on to the arm of the chair. Now she has to tell Everleigh about Will. Or should she just tell Ceryn? No, Everleigh would never forgive her. She has to know the complete story.

"I have to tell you something, but you have to promise not to fly off the handle. It's what your brother wants. Please."

"Will?" Everleigh knows.

Ginata nods her head. "He's only in the tower, but..." She hangs her head, crying. She cannot bear to say it.

"What?" Everleigh's voice is harsh, and everyone has moved closer to hear. The door pushes open, and everybody jumps.

Finn and Weaver wince as they slope inside. "Sorry."

Weaver takes in Ginata's presence and the sick look on Everleigh's face. "What now?"

"Millard's taken Will. He's in the tower."

"There's more, but Ginata won't say."

Ginata sighs and holds up her hands. "Fine, but Everleigh, promise to stay calm."

Everleigh nods.

"Look, he's only taken him to get you out of hiding, so you have to promise to stay hiding. To stay safe..."

"Tell me."

"He says he will send messengers to all the villages tomorrow to spread the word that if you don't come out of hiding, by noon, he'll hang him."

Everleigh doubles over, hand over her mouth, rushes out of the door and retches into the bushes.

They all follow her out.

"I can't, I can't, I can't lose him too."

She's on her knees, sick dripping from her mouth and still every one of them would die for her, is desperate for her to be their Queen.

"I have to go to him."

"No!" More than one voice shouts out, but Everleigh shakes her head.

"I cannot let him die. I cannot see one more person I love die."

Ceryn kneels next to her. "We'll all go. In the morning. Don't rush off like a fool. Think like a Queen."

They both stand up. Ceryn ushers her back inside and they all congregate around her.

"We could all do with a good night's sleep..." Della says.

"We need a plan," Weaver says.

"I'll be happy to help kick Millard's ass after what I saw earlier." Ceryn grimaces.

"I can help, if you need me to." Finn looks almost embarrassed offering his help; he knows he's no match for Ceryn and Weaver.

"We'll all have to work together. We have to rescue Will."

# Ceryn

WE TALKED AND PLOTTED and argued and planned until Ginata realised how late it was and panicked. Weaver offered to ride her back to the castle on his horse, and the rest of us went to sleep. I reckon he might fancy her. I'll ask him later.

I know Everleigh wants to kill her brother and I want to as well.

My hand is itching to strangle him. The way he killed that girl yesterday. I know I didn't like her, but I didn't want her dead. He just did it; like it was nothing. Like she was nothing.

I pace the path outside. We are waiting around for someone to come to the village and announce Will's hanging. It will probably be some King's men and a herald, so we're keeping Everleigh hidden for now. Everyone's eating, but I feel too sick.

My stomach is twisting and leaping, ready for a fight.

"Hey."

"You're not eating either?"

I know Weaver is like me. He'll feel too sick. The anticipation and excitement that comes before a fight or a battle.

He shakes his head. "Can't."

"How was Ginata last night? When you took her back to the castle? Did she say thank you?"

"Behave."

"What?" I try to make my voice innocent, but Weaver knows me better. He punches my arm. I laugh, but don't press the issue.

We need to get our heads ready for today. We have made a plan. Kind of. We'll wait for the announcement. Then we'll all go to the castle, but me and Weaver will stay hidden. Everleigh will talk to Millard but use some magic to keep him back. Like a fire or a storm or something. She doesn't really know what she can do, so we'll see.

Then Weaver and I will lamp Wolf, get him out of the way, so he can't do Millard's dirty work. Then we'll wait for the rope to go on Will and shoot it down, or something. And then we'll capture Millard, somehow and...

It's not the best plan I've ever worked with and like me and Weaver told everyone, plans don't always go according to plan, but, we are all going to go and somehow, we'll rescue Will. It would be nice if we got hold of Millard too. But I reckon he's a slippery snake and might get away.

Getting hold of Wolf will be good, and we can do that while Millard is talking to Everleigh. We are trying to convince Addyson to stay here. She's too young to get in the middle of this fight.

But if she's anything like I think she is, she won't listen.

The door opens, and Finn comes out and grins at Weaver. They've become excellent friends since we got here and it's nice for Weaver, with Archer gone...

I can't think about him today. It's too sad.

We need to fight today. We need to battle today. We need to win today. I can't be moping around or distracted.

I go inside the cottage.

Everyone is quiet. Tense. Addyson looks like she's been crying.

"What's up?" I ask.

"Everleigh says I can't come today."

"You shouldn't."

"I'm nearly twelve. I'll be fine."

"I watched your brother kill someone yesterday without a second's hesitation. He killed your brother, his own brother. He didn't care. If he gets hold of you today, he'll kill you."

"He wouldn't."

"He would. He locked you up, but you got away. He'll be so angry..."

"He won't hurt me."

"It's not just that. Have you ever been in the middle of a fight? A proper fight to the death?"

Addyson shakes her head.

"It's scary. There's shouting and screaming and swearing, and thuds and clashes of swords and blood. So much blood. Half dead men dragging themselves across the floor towards anyone who might help them-"

"That's enough!" Della rushes to Addyson's side. She's gone white, and she's crying.

"Sorry. But I thought she should know."

"She should." Everleigh's voice is firm. "Addyson, I love you and I need to keep you safe. I don't know what Millard will do today. He might capture me; he might kill me."

"No!"

"He might."

"Not if I can help it."

Everleigh smiles at me. "You wanted to kill me yourself when you met me."

I lower my head, embarrassed, but then I laugh. "People change."

And I have. So quickly. I hated Everleigh before I even met her, and when I saw her I wanted to hurt her so badly. But now we're on the same side. The same team.

The morning drags and just as we are wondering if Millard has changed his mind, there's a clatter of horses and the noise of the herald.

Everleigh turns white, but we shut her firmly inside and rush out. There are three little cottages across and down a fair bit from Ginata and Della's cottages, but I can see the owners are all outside, listening like us.

There are ten horses with liveried guards atop and the herald, blowing his little bugle. "Announcement from the King. He will hang the fool today at noon, unless his sister, the Kingmaker,

Everleigh, makes herself known. For those who hide her, leniency. For the fool, his life."

They ride off and repeat the words further away. They will continue doing this all morning.

Noon.

It doesn't give us long.

We wait until the last rider is out of sight before going inside.

Everleigh is crying. "I heard. They'll hang him at noon."

"They won't, because we'll rescue him. We just need to make sure you're safe too."

Addyson speaks up. "I'll stay here, then."

I give her an enormous hug. It's hard to feel left out, but she needs to be left out of this.

The tension is thick again. We are all quiet. Lost in our thoughts, worries, concerns.

"I'll stay too," Della says and I agree with her. She was only ever an extra pair of hands.

Weaver and me will be the main fighters, Everleigh will distract Millard and we have to risk taking her so he doesn't kill Will. Ginata will give us any aid or information without blowing her cover. We don't really need Finn, either, but he's sweet traipsing after Weaver and I won't offend him and that shows exactly how much I have changed!

Offending people has always been my favourite thing to do.

# 28

WILL WAKES UP IN THE tower, surprised that he even got to sleep. He is alive which is good but he has a feeling of doom and fear which is not good.

What will Millard do? He wants to draw Everleigh out of hiding, to kill or capture her. Surely, he needs Will alive to do this? But he could hurt him, parade him around with his injuries on show, who knows? Not him.

He can only sit and wait. All the foolery is gone from him; he doubts he could make anyone laugh if a knife was at his throat. What will this day bring? His freedom or his death. He's sure enough that it will be one or the other.

MILLARD WAKES UP REFRESHED and excited. Today is the day, he is sure, he will kill or capture his little sister and then he will have free reign over the Realm and all who live within it. This is all he wants, and it's not a lot to ask. Girls have never ruled before and regardless of some stupid prophecy he doesn't see why they should start now. Everleigh could have lived alongside him as a royal sister, a princess, married to some good and wealthy man, maybe someone from the North of the Realm. Everyone would have been happy, but no, she had to be awkward and greedy; hankering after everything that is rightfully his. He didn't kill his brother to give away his throne to a girl. It's just ridiculous.

GINATA DREAMS UNHAPPY dreams of hurt and betrayal, love and lust and wakes in a sweat. Today is the day she will redeem herself and atone for a sin she committed without choice, a sin that was foisted upon her. She will help Everleigh kill or capture her brother and end the day by placing the crown upon her head.

JUST BEFORE NOON WOLF and Brett come for Will. "Come on, fool. Let's see how funny this is." Wolf revels in doing Millard's bidding. The more heinous the better.

Brett takes hold of one of Will's arms, but doesn't pull him as hard as Wolf does.

Out in the courtyard they present Will to his future; the hangman's noose.

Will keeps his face blank, refusing to breakdown or cry. He has to believe he will be rescued or he'll go mad.

They set the wooden frame for the hanging up overnight, Will vaguely recalls the hammering he heard from the tower and dismissed as nothing important. Will Everleigh come? He knows she will and wants her to; he wants to be safe. But he wants her to live and rule more. If rescuing him leads to her being imprisoned in his place, then he would rather die.

And he might.

Millard comes to join them, all looking at the wooden frame and the thick rope hanging down, the noose ready for a neck of Millard's choosing; he's nodding his approval. "Morning, Will."

Will bows low. "My King."

"My fool. I know my sister. She'll come, and you won't hang. I'm sure of it. I have no desire to kill you. I find you funnier than your father – and that is a compliment indeed."

Will bows his head in thanks and smiles at the farcical nature of needing to thank the man who wants to hang him.

"We must set it up to look real, though. The villagers love a show."

The courtyard is already half full of men, women and children thrilled to watch a good killing. It's a long time since there's been a hanging in the courtyard; the old King wasn't one to dole out punishments for public delectation and neither is Millard, really. If someone deserves to die, then they deserve to die now, not in a day or two when the wooden tower has been erected, and the villagers informed of the show to come.

"I understand." Will looks directly at Millard but sees nothing in his eyes but a glint of mischief; he's enjoying this.

"String him up, Wolf."

Millard steps back, and Wolf steps in. Will offers no resistance but Wolf still drags him roughly to the tower, hauls him up onto a small wooden stool, and slips the rope around his neck, pulling it tight enough that Will wonders if he'll choke to death before the stool is pushed away. He knows that's not how it works, but the reality of the situation is making his brain fuzzy.

His neck is bent at an uncomfortable angle, so he's staring at his feet. If he lifts his head, he can see the crowd, and the first time he does so, a barefoot boy throws an apple at his head and the crowd burst into laughter. He keeps his head down, determined not to look up again until this is all over, but he lifts his head again when he sees his father's feet.

He doesn't even know how he knows his father just by his feet, but he does.

"Son, what is wrong with this King?"

"He's definitely mad. But I'm all right. I know Everleigh won't see me die."

"She saw her brother, her father, Halfreda and that boy she loved die."

"And Lanorie."

"Well, then."

"She'd have saved them all if she could."

Will's father doesn't answer, just kisses the top of his head. "I would save you if I could, son, and that's as much use to you. I'll go now, I will drink the day away. Hopefully, at night fall it'll be you that finds me passed out drunk down at the inn and throws me in my bed. I love you. Always have. Always will. But I cannot stay and watch this."

"I understand. Have one for me, too."

Will's father laughs. "I will, Will."

His shoes shuffle away and Will watches his tears drop onto the dusty floor where his father's shoes had been. He hopes he will be the one to find him drunk and unconscious.

GINATA IS WATCHING Millard and Will from near the castle wall. She's not ready to face either of them yet. She took breakfast alone in her room, which she hasn't done before, and now she's watching for any sign of Will's rescuers. She wishes she was with them, instead of on the other side. She's not even sure if she should go to Will's side or if Millard will see it as a betrayal. She makes her way over to her King.

"Morning Ginata. How great is this?"

"It's certainly a clever idea."

"Do you think it will work?"

"I think if Everleigh hears about it, she'll come. What will you do?"

"Take her prisoner."

"Kill her? Kill him?"

"I won't kill Will. I wish I didn't have to use him like this. It's the handmaiden's fault. She shouldn't have tricked me. But I don't know about my sister... what would you do?"

"I think letting Will go free is an excellent idea. He's a good fool. I cannot judge what to do with your sister, my King, but I will say that she is beloved of the people. And it never hurts for the man with the ultimate power to be seen as kind, to be forgiving."

"What's the point of power if I don't use it?"

"You use it, you used it yesterday, but Everleigh is different to her handmaiden. Everleigh is the Kingmaker."

"Was the Kingmaker. Some say she should be Queen."

"Do they?"

"Don't you agree?"

"I have said before that it was what Halfreda wanted, but I also believe we have the power to change things. We don't have to do what a prophecy says."

"You don't think it's inevitable? That she will be Queen regardless of what I want?"

"I don't know, my King. I wish I had answers for you. My powers aren't what they were, I'm nowhere near the level of Halfreda..."

"I am sure you will get better in time." He touches her cheek briefly. "Right, is there any sign of my lovely sister? Wolf!"

Wolf rushes over to them, shooting a sulky look at Ginata and shaking his head. "I can't see her yet. I think we should get you up on the platform, start talking, see if we can flush her out."

"Outstanding idea. Do one last sweep around the perimeter of the castle with Brett and then we'll start." Wolf bows and backs away, looking around for Brett.

"My King, may I speak to Will, to reassure him?"

"If you like."

Ginata leaves the King's side and walks over to Will. He looks pretty pathetic, standing there with the noose around his neck, his clothes wet from the ale and food people have been throwing at him.

"Will." Ginata's voice is soft, and he lifts his head a little. It hurts to hold it up, his legs are buckling, and he is desperately trying to stay upright, not to hang himself by accident.

"Any sign of anyone?"

"Not yet, but you know they'll come."

They are both silent and sad and wishing for the end of the day to come, whatever it brings.

# Ginata

I CANNOT THINK OF ONE thing to say to cheer either of us and so I give up. What we need now is the cavalry.

I kiss the top of Will's head; he smells of ale.

I head back over to Millard, the sick feeling in my stomach intensifying. What sort of man is he? And why is he sneaking in to my dreams?

"Wolf's been ages. I will start without him. Tell him to join me if you see him."

I nod, and a shiver of excitement goes through me. Wolf's not back; have they got to him already? I cannot stand being out of the loop like this.

The crowd is rowdy, but not violent, and I am desperate to see Everleigh, to start this thing and finish it. I don't know if our plan will work, but we have to try. When Everleigh is Queen, I can forget about Millard.

For now, I cannot. He is standing next to Will on the platform of the wooden tower, calling out to the crowd. "My people, my agreeable people. Welcome, welcome."

The crowd gives a roar of approval; how quickly they forget. Three days ago, they would have had this King's head if they could. The disgust for him had been palpable, the barely contained fury, real. Three days later he's their best King for giving them a spectacle to watch. One small group have pulled up stools and are eating bread and meat.

Come on, Everleigh. Come on Ceryn – she'll give Millard a run for his money. Come on, Weaver. I cannot stand this waiting and I know exactly how Will must feel: sick, sick, sick.

"I am saddened to be here today. But my fool isn't a loyal fool and so..." Millard gestures at the noose; he cannot tell the crowd the truth; they would mob him, but now they happily boo and hiss at Will.

It leaves Millard stalling for time as he waits to see if his sister shows. I, of course, know that she will. Unless something has gone drastically wrong, but I don't feel that.

Truthfully, I feel nothing. I am of no use.

I hear the first call of Kingmaker before Millard does and I turn my head. The crowd is parting, like they did in the coronation, and there she is.

The Kingmaker who will be Queen.

Della has dressed her in one of her own dresses but altered it and it suits her perfectly. The colour is a soft pink, and it makes her look beautiful but vulnerable too, which is good. Her lovely long hair is loose, and the soft curls also add to her vulnerability. She looks young and ethereal.

Just behind her I see Weaver and Ceryn. Ceryn grins and nods at me before walking to my side, letting Everleigh continue onwards.

"All well?" I ask her.

"Yes. We've got Wolf. Easily. I walked towards him, pretending to have hurt my ankle, and Weaver came behind him. Cracked him over the head with an axe handle – he'll live."

"More's the pity."

They smile and turn as Everleigh speaks to her brother.

"Millard."

I note that she doesn't call him King, nor does she bow to him. She stands directly in front of him, though he is on the platform and she is on the floor. I see Will lift his head, despite the pain, to get a look at her and the smile on his face is filled with love and relief.

The crowd is murmuring, unsure of what's going on.

Ceryn and Weaver have their hands on their bows and an arrow ready each. No one in the crowd even notices; all eyes are on Everleigh and the King.

"Ah, sister."

Millard surprises me then and pulls the noose off Will's neck. He must be so sure that Wolf or Brett or one of his guards will grab Everleigh that he's happy to free his bargaining chip, and yet there's no sign of them. Will bows to Millard and then jumps down off the platform, rubbing at his neck. He comes to me and I squeeze his hand. We cannot talk or relax or rest. We aren't all safe yet.

Ceryn lowers her bow. "I don't trust him."

Weaver nods. "Stay alert."

"Sister, I have freed your friend but I want you in return."

The crowd's murmurs are turning more hostile. The love the Realm has for Everleigh, a tragic figure all her life because of her role as Kingmaker, is still clear and it cheers me.

"Brother. You have something that I want."

"I've already freed your friend."

"Not Will, though I thank you for keeping him safe."

"What then, sister?" Millard is looking nervous. He's not focussing solely on Everleigh; his eyes are darting around the crowd and I can tell that he's unhappy with what he sees. We have hurt Wolf, so does that mean the other men have had no orders? I can see some of them on the outskirts of the crowd, but none are close, none are near enough to be of any use, I don't think.

"What's he playing at..." Ceryn mutters the words but they're not really a question.

Everleigh takes a step towards her brother. "My crown. I want my crown."

He laughs then, a strange sound, and the crowd join in. They don't understand this power play and are waiting to see what will happen.

"You will never be Queen."

Everleigh ignores him and looks up at the sky – blue and clear, some wispy white clouds. I can see her lips moving and I feel the air turn thick; she's summoning a storm. She's going to bamboozle him with her powers.

"You two get in position and when he's distracted, grab him."

Weaver shakes his head. "If we do, his men will attack us. We need to wait and see what happens..."

I nod, unhappy but accepting that both him and Ceryn know how to fight better than I ever will.

"Sister, what are you doing?"

"Brother. I am doing something you can't."

Millard doesn't answer her, just humphs, watching the sky.

"I am controlling the Realm, not just the people within it."

With those words, she flings her arms into the air and the rain lashes down on her upturned face. I grin at the drama; she's getting the hang of this.

Millard shrugs. "So, it's raining."

Everleigh lifts her face to the rain again and says something out loud, the weather stealing the sounds as she speaks them.

Lightning bolts split the sky, causing the crowd to call out and many of them to back away. Everleigh is still muttering as thunder cracks overhead.

I am so proud of her at this moment that I forget about any connection Millard has tried to forge with me and I am almost jumping and clapping my hands for her. Will is the same. "He doesn't know what to do!"

Everleigh calls more lightning and almost as though her hand is controlling the charge, and maybe it is, she points at the wooden platform that Millard stands on and the lightning strikes – she aims to the left of him, to the wooden tower, and the fire sparks up immediately.

She moves closer, whispering and gesturing as the flames take hold, despite the rain. Impossible, but true. The fire erupts, and Millard shrieks and jumps down, batting at an errant flame on his arm.

"*Witch*."

"Queen."

"Seize her!"

## 29

AT MILLARD'S WORDS his men rush forward at Everleigh, but the roar of the fire or the change in the weather or the fact that these people love their Kingmaker turns the crowd even more hostile. As Millard's men charge, the horde turns and suddenly the village men are fighting the King's men and fists are flying; they reach for swords and Everleigh ducks under arms and around battling bodies to jump on the platform; the fire blazing behind her.

Seeing that Everleigh is safe, for now, Ceryn and Weaver raise their swords and join the fray, helping the villagers to protect their Kingmaker and future Queen, keeping the King's men away from the flaming platform.

"Come on, brother. Come on, King!" Everleigh screams at him and he turns to look at her. "If you want to keep your crown so badly, come and fight me for it."

Millard pauses, looking from his sister, to his singed skin, to the men fighting around them. "I've got the crown. You cannot win this, not through fighting or foul weather or anything else. Brett!"

Brett turns to look at the King and gets punched clean in the side of the nose. He turns to his assailant and punches him back before running to Millard's side, wiping his bloody nose on his sleeve.

Millard looks at Everleigh. Will has joined her. "String him up and take her to the tower. I'll deal with her once Ginata's fixed my arm."

Millard walks away as though fighting Everleigh and battling for his crown, is beneath him.

Will takes Everleigh's hand and they leap through the smoke. They cannot wait for Brett or anyone else to catch them. Once again, their plan has gone awry, and damn Millard still wears the crown.

Millard calls to Ginata, and she hesitates; she wants to follow Everleigh, be part of the squad that saves their Queen but Millard calls for her again and duty trumps desire. "Ginata, please, help me get out of here."

It's typical that he doesn't stay to take part in a fight that he started, but wants to duck out of the way to safety, letting his men take the fall, and sending someone else to take Everleigh prisoner.

The throng of fighters is screaming, yelling, shouting, the observers making a run for it and part of Ginata is glad to be out of it. She just wishes their plan had worked.

As she follows Millard she can see that he's injured. "I'm burnt."

She can see the singed edge of his clothes where the skin has bubbled.

"She tried to set me on fire. She tried to kill me."

"I'll fix you."

"She will die. When I get my hands on her, she will die. Where the hell is Wolf?"

EVERLEIGH AND WILL run, the rain impeding their vision; the fighting expanded beyond just the courtyard, the sound of thumps and punches masked by the rain but the yelling and crying out loud enough to be heard, the throng of battling bodies getting in their way.

They know Brett is on their heels, maybe even more of the King's men. They can't stop. They weave through the courtyard and then jump over a wall. Will risks a quick look backwards. "He's not there."

They tuck their backs against the wall, catching their breath, composing themselves for a minute.

"He's done it again. Damn him, Will."

"It's fine. We'll try again, and again, and again until we get that crown on your head."

"Is it worth it? What if I just surrender? No more death, no more battling. Just let him win."

Will takes Everleigh's face in his hands. "Everleigh. You have to be Queen. Your brother killed his own brother to get the throne. If you weren't fighting to win the crown, if he was left to his own devices, what do you think he'd do?"

"Kill anyone who disagreed with him. Kill anyone he took a disliking to. But it's so hard. I can't do it..."

"You can and you will. The prophecy says you will reign. Who knows why? Maybe this fight with your brother is just the beginning, maybe in the future we will need a powerful Queen more than we do now, who knows... but you cannot let him win."

"But I don't know what to do."

"We'll go now, we'll reconvene, make a plan."

"Our plans don't work. I've tried killing him in his sleep and asking him to fight. I just want that damn crown. What am I missing?"

"Something, but now's not the time to worry. Come on."

They stand up to run to the safety of the cottage and Brett cracks Will over the head, and he drops. Brett looks at Everleigh who is paralysed with fear, remembering their previous meetings.

He mouths the word sorry, then throws a black hood over her face, before bundling her, kicking and screaming, over his shoulder.

He checks that no one is looking and runs into the woods, leaving Will on the floor, alive, but unconscious.

GINATA TAKES MILLARD'S hand as she leads him through to her rooms. Burns are nasty and the sooner she gets to work on him, the more chance there is of a scar being smaller and less angry looking.

"Why is she doing this, Ginata? Why is she so eager to get the crown?"

"She thinks it's hers." Ginata's voice is dull. Suddenly, she cannot stand this battle for power, this dance between the two of them. This feeling of being on the other side, the outsider.

"What do you think I should do?"

"Maybe stop chasing her. Stop attacking her. Stop threatening her. Maybe she'll leave you alone..."

Millard shakes his head. "She tried to kill me today. Burn me to death. Imagine how much that would have hurt?"

"I can only imagine, my King." She gathers the things she needs to attend to his wound. The burn is nasty, some material of his clothes burnt into his skin where the fire has melded the two together.

"I will have to kill her. I know she's beloved and the people love their Kingmaker and she thinks she should be Queen, but really, people don't understand what it's like to be me, to be King, to be in charge. I took tremendous risks to get this throne. I killed my brother. That wasn't easy. I loved him, but I needed the power more. I killed Halfreda, she'd looked after me since I was tiny. Such sacrifices..."

Ginata has her back to Millard sorting out her lotions, and while he prattles on she tunes out. Everleigh needs to be Queen, but their plan has been thwarted again. This raving King thinks he's hard done by but what can she do? She is torn between wanting to knock him out and kiss him until he's quiet.

She hears a massive thunk and whips around to see Millard slumped in the chair and Ceryn holding a stone bowl, the one she uses for grinding herbs and seeds, above his head, a massive grin on her face.

"Everleigh and Will got away. One of the King's men's chasing them but they had a good head start. Weaver's fighting off the King's men and I followed you up. Help me tie him up. Hell, no, I'll tie you both up, for now, just in case."

"What have you done?"

"Whacked him. He's not dead. Though..."

"No, don't kill him. Everleigh needs to see him."

"She'll be glad if I kill him."

Ginata shakes her head. "No. Everleigh has to make that decision, not you, or me."

Millard murmurs something unintelligible and turns his head slightly. Before he can come to, Ceryn hits him again, not as hard as the first time, but he collapses back down. "Quick, Ginata, have you got rope?"

"Yes." She roots through her drawers and finds a thick coil of rope. "What do we do now?"

"I'll tie you both up, fetch Everleigh and we'll do an exchange. His crown for his freedom."

"Ceryn. That might work."

"I know and it was great to whack him too!"

Ceryn moves Millard onto the floor, and Ginata sits with her back to him. "Do I really need to stay with him?"

"If something goes wrong; we still need you on the inside."

"But we've got him now. I don't think anyone would look for him here. Get Everleigh quickly."

Ceryn ties them up, but leaves Ginata's wrists slightly loose, not loose enough to cause suspicion if someone finds her, but enough that she's not in pain.

"I'll be back as soon as I can."

# Ceryn

I AM HUMMING AS I WALK; oh, it was satisfying whacking that dirt bag over the head. Twice. I wish I could kill him, but I know it's up to Everleigh to decide.

Out in the courtyard the fighting has ended. There are split lips and broken noses, and a few dead guards. Weaver is doubled over, back against a wall, blood dripping onto the floor.

"Will you live?"

He grins as he looks up at me. "Of course." He spits a gob of blood onto the floor, his nose and his lip are bleeding and there is blood on his sword. "I didn't kill anyone, but I put a few out of service."

I grin at him. A few injured guards are nothing to what I've done. "I've got Millard."

"What? Where?"

"I whacked him over the head, like you did with Wolf, but I've tied him up, with Ginata, in case." I shrug; he'll know what I mean.

"Fantastic. Where?"

"He's in Ginata's rooms, I followed them, he's injured and she was going to fix him. I whacked him with a stone bowl thing. Twice."

"Is he dead?"

"No. I'll find Everleigh, come with me." I shake my head. "No, go to Ginata's rooms and watch them till I get back. Just in case."

"Brilliant idea. Where is it?"

I give him the best directions I can remember and head through the mass of groaning, bloodied bodies, thinking if Will and Everleigh had any sense – which they do – they'll head for the cottages.

Despite the bloodshed and the plan going wrong, I am happy. Della and Addyson are safe. I've not seen Finn, but I can imagine he ran back to the cottages when the fighting started, and I don't blame him. He's not a fighter.

We are all safe and well and considering how things played out, that's not too bad. I wish we'd got Wolf tied up like I tied up Millard, but there was nothing around to do it with. We threw him down a ditch, after I kicked him, and hopefully he'll stay there for a bit. I don't think he'd look for Millard in Ginata's rooms, anyway. At least not straight away.

I still need to be quick though.

I jump over the wall, heading back to the cottages and land on something. Hell, it's someone – it's Will. He's got a bloody wound on his head, but I can see he's alive from his colour. "Will!" I shake him. There's no sign of Everleigh and Will is hurt. That means something went wrong.

"Will!" I shake him harder. "Will! Where's Everleigh?"

He moans and groans but doesn't wake up. "Will! Where's Everleigh?"

He can't answer my questions, so I roll him closer to the wall. I'm no healer, but I don't think he's in any immediate danger and I have to find Everleigh.

I can't; she could be anywhere. I scream out her name in case she's close by, but there's no reply. I scream it again. Where the hell is she and who took her? One of Millard's men, I know that much. Damn Millard. I contemplate going back to the castle, kicking the life out of him, but I don't think it will help. If someone has taken her, then it's him they'll bring her back to.

Maybe she's already in the King's rooms. Only I don't know where they are. The castle is enormous, and I barely found my way out of Ginata's rooms to the courtyard.

I close my eyes for a second, try to think of the best thing to do. Then I run to the cottages.

When I burst in Finn, Della and Addyson all jump out of their seats. "I need help."

"What's happened?"

"I can't find Everleigh. She was with Will, but Will's hurt."

"Where is she?" Addyson bursts out crying and I want to join her.

"I don't know. I don't know."

"Has Millard got her? Is she dead?"

"No. I've got Millard."

"What? How?"

"I followed him and Ginata and cracked him over the head."

"Has Wolf got her?"

"I don't think so. We cracked him over the head and threw him down a ditch."

"But he could have got up?"

"He could have... let's just go. I thought if someone took her they might have taken her to Millard's rooms. But I don't know where they are."

Addyson takes my hand and the four of us rush back to the castle. I tell them everything I know on the way. The way Millard let Will go free. The way Everleigh made it rain and set the wooden hanging tower on fire. How Weaver knocked Wolf out. How I knocked Millard out. And hit him twice. How Will is hurt. There's too much to say, and we have to be quick.

Will is where I left him and still breathing and so we abandon him again, and head to Ginata's rooms first. There are a few stragglers still sitting around the courtyard, groaning and nursing their wounds, but anyone who could get away has gone and there are only two bodies, both Millard's men.

Addyson leads the way because I can barely remember. We go through Ginata's rooms and into her work room and I can see that Millard is still unconscious. If we could just find Everleigh we would have everything we want.

Ginata holds her hands up. "Untie me and I'll get a sleeping draught for Millard. He won't wake for hours. Where's Everleigh?"

"She's gone?"

"What? Where?"

"We don't know. We found Will, but they have knocked him out. There was no sign of Everleigh."

"We've lost her?"

"Unfortunately."

"Now what?"

We are all silent. I feel sick that we've lost Everleigh. She could be dead already.

"We could put him in the tower..." Addyson suggests, her voice quiet. "It's what he did to me."

"That would be good, but we don't have a key." I ruffle her hair, and she smiles up at me.

"We need him somewhere we can leave him without worrying. While we look for Everleigh."

"What about the cottage?" This suggestion from Della. "No one would look there."

Ginata looks worried. "True, but if he wakes up, then he'll know I'm not on his side."

"Is that so terrible?" I ask.

# 30

GINATA DOESN'T ANSWER, and Ceryn gives her a strange look. "This is everything we wanted. Millard out of action and Everleigh on the throne."

"Yes, but Everleigh's not here."

"Whoever took her, took her for Millard..." Weaver thinks the same way as Ceryn. "So, they'll bring her back to Millard."

"So where do we go, what do we do with him?" Della asks.

"We go to his rooms." Ceryn and Weaver grin.

"We'll be safe there. No one can sneak up on us."

"And then when whoever has her, brings her, we'll attack them and crown her."

"That's a bloody superb idea."

"Brilliant."

"And if Wolf comes, he'll never expect us to be there and we can attack him again. Tie him up this time."

"No one will expect us to be there."

"Do we know who took her? Who chased them?"

"It was Brett," Ginata says. "The one with the bandaged hands."

"He'll have worse than that when we find him. Right, let's move Millard, before anyone comes looking for him."

Ceryn uses her dagger to cut some ropes off him so he's easier to carry and for a second everyone just stares at him. This is the King of the Realm; knocked out, tied up and drugged. What they have all been a part of is an act of treason, and without Everleigh there to take over his reign it seems far worse of a crime.

Addyson kneels in front of him, her older brother. She touches his face and then touches his crown. Then she takes it off his head. "For Everleigh."

The silence is thick, it's too upsetting, too sickening, that Everleigh is missing, could be hurt, could be dead. That they finally have the crown, but not the head to wear it.

"Right, let's go."

Finn and Weaver carry Millard easily from Ginata's work room to his own room, and Ceryn ties him back up. She pulls the ropes extra hard and gives him a kick on the shin before turning away. "What if I look for Everleigh and you boys fetch Will to Ginata? Addyson – you wait in Ginata's rooms with Della."

"Why go looking for her? We think they'll bring her here, whoever has her."

"What if we're wrong?"

Weaver nods his agreement. "I'll come back and guard Millard?"

"Let's hide him first, in case anyone comes in. Put him in this closet."

They shove him in a closet where there's less chance of anyone coming across him by accident.

Ceryn nods and the plan made, they all walk away from their crownless King.

Back in her own room, Ginata paces while Della and Addyson sit on the window seat, crown on the table near them. She can hear them chatting to each other but can't hear what they are saying. She envies their closeness; she has no one that she's close to since Halfreda died.

She's stuck in this limbo between helping Everleigh but being separated from her, serving Millard and having such conflicting feelings about him.

Leaving him just now, trussed up like a chicken and helpless felt worse than wrong; it felt like a betrayal. But helping Millard and not Everleigh is another type of betrayal. She takes a slug of ale from the cup on the table, her mind made up.

Her hand is searching among her potion bottles before she knows what she's doing and she ignores her inner voices as they argue.

"I'll watch for them in the corridor," she announces her intention to Della and Addyson, but they barely glance her way.

She has no idea how much time she has as she runs along the corridor to Millard's rooms, but she knows it's not long. She bursts inside and shuts the door behind her, resting against it, heart hammering, stomach twisting.

She throws open the closet door; Millard looks like a victim; his handsome head empty without his crown, his thick hair ruffled with the indentation of the heavy gold. His rich clothes make him look pathetic because he's tied up and vulnerable.

She looks at the bottle in her hand and takes a deep breath. What is she doing?

Making things fair, giving him a chance.

Serving her King.

Betraying her Queen.

She walks slowly to his side. If Weaver comes back now, it's all over; Everleigh and all the others won't want anything to do with her. They will kill her as a traitor when Millard is killed or, at best, lock her up; her betrayal of Everleigh and her cause complete.

Or, before she crosses that line, she could go back to her rooms and wait for Will, patch him up and keep herself and her feelings separate; become an observer of all that's going on rather than a participant.

What to do?

She pulls the dagger from her boot and slices at the ropes that bind him. She holds his head back as though he's an infant who cannot help himself and she pours the tonic that will wake him up into his mouth.

Deed done, she rests her hand on his cheek for a second, before turning away from him and rushing back to the corridor to wait for Will. Only seconds after she gets her breath back, Finn and Weaver come around the corner carrying him.

"All good?" Weaver asks and Ginata nods.

"Help me get him laying down." She wants to keep Weaver from Millard's rooms for as long as she can. Give her King a chance to come around and make an escape.

"I think he'll live," Weaver says.

"Thanks. Do you think Della and Addyson should go back to the cottage? Maybe you could take them?"

Weaver frowns. "I should guard the King."

"He's tied up and hidden. I just fear for their safety, walking back alone. Even with Finn."

Finn laughs, and Ginata touches his sleeve. "No offence."

"None taken. I know I'm no noble warrior."

They smile, a moment of lightness welcome to them all.

"I don't want to leave you though, Ginata."

"I'll be fine. None of the King's men would do me any harm, and most of them are off somewhere licking their wounds. It was quite a fight out there today."

"You're right. Yes, it'll be safer for Addyson away from the castle. The King's men won't bother you if they see you, but they might try to hurt or imprison her again."

"I'll sort Will out. He seems fine. There's a lump on his head but no fresh blood. He just needs a tonic and some rest."

After hugs and promises to be careful, Weaver, Finn, Addyson and Della leave Ginata and Will and while Will snoozes, oblivious to all that's going on, Ginata sits with her head in her hands.

Right or wrong, she's done what she's done, and now it's time to live with the consequences, whatever they may be.

CERYN IS SCREAMING out Everleigh's name as she rides through the woods, past the river, up to the top of the forest, looking down over the castle and the villages beyond.

It's not fair that they've got Millard prisoner; that Addyson took the crown off his head and they have nowhere to put it. "Everleigh!" Her voice is hoarse from shouting, but she keeps shouting and searching and shouting and searching. It's what Archer would have done if he were alive, and she has to honour that. Besides, she had a choice to go home and leave Everleigh to fight her own battle for the throne, but she didn't want to. She has to be here helping and until she finds Everleigh, she will keep shouting and searching.

WEAVER HEADS UP THE little group, Finn and Della either side of Addyson. It's right to get her away from the castle, and with Millard tied up and unconscious and hidden, there is less urgency than there might have been, but he still wants to be quick. There's still tension in the air and a feeling of unrest around the castle.

The courtyard is still quiet, though a few little maids are quietly going about their business. Life always goes back to normal, but Weaver is ready, hand on his sword, in case.

They leave the castle behind them, happy to move away from the memories of the day; Everleigh being taken and Will attacked, all the fighting, the horror of it, the hollow victory of taking Millard's crown and having nowhere to place it.

They walk along quietly, each one lost in their own thoughts, memories and troubles.

What happens next is a question none of them can answer.

# Everleigh

BRETT WHISPERS HE IS sorry and then throws a hood over my head and carries me away from the castle, from Will, from any rescue.

Sorry for what? I cannot help but think of what he wanted to do to me before and I am trying not to be sick in this hood. If I do, I am likely to choke and die and I won't go out like that.

I want to fight so badly but my body is limp and I am not so stupid as to not recognise that I am helpless.

Imagination is no friend to anyone in trouble; I am imagining Brett taking me to the tower; or attacking me in the woods again, like he did before, but succeeding; I picture him killing me and proudly taking my body to my brother to show him how clever he is and how deserving of praise. Will he hit me, hurt me, touch me, kill me?

I am sweating and shivering and more scared than I have ever been in my life. Even when I imagined Halfreda slitting my throat, I wasn't this scared; I had planned for that my entire life long; I had pictured it and prepared for it as best I could and I knew with the entire Realm watching I would not scream and cry and dissolve into tears; I had decided to die like a brave Kingmaker, head held high, throat exposed...

But this, this is different. I don't know what's coming. Brett ready to attack or my brother crowing with victory or more of the King's men wanting to aid and assist Millard in anything he chooses, no matter how nefarious.

I am not sure what will be worse; facing Brett or my brother.

At least my brother doesn't have any designs on my body, doesn't fancy himself as the right man to awaken my inner desire and convince me to abandon my innocence.

Millard will kill me. I don't think he'll lock me up, maybe before but not now, and maybe death would be preferable to what Brett might do.

So, some sort of horrible ending awaits me when I get to wherever we are going and a little bit of me hopes that Brett will just keep walking. Keep walking and I can close my eyes and pretend I'm somewhere else, doing something else, laughing or joking, that maybe it's a week and a half ago and my father lives, Halfreda lives and Archer lives.

Tears flow down my face at the thought of all that I have lost and a little helpless, weak bit of me thinks death would be welcome. At least I could stop fighting, stop battling, stop.

Forget about how lonely my life has become, how helpless and hopeless. How much I miss my father, Halfreda. Archer.

I hope that maybe whenever we get where we are going, he will leave the hood over my head and I will never really know what my fate is.

Brett is slowing down and the snakes in my tummy unfurl and squirm free, the bile rises in my throat and I swallow it down, the bitter, acrid taste making me wince.

He sets me down and whispers, Walk, to me, and putting his hands either side of my hips, in a far too intimate gesture, he guides me forward.

My feet are refusing to work properly, the fear and the upset making me stumble and stagger. What if I just lay down and refuse to go further? Will that start an attack sooner or give me a temporary reprieve while he decides what to do with me?

He pushes my head down and I feel the surrounding atmosphere change; I think we are in the caves at the farthest edge of the river; the air is dank, oppressive and our treads are echoing.

The end of our journey is coming. I can feel it. We are walking more quickly, with purpose. Brett is taking me to where I will end up.

At his feet or my brother's, I cannot stand the not knowing, the lack of sight making every other sense heightened.

I can smell Brett; he smells like he needs a good wash; he smells nervous, if that makes any sense. I can hear my breathing, shallow and too fast, panic overcoming me and threatening to send me into a meltdown.

I can sense other people in the cave, hear breathing that's not mine or Brett's, and my knees buckle, no longer able to hold me up. As I drop to the ground, I feel the dirt and stones under my palms, and I know this is it; I am about to die. Or be violated. Or both.

I feel Brett tugging at the ties that gather the hood around my neck and I flinch from his fingers, drawing my whole body inwards like I might disappear from his sight completely – from the sight of whoever else is here with us.

There's a whoosh over my ears as he pulls the hood off and I push my hair off my face, wiping away the tears and sweat and squinting as my eyes adjust to the gloom.

I was right, Brett has brought me to a cave; I can remember playing here with Addyson and my brothers before they both went mad.

And I am right that there are other people in the cave, but I am not sure if the trauma of being taken has addled my brain somehow.

Brett is grinning at me, standing placidly by the side of two men I recognise.

The first is Halfreda's teacher.

My eyes come to rest on his smile, and his lovely eyes, and then I look to the right of him. And I feel like I will faint, yes, I will faint, because standing next to him, bruised and a little battered-looking, standing not quite as strong and upright as he used to, but with his bright red shock of hair exactly as I dreamed about it and his smile and his face and his eyes and himself so, so perfect, and alive... is Archer.

# SEIZE THE CROWN

## THE END

Made in the USA
Las Vegas, NV
18 March 2022

45838556R00152